'If you like your crime dark and unafraid, then look no further than Johana Gustawsson. *Block 46* is brutal and sexy, exquisitely written, and unforgettable. Gustawsson doesn't shy away from anything; she'll take you where other crime writers might not dare wander, vividly and accurately describing the most brutal of crimes, taking you inside the heads (and hearts) of those on both sides of the investigation, and all this conjured up with the most beautiful prose. The ending left me pacing the house. That's all I'll say. Read it' Louise Beech

'Multi-layered, superbly plotted, brimming with mystery, tension and bone-chilling violence, and with two very different – but equally fascinating – lead female characters, *Block 46* is not for the squeamish or faint-hearted … Disturbing, moving and utterly mesmerising, this is a book that has the power to shock and the artistry to impress long after the last page has turned' *Lancashire Post*

'This debut by journalist Johanna Gustawsson is written with an assured hand, woven intricately where the strands knot into a breathless and startling dénouement' Shots Mag

'Without hesitation this book has already made it to my top reads of 2017. Why? Because it's a rich and harrowing story of the psychology of evil, good versus bad, death versus life; it's complex, fast-paced, and disturbing, all the elements that make a crime read stand out from the norm. Gripping from the first page, *Block 46* will keep you on the edge of your seat all the way to its shocking conclusion, that I can guarantee' The Book Review Café

'The type of book you can't put down. Don't start it at night like I did … not that you will be able to sleep after reading it. Outstanding' MrsLovesToBake

'Gritty, bone-chilling, and harrowing – it's not for the faint of heart, and not to be missed' Crime by the Book

'The subtle weaving of powerful emotion, murderous intent and the tracking of a deranged killer, all underscored by Gustawsson's influences from French and Scandinavian fiction, all co-exists and blends perfectly into a brave and beautifully realised book. Disturbing and compelling, *Block 46* is an intensely unique read. Highly recommended' Raven Crime Reads

'The writing is crisp, taut and intelligent, the plotting is tight, bold and skilled, and had a profound effect on me as a reader. It's one of those books that linger well after you finish and challenged me to think in a deep way' Novel Gossip

'If her future novels are as fascinating as *Block 46*, I will be first in line to read them' Segnalibro

'The type of brilliantly insightful crime thriller that doesn't come along that often' Liz Loves Books

'The author spins a wicked tale of terror, pain and deception. It is an absorbing combination of history and crime, with a touch of Nordic noir and a nefarious mind behind it all' Cheryl MM

'If you read only one book I've recommended this year, make it this one – emotive, thrilling and beautifully written' Keeper of Pages

'Harrowing, unflinching and brutal; it's also brilliant, gripping and completely and utterly unputdownable!' Rather Too Fond of Books

'Very well written, with strong and believable characters and plenty of twists and turns' If Only I Could Read Faster

'There are so many elements of this story that just reached out and grabbed me. Apart from it being extremely dark and disturbing in parts, it has everything I love in a crime novel' By-the-Letter Book Reviews

'Sheer perfection' Novel Deelights

'I found the story strong enough to work out well as a series but the Buchenwald storyline made this book so much more than a usual crime novel. This was an account that needed to be told and has catapulted it into my top ten list of books read. Not just in 2017 but my all-time top ten' Steph's Book Blog

'Definitely one of the best I've read so far this year' A Crime Readers Blog

'It is beautifully written and skilfully conceived … a gripping and gritty read that deals with issues that take you further than a crime novel. As an examination of evil, it is a chilling but unforgettable read' Books, Life and Everything

'Raw, shocking and brutal, this beautifully layered story will not only fill your waking hours but your dreams too. What an incredible book!' Ronnie Turner

'Wow. This book. As dark as this is at times, it is also so beautifully crafted that it is one of those I will remember for some time' Jen Med's Book Reviews

'Dark and disturbing, this book has left me with much to think about … the best book I have read so far this year!' Reflections of a Reader

'A book that will leave you speechless and quite disturbed, horrified and traumatised, yet wanting more. I feel very strongly about this book and I so hope it gets all the accolades it deserves' Swirl & Thread

'Chilling doesn't even begin to describe it. Steadily, the two main plotlines weave together, with a few twists thrown in for good measure, leading to a climatic "don't go in there" moment … impressive' Joy Kluver

'Johana Gustawsson gives French Noir new meaning with this phenomenal and unforgettable story' Chocolate 'N' Waffles

'The brutality and courage are described here with equal passion, which at times stopped me reading. I don't think that a book I have read has ever captured the essence of pure fear that came from these pages, word for word' Books from Dawn till Dusk

'A dark, unsettling, harrowing novel that will make you stop and think. I loved the twist and would read another novel by Gustawsson in a heartbeat' damppebbles

'Looks at evil in a unique and memorable way and the quality of writing makes it hard to believe that this is Johana Gustawsson's debut novel' On-the-Shelf Books

'The story was engaging, the plot intriguing and the dénouement played out really well' From First Page to Last

'A totally compelling read' Crime Book Junkie

'It's not often I find myself struggling to find the words for a review. But I am with this one. *Block 46* is brutal, honest and emotionally harrowing but it's so worth reading!' Bibliophile Book Club

'This book will end up being one of my favourite reads of the year. Hands down.' Clues & Reviews

'The author's astute and uncompromising style suggests she is one to watch' Never Imitate

'*Block 46* was so much more than I had hoped for in a serial-killer thriller. It's probably one of the most memorable debuts I have ever read. Heart-breaking and hard-hitting in equal measure, this book had it all for me and I was an emotional mess by the end of it' My Chestnut Reading Tree

'This is one thriller that will haunt you for some time after you have finished reading. But it is a five-star read' The Last Word Book Review

'Tension seeps off the page and into your soul' Books are my Cwtches

'Absolutely blew me away' The Bibliophile Chronicles

'A debut novel that will knock your socks completely off!' Emma the Little Book Worm

'A gripping psychological thriller with a clever and engaging resolution, but it also does what the most intelligent fiction can do – it reaches into the past and tells us that there are some lessons we must never forget. I absolutely loved *Block 46*' Hair Past A Freckle

'A thoughtful and tightly plotted book that's both moving and thrilling, an absolute page-turner that delivers in spades' Mumbling about…

'While covering some dark subjects, this is an excellent read, and it becomes more and more compelling throughout … I can't wait to read more about Roy and Castells' Blue Book Balloon

'Artfully weaves suspense and mystery together. I am in awe of the final result' Jena Brown Writes

'Remarkable' Greenacre Writers

'A truly thought-provoking read that's set within a superbly crafted plot … keeps you guessing until the brilliantly terrifying end that has you shocked at the clever and ingenious twist!' Miriam Smith

'What Johana has also done in this book is make us, the readers, realise how important it is to learn about what happened in these times, to ensure that this atrocity never happens again' Hooked From Page One

'It threw up the classic reading dilemma – so good I want to reach the end to find out what happened; but I don't want to reach the end as I was enjoying it so much' Grab this Book

'She's got a new fan here!' The Belgian Reviewer

'What Gustawsson does is mix the bloody reality of *Schindler's List* with Scandi Noir and in doing so produces a very enjoyable and original novel…' The Library Door

'Bloody brilliant!' Emma's Bookish Corner

KEEPER

ABOUT THE AUTHOR

Born in 1978 in Marseille and with a degree in political science, Johana Gustawsson has worked as a journalist for the French press and television. She married a Swede and now lives in London. She was the co-author of a bestseller, *On se retrouvera*, published by Fayard Noir in France, whose television adaptation drew more than seven million viewers in June 2015. Her solo debut, *Block 46*, became an international bestseller, with *Keeper* following suit after its publication in France in 2017. She is working on the next book in the Roy & Castells series.

Follow Johana on Twitter *@JoGustawsson* and on her website: *johanagustawsson.com/en/*.

ABOUT THE TRANSLATOR

Maxim Jakubowski is a highly regarded translator from French and Italian. An ex-publisher, and one-time owner of the Murder One bookstore, he is also a writer and editor of crime, mystery and erotic fiction, and has published nearly one hundred books. A regular broadcaster on TV and radio, Maxim Jakubowski reviews crime fiction for the *Guardian*. He also contributes to *The Times*, the *Bookseller* and the *Evening Standard* and is the literary director of the Crime Scene Film and Book Festival, held annually in London. For many years, he has edited anthologies of the best British mystery stories of the year and the world's best erotica, which have become bestsellers in the UK and America.

KEEPER

An Emily Roy and Alexis Castells Investigation

JOHANA GUSTAWSSON

Translated by Maxim Jakubowski

ORENDA
BOOKS

Orenda Books
16 Carson Road
West Dulwich
London SE21 8HU
www.orendabooks.co.uk

First published in French as *Mör* by Bragelonne in 2017
This edition published by Orenda Books 2018
Copyright © Bragelonne, 2017
English language translation copyright © Maxim Jakubowski, 2017

ISBN 978-1-912374-05-2
eISBN 978-1-912374-06-9

Typeset in Garamond by MacGuru Ltd
Printed and bound by Nørhaven, Denmark

For sales and distribution, please contact *info@orendabooks.co.uk*

For Mattias,
my BETTER half

KEEPER

He unbuttoned the jacket of his pale grey suit with careful delibera-tion, straightened his narrow tie and sat down to face the judge. Sorry. Madam Justice.

His eyes zeroed in on the heavy pearls dangling from her distended ear lobes. As big as his thumb. His lawyer had advised him to wear a sober, dark suit. For the tie, something more classic. With a looser knot. Just a 'suggestion'.

He couldn't give a damn about the suit, per se. It was having a choice in the matter that he found exciting. This was one sliver of power he could exploit to the hilt. Savour it right down to the bone.

The judge started to speak. She shook her head, and her earrings swayed as if they were slow dancing. Ear lobes lolling like tongues.

Lobes and mash, home-made style…
Beat two egg yolks and dip the lobes in.
Toss them in breadcrumbs.
Fry them up in parsley butter.
Drizzle them in olive oil and serve with mash.
Lobes and mash, home-made style…

He leaned in to bring his mouth closer to the microphone and give Madam Justice an answer. Spelled out his surname. Paused to brush away a speck of dust from his left shoulder with the back of his hand. Carried on with his given name, date of birth and profession, his mind dwelling on the curious habit he had of unbuttoning his suit jacket when

*he sat down. A fashion adopted by pupils at Eton or, more accurately,
those elected to the in-crowd of their exclusive 'Pop' club. Though perhaps
this particular idiosyncrasy went all the way back to King Edward VII,
whose fullness of figure demanded the extra space when His Majesty sat
on His Royal Backside.*

*The judge had just asked him to speak. She straightened the lace collar
of her robe and shifted some files across her desk.*

Lobes and mash, home-made style…

*He coughed into his hand. Appreciated the absence of handcuffs.
Reflected on how a cage would soon replace them. An image flashed
across his mind, slotting into the space between himself and Madam
Justice with her lolling ear lobes. A vision of himself hanging from the
bars of his cell like a monkey. Still wearing his suit.*

He laughed. The sound of it echoed harshly back at him.

*Though he was laughing, he shivered as a thin film of sweat spread
across the nape of his neck.*

'It's not my fault,' he mumbled, as if to himself. 'It's not my fault…'

*The judge interrupted him. He couldn't make out the words, just the
music of her speech. A crescendo building to a climax. A question.*

*'It's not my fault,' he continued. 'Hilda was the one who started it …
It all started with Hilda…'*

KARLA HANSEN SLIPPED HER MOBILE into the back pocket of her jeans, zipped up her jacket and pulled on her rain boots. She threw her Converses into the boot of her estate and set out into the woods.

The sun was already rising in the sky with casual ease. In July, it shone proudly for seventeen oh-so-blissful hours and seemed to revel in its summer reign as much as the Swedes basked in its glow. It had been a frigid winter that year, lingering oppressively all the way through to May like a house guest who refuses to leave, shooing spring away until a Divine hand intervened to throw back the frozen curtain and clear the air. Hallelujah.

Karla's every step was marked by the sound of snapping twigs and the muted splash of muddy puddles, the remnants of yesterday's squalls.

Like every morning when she awoke, her brain was switched to 'Post-It factory' mode, as her husband, Dan, liked to tease. And her to-do list went on, and on and on. Summer had barely begun, and already it was time to think about autumn. She would have to sign her daughters up for their extra-curricular activities once school started: judo and soccer for Pia, the eldest; contemporary dance and theatre for Ada, the youngest; Spanish for both of them. They would no doubt complain about the language lessons, but they didn't have any choice in the matter. Dan would rather they learned French, but the girls had kicked up a fuss (they were allowed one veto a month, and used and abused the privilege). Reason given: the teacher was a slave-driver. Real reason: there was no way they were going to get up at eight in the morning on a Saturday.

Karla also had to call the electrician back and run into Ica to pick up lunch: some steaks, flour, strawberries and *vaniljvisp*, the delicious vanilla cream that always whipped up so nicely for dessert. No, she would ask Dan to do the shopping. And he could sort out the Spanish lessons as well; she would text him a bit later.

Dan wrote young-adult novels. Or rather, novels for young women, or women who wanted to feel young again. Stories about wicked witches, conniving queens, fearless warriors and fearsome dragons, all fighting among themselves to rule over kingdoms with unpronounceable names. Karla's little lists were her way of bringing him back down to earth every day and reminding him what a wonderful husband and father he was. How else could she rival all those doe-eyed groupies who drooled over him? Flattering his ego and keeping his feet on the ground, that's what she did. Blatant manipulation, her colleagues at work called it. Manipulation? No, that's what marriage was all about, she reasoned with a smile, never daring to admit she was deadly serious about the whole thing.

Karla slowed her pace. Through the rows of quivering birch trees, she could see the shores of the lake – Torvsjön – awash with the bloodlike hue of dawn.

'I'm sorry, but the lake is off-limits this morning,' said a deathly pale officer in uniform, blocking her way.

'So I see…'

'I'm going to have to ask you to turn around.' The young rookie's breath stank of vomit.

'You've just thrown up your breakfast, haven't you?'

The young man swallowed hard and glanced down at his muddy boots in embarrassment. Then he pulled himself together and barrelled his scrawny chest as best he could. 'Madam, I must ask you to…'

'I hope you haven't puked all over my crime scene.'

'What? But…'

'I'm Detective Hansen.'

The officer opened his mouth. Closed it again.

'Ah ... I ... sorry ... I thought...' he stammered, his cheeks reddening.

'I know I'm not what you were expecting: all tits and no balls. Don't dwell on it, though. Where's all the action around here, kiddo?'

FREDA WALLIN WAS WOKEN UP by the ugly din of screaming, barking, whistling and laughing. A familiar scene was unfolding a few streets away from her modest lodgings: lambs being led to the slaughter at the Spitalfields abattoirs 150 yards away, bleating for their lives, as if they could sense the sorry fate awaiting them, while the jeers of vulgar passers-by as excited at the sight of blood as they were a whore's bare leg echoed like a beating drum.

Soon, all that would be left of the poor creatures would be their entrails littered across the Whitechapel pavements, their blood running down the streets in torrents and a stench of death so suffocating it felt like a kiss from the Grim Reaper himself.

Freda yawned, threading her fingers through her hair.

'*Helvete!*' What the hell?

She'd rolled in at midnight and forgotten to rub Keating's powder into her scalp. She pressed her nose down into her mattress and sniffed every square inch of its surface. It smelled rank, but not of rotten raspberries, thank goodness, so it was unlikely there were bed bugs. She pulled off the bed sheet and shook it out, just to make sure.

She'd come home too late: she shouldn't have gone down to the Shadwell docks for a gander at the fire that had broken out. She'd been having a drink with Liz Stride at the Ten Bells. By ten o'clock, Liz had already earned enough to pay for a room on Flower and Dean Street, so she'd dragged Freda along with her to the docks.

The spectacle had turned out to be as sinister as it was hypnotic. The flames had roared up into the sky, devouring the clouds and the night, casting their light over London at its most appealing: when the city was silent. During the daytime, the incessant clamour in the streets was a blight on the city. Horses and their neighing, the clap of their hooves on cobblestones and the jingling of their harnesses. The cheery calls of market traders, muffin men and coffee sellers, the exasperated cries of women splashed with muck by hackney carriages, the tears and barking coughs of children all swallowed up by the music of the barrel organs. London, in the daytime, was a fair, fresh-faced, buxom maiden whose charms were tainted by her toothless grin.

'Freda!'

Her neighbour was knocking at the door to get her out of bed. She owned an alarm clock, passed on by her old boss, which meant Freda had no need to pay for a knocker-up. Her neighbour lived in a room as small as hers, but with six children. When her husband died – crushed by a falling crate at the docks – she was already expecting a seventh. She had prayed no end for the baby not to live and the devil had heard her call: the poor thing was stillborn.

Freda rose, plucked a couple of drowned cockroaches out of her washbasin, chucked them into the hearth and splashed some water on her face. She slipped on her woollen stockings and two cotton skirts over her flannel underwear and laced up her corset as best she could before buttoning her blouse and stepping into her linen dress.

She then folded four large sheets of newspaper and slipped them into the left-hand pocket of her coat. The rough paper was hard on the skin of her backside but, as Liz would say, better that than wandering around all day with shit smeared across her bum. From the right-hand pocket, she pulled out her dust-dirtied handkerchief and switched it for a clean one she had set out on the back of the chair. She shook out her boots to make sure no vermin had holed up there during the night, however short it had been, and pulled them onto her feet.

'*Murder!*'

Freda ran to the window. A crowd was gathering down in the street, on Buck's Row.

'*Murder! Murder!*' a young boy was screaming, using his hands as a loudspeaker.

Freda quickly slipped on her coat, donned her straw hat and ran downstairs to the street.

HECTOR NYMAN DUCKED UNDER the blue-and-white tape strung between the spindly tree trunks and forged a path through the twenty or so jumpsuited officers digging around the undergrowth.

Björn Holm, the head of the SKL, the crime-scene unit, took off his mask and unfurled his moustache the same way you'd stretch your legs after a long journey.

'Well, if it isn't Detective Hutch putting in an appearance!' he teased Nyman. 'Say, blondie, aren't you supposed to be on holiday?'

'Not until August. I'm going to top up my tan in Greece.'

Nyman picked up a plastic pouch from a trestle table, tore it open and pulled out a hooded crime-scene suit, slip-on shoe covers, a pair of gloves and a mask.

'Why such a crowd? Is it market day or something?' he wondered as he slipped into the regulation outfit.

'We had to bring in the cavalry. Hansen will explain.'

'So where is she, then, my Starsky?'

'Over there. She's taking a dip,' Holm said, pointing with his chin to the lake over Nyman's shoulder.

'The usual smell?'

'Doesn't smell of roses, at any rate. I reckon you'll be sniffing your Vicks, Nyman…'

With a grimace, Hector Nyman turned and parted the sea of white jumpsuits surging their way back towards him.

A few minutes later, the shoreline of Torvsjön lake emerged through a veil of birch trees, and Hector soon caught sight of his partner, Karla Hansen. Already out of her crime-scene garb, displaying endless legs clad in rain boots, she was talking to a gaunt man he didn't recognise and barking into her phone at the same time.

She waved as soon as she saw him. Hector hurried over to join her.

'Let me guess, Holm's been taking the piss again and there was no need for me to put this damned thing on, right?' he groaned as she hung up.

'Yep, you've missed the boat, Nyman. The SKL's just finished down here. We were only waiting for you to help move the body. You can strip off now.' Karla Hansen gave him a cheeky wink.

'Ooh, such dirty talk, Hansen. And at such an early hour too … How the hell does your husband keep up with you?'

'I have to spank him.'

Hector Nyman shook his head, unsure as to whether she was joking.

'Oh, really! Now all I can think about is you in a kinky leather catsuit…'

'You'll get over it, Nyman. Just set your mind to something else,' his partner replied, tapping the side of her head. 'Oh, let me introduce you to our new medical examiner, Nicholas Nordin.'

Nordin had been standing there all the while, lost for words.

'Nicholas will be replacing Birgit for the next year,' she continued.

'Really? What's up with Birgit?'

'She's on mat leave.'

'Again? How does she keep shitting out all those kids?'

'You should think about having kids of your own, Nyman. Combine pleasure with something useful, for once.'

'You sell it so well, Hansen. Jeez, I can't wait.'

'Well, say hello to Mr Nordin here, then we've got something to show you.'

'How nice, a fresh body. Just what I need to get in the mood.'

With a tentative smile, the medical examiner offered the detective a bony hand to shake. Their latex gloves squeaked as their palms made contact.

'Let's go,' Hansen said as she stepped away.

They walked in single file along the water's edge, flanked on one side by dense shrubbery and on the other by a fringe of pebbles, slippery from the lake's moist tongue – all the way to a decapitated tree trunk that was teetering precariously on the shore, its knotted roots clinging to nothing but a skirt of tall grass.

'Are you OK, Nyman?' Hansen asked.

Hector nodded a careful yes, his eyes fixed on the body.

The young woman was naked, sitting on the ground with her back against the dead tree trunk, legs wide apart, arms by her sides, the palms of her hands turned to the sky. Her head lolled forward, her chin nearly touching her chest. Parted down the centre, her long blonde hair was splattered with mud and drawn back behind her shoulders to reveal her bust. Here, two dark red craters now sat where her breasts would have been. The killer had also cut big chunks of flesh out of her thighs and hips.

Hector forced himself to swallow a few times to stem the bile rising towards his throat.

'Wait, that's not all,' said Hansen, as she kneeled down by the corpse. She gave Nordin a nod, and he came over to the other side of the body to hold the head and arms steady as she leaned it over towards him.

An expletive escaped through Nyman's clenched teeth. Karla wasn't kidding: there were two cavernous wounds where the woman's buttocks should have been.

ALIÉNOR LINDBERGH GULPED another mouthful of coffee.

She had arrived at seven that morning, leaned her bike against the low stone wall and sat on the front steps of the building at 14 Arvidstorpsvägen. She'd eaten her banana and her three thin slices of *tunnbröd* and *prästost*, the only Swedish cheese deserving of the name, as she went over every step of her plan in her mind. Again and again.

For the last month, she'd been cycling in from Skrea Strand to 14 Arvidstorpsvägen. Always at the same time every day to provide for every contingency: the flow of traffic, the correct type of clothing for the weather, the weight of her backpack. After trying on a number of options, in the knowledge that this Thursday morning, the temperature would be 17 degrees by six-thirty, she had opted for a pair of pleated trousers, a blouse, a cotton cardigan and some canvas slip-ons. She had tied her hair back into a ponytail, so that it would be out of her face on the ride, knowing she'd feel the odd strand brushing the back of her neck. She'd also brought some supplies and a few toiletries she couldn't do without.

In twenty-two minutes' time, she would put her Thermos flask away in her backpack, wedged between the rolls of toilet paper and the box of Annas *Pepparkakor* – the only biscuits that truly tasted like gingerbread – and then she would enter the building.

Twenty-two minutes. Her heart was racing. Aliénor closed her eyes, took a deep breath in through her nose, exhaled loudly through her mouth and repeated the exercise until the palpitations stopped. She opened her eyes again and ran through the list in her mind, which was usually enough to keep any rising anxiety at bay. She could picture the sheet of paper floating on the breeze, tethered only to the clouds. She mentally read out the rules she had written down in industrious capital letters until a pleasant set of chimes sounded. Eight twenty-seven am. It was time to pack her things away and get going.

She pushed the glass door open. The entrance hall was empty; only a solitary shaven head peered over the light wooden front desk. That would make matters easier.

'Good day. My name is Aliénor Lindbergh. I have an appointment with Lennart Bergström.'

The young officer looked up, his face a mask. Without taking his eyes off her, he held a phone to his ear and announced her arrival to Kommissionär Bergström. The man then lowered his head as he hung up, affording Aliénor a bird's-eye view of his shining cranium. Good, she wouldn't have to make small talk. She took a few steps back to discourage any further dialogue, should he change his mind and start on about the weather. She just couldn't understand how people could enjoy that kind of conversation. *Cold today, isn't it? What's with all this rain? What a hot day!* It was all relative anyway: a Swede and a Mexican would certainly have differing views on the matter. Her French teacher had once told her how she had burst out laughing reading one of Mankell's novels in which Wallander commented how pleasant the twenty or so degrees of a Swedish 'summer' were.

'Aliénor Lindbergh?'

Aliénor turned around. She had been expecting the commissioner to come down the corridor to the left of the front desk, but he had emerged through a door behind her, by the main entrance.

Lennart Bergström frowned slightly. Aliénor realised she was standing there wide-eyed. She pulled herself together and clenched her cheekbones into a tight-lipped expression of courtesy. Her nice-to-meet-you smile.

'Lennart Bergström. Delighted to meet you.'

With his imposing frame and his short grey-streaked beard, Kommissionär Bergström looked just as he did in the photos that had circulated in the media during the Ebner affair the previous year.

Aliénor shook his outstretched hand. 'Likewise.'

She found the contact of his calloused palm unpleasant and abruptly let go, triggering another nice-to-meet-you smile to make up for what her father would have called her 'uncivilised' reaction.

The commissioner relaxed. 'Come with me,' he said, leading the way.

They walked down a corridor that led into an open-plan space, then zigzagged through a little maze of empty cubicles until they reached a door in the back wall. Bergström stepped inside and settled behind a desk; Aliénor sat across from him. The chair felt as hard as the front steps of the police station, and squeaked every time she shifted. She slid forward to the edge of the seat to silence it.

'I was just reading through your email and the public prosecutor's,' Kommissionär Bergström began.

'You mean you read them again right before you came to get me?' Aliénor interjected.

The commissioner didn't answer. Aliénor realised she'd made a blunder. She recognised the spark of surprise that often flashed across people's eyes and could so easily turn to antagonism.

'You're a student of criminal law and legal psychology.'

'Yes.'

'And you come warmly recommended by the prosecutor…'

'Yes, he wouldn't have solved the Pedersen case without me.'

The commissioner looked around at the untidy office. 'Aren't you worried you'll get bored working with us after your year as a trainee with the public prosecutor's office?'

'Eleven months.'

'Excuse me?'

'My traineeship with Hans Møller lasted eleven months. No, I won't be bored.'

Lennart Bergström covered his mouth with his hand, trying to hide his laughter. Aliénor was unsure whether she should laugh as well. She chose not to. It was safer that way. Besides, it might have been a yawn he was trying to stifle.

'You worked eleven months with Møller, so you know how it goes,' he continued. 'You'll have to sign a confidentiality agreement and you won't be allowed in the field. You'll report to me for the entire period. If things get too much for you, you come to see me. OK?'

Aliénor shifted in her seat. She didn't understand Lennart Bergström's question. What was she supposed to call him, anyway? Kommissionär? Bergström? Kommissionär Bergström?

'A police station is much busier than the public prosecutor's office. Even in a place like Falkenberg. If at any time you find it … difficult to be here, just come and see me. We can always find a solution.'

'I won't have any difficulty being here. I'm ready.'

'So you'd like to join us in September?'

'I'd like to observe all the stages of an investigation and how the station functions from September to December. But I'd love it if I could actually start work here today.'

'Today?'

'Yes, today, Thursday the sixteenth of July. As I mentioned in my email, my time with Hans Møller's office was complete at the end of the day yesterday, the fifteenth of July, as per my traineeship agreement. So I can start here today.'

'But Møller talked about September to me,' Bergström persisted, peering at his computer screen.

'That's correct. But my email did stipulate my wish to start on the sixteenth of July. And you did write back to indicate that was fine.'

'I'm sorry, Aliénor, I must have read your message too quickly. I'm away on holiday starting tomorrow, so there's no way I can have you start before September.'

Aliénor's heartbeat began to quicken. She'd had it all planned out.

'Surely Detective Olofsson won't be taking his holidays at the same time as you. I could report to him in your absence,' she ventured.

The squeaking of the chair was getting to be unbearable. She shot to her feet. The commissioner did the same.

'Aliénor, I'm very sorry, but I can't leave you with Olofsson. Møller asked me to … look after you. Detective Olofsson would be the wrong person…'

There were three sharp knocks at the door. A set of blue-lined eyes and an aquiline nose peered through the crack of the half-open door.

'Sorry to disturb you, Kommissionär. Your line was busy, so perhaps you didn't hang up properly. There's a very urgent call for you from prosecutor Møller…'

'Isn't he at his holiday home in in Piteå?'

'Yes, sir, but … it's very urgent…'

Lennart Bergström closed his eyes for a moment and nodded tiredly.

'Thank you, Hannah. Aliénor, can you give me a minute? You can stay.'

The phone rang just eight seconds after Hannah's departure. The commissioner didn't utter a word after his *'Hej, Møller'* in greeting, but his face said it all. His lips tightened in a downward curve, wrinkling his chin, and he kept clenching his jaw.

Aliénor was all too familiar with that expression: Lennart Bergström clearly didn't like what Hans Møller had to say.

TWO WRETCHED LADIES of the night were fighting over a square of pavement in front of the Ten Bells. Truth was, the pub drew quite the crowd, so soliciting right outside the door was an easy road to the four pence they were all so desperate to earn. That was the cost of a bed for the night in a lodging house, on a mattress teeming with vermin and sheets that hadn't been changed in months.

The two unfortunates were clawing at each other's hats and faces like gutter cats. One tore the other's blouse clean open, unhooking her tattered corset. One flabby breast flopped out like a teat, provoking a peal of laughter from the drunken crowd pouring out of the pub.

'That's nothing. Just wait till you see Mary Kelly get her claws out!' Liz sniggered, weaving her way to the bar.

Freda followed Liz, trying to suppress the urge to throw up. It had been three months since she had arrived in England – three months of Liz dragging her along to all sorts of pubs after their day's work. And still she couldn't get used to all the stomach-churning smells. The air in the Ten Bells was heavy with the bitter stench of beer and gin, the stink of filthy clothes and the stale smell of bodies exhausted by long hours of toil. None of the regulars was in the habit of changing clothes for the pub; they couldn't afford to. These lost souls wore their worldly wares on their backs: their rags and probably a handkerchief, a comb and a handful of sugar. What little money they had earned that day would quickly be spent on gin. The careless would end up sleeping outside, on the same pavement where the two whores were fighting.

Everyone drank in Whitechapel: men, women and children alike. Alcohol was the best way to deaden the body and soul and cloud the fact that tomorrow would be just another today.

Liz suddenly jabbed a rotund, sorry-looking young man in the ribs with her elbow. 'Hey, fatso, if yer want to touch what's underneath 'ere, it'll cost yer four pence! Or keep your hands around your glass.'

'Where's your room then, lass?'

'My room?' Liz burst out laughing, making no effort to cover her toothless mouth. 'Where does this clown think we are, in bleedin' Mayfair? My room's up against the wall of the Ten Bells!'

'Standing?'

'Standing, sitting, on all fours, any which way you like, love, you're the one who's payin'!'

Freda blushed, since her friend wasn't going to. When she had met her at the Swedish church on Prince's Square, Freda would never have guessed that Liz did more than just housework and cleaning in the tenements at 32 Flower and Dean Street. When he had introduced them to each other, the pastor had pointed out their common origins: they had both lived in Gothenburg and grown up on the west coast of Sweden, Liz in Torslanda and Freda 100 kilometres to the south, in Falkenberg. The man of God was hoping to find a shepherdess for his little lost lamb. Liz had been arrested by the police nearly a dozen times over the past couple of years, and the pastor was hoping Freda would help guide her back onto the right path. But the problem was, there was no right path through Whitechapel.

Liz picked up their glasses. On their way to the back of the pub, they passed a small boy clinging on to his mother's fraying shawl. The woman giggled uncontrollably while a man Freda doubted was her husband drowned her in kisses. Bare-headed with dead-tired eyes, the poor mite was sucking his thumb under a shower of beer.

Liz found a free corner at a table. Freda set down a small flask in front of her friend. 'I brought you some Keating's powder,' she said.

'Oh, you're a love, thank you!' Liz gushed, cupping her friend's cheek with a rough hand. 'It's not like a couple of bed-bug bites are going to kill me, though!'

She swallowed a mouthful of gin and continued. 'Oh, and did you hear, they found poor old Polly Nichols on the street just down from yours?'

Freda went pale. She ran her tongue across her lips, which were burning from the alcohol. 'Dear God, Liz … I was actually there … I saw the wretched soul … lying in the street, her dress hitched up to her stomach, her body still warm … The constable thought she was just drunk and he was about to pick her up when he saw her throat had been slit from ear to ear. I swear her head would have toppled off if he'd tried to move her.'

'Forty-three years old, poor Polly, can you believe it? Only a year younger than me! It's so sad … leaving five kids behind and all. Not that she did much in the way of caring for them, mind, as she was dead drunk from morning to night.'

A dark cloud cast a shadow over Liz's normally jovial face. Beneath the veil of misery, Freda could see the remaining traces of a beauty ravaged by alcohol and poverty. Had her mother still been alive, Freda thought, she would have been the same age as Mary Ann Nichols – or Polly, as everyone called her. She felt a twinge. Freda was eighteen. She hadn't left Sweden to end up like Polly. Nor like Liz. She hadn't fled the Swedish countryside, its frigid winters and its dead-end life, to perish on the filthy, godforsaken streets of Whitechapel.

'Don't think I'm casting the first stone at the poor woman. What else is there to do here but drink, anyway? Here's to your good health, Polly, may you rest in peace!' Liz raised her glass and drained it in a single gulp.

'It's a gang, I'm telling you,' Liz continued. 'They're trying to frighten us and take our money, and we've barely got enough to keep a roof over our heads as it is.' She unbuttoned her shirt, flashing her cleavage to a red-haired man with a bushy moustache who was ogling Freda drunkenly. The man looked away and Liz turned back to her friend.

'And you know she's not the first, don't you? No, Polly ain't the first to be knifed to death around 'ere,' she went on, playing with her empty glass, rolling it around on the table. 'There were two others before her. One in April and another at the beginning of this month.'

Freda suddenly felt a lump in her throat. Was she the only one who was afraid?

'Oh, it's a hard life, my dear Freda, but we'll be fine, you'll see. As if we didn't have enough shitty problems already, though … Who knows who's going to be next? Because the way these murderous bastards are playin' around, they're not about to stop any time soon, are they?' she opined, as she sidled off to the bar for another round of drinks.

KARLA HANSEN AND HECTOR NYMAN sat down across from Bergström.

Prosecutor Møller had called Karla on her way back to the police station in Halmstad and imperiously suggested she drive up to Falkenberg: Bergström was now in charge of the investigation. She hadn't even had a chance to catch her breath before Møller hung up on her.

Of course, she reflected. *Of course Bergström would be put in charge of the investigation. Who else but the star of the show from the Ebner case?* But this one should have been hers, and now she was having to pass it on. She felt a cold rage take hold of her, turning her into a savage beast determined to sink her teeth in as soon as the commissioner opened his mouth in an attempt to justify the turn of events.

Hector could sense the fury building in his partner and wisely kept quiet.

'Well, it appears the Torvsjön affair has fallen into our laps,' Bergström began.

'So it seems,' Karla snapped.

The commissioner glanced at her for a second, taken aback by her attitude. 'Anyway, here's what I suggest—' He was interrupted as a burly man, muscles on obvious display through his tight T-shirt, strode in to his office without knocking.

'Kommissionär Bergström, I ... Nyman?' he paused, opening his arms out wide as he caught sight of Hector. Nyman stood up, and they clapped each other on the back in a fraternal embrace.

'What the hell are you doing here, Nyman?' asked the body-builder, his hair slick with gel.

'Well, it seems you're the ones fishing for clues now in the case of the lady of the lake.'

The newcomer roared with laughter, revealing a rack of suspiciously white teeth as he wagged a finger at Nyman, whose dry humour had clearly hit home. He cast a glance at the commissioner, who was glaring at him. 'Hector and I are on the same hockey team,' he explained, his spirits still running high.

Bergström sighed heavily and nodded without a word. Then he continued. 'So, Olofsson, you already know Hector Nyman. And this is detective Karla Hansen. Karla, this is detective Kristian Olofsson. When you interrupted us, I was about to explain to them that in light of their own commissioner's health, I was asked to take over the investigation.'

Karla shifted on the edge of her uncomfortable chair. 'I don't understand; what are you talking about?' she asked, somewhat taken aback.

Bergström knitted his brow. 'Møller hasn't told you about Johansson's accident?'

Karla shook her head.

'Kommissionär Johansson has broken his pelvis.'

'His pelvis?' Hector echoed, a dubious look spreading across his face, but with the hint of a smile.

'Yes … surfing,' Bergström explained.

Nyman burst out laughing.

Recently divorced, the head of the Halmstad police station was now racking up the strangest bucket-list experiences for a man just shy of retirement. It had been one thing after the other: skydiving, trekking in the jungle, tango lessons, you name it. Everyone was wondering when the old man's mid-life crisis would fizzle out and he would go back to golfing.

'So Møller has asked me to oversee the case,' Bergström continued. 'But far be it from me to take the nuts and bolts out of your hands, Hansen. The investigation is still yours.'

Karla felt as if a bucket of ice water had been dumped on her head. She had got the wrong end of the stick. Bergström wasn't out to steal her glory. And to add to her embarrassment, the commissioner had been quick to pick up on her petulance, though he didn't appear to be holding it against her.

Karla knew she had a tendency to shift into battle mode much too hastily, even before she sized up the enemy. Brandishing her weapons, baring her teeth, sometimes sinking them in … warding off anyone who deigned to see her as just another woman.

Her critics were of the opinion that she owed her progress through the ranks to her looks. 'Tits for brains', as some would cruelly put it. And it wasn't as if her most vocal critics were men. 'Too pretty for the job', one of her superiors – a woman herself – had even jibed. The forked tongues of the supposedly weaker sex were the worst of all.

Swearing she would keep her impulses under control next time, Karla drew herself up in her chair – as far as all one metre and seventy-six centimetres of her (five feet nine inches to you and me) would allow.

'Nyman, I want you to take over Johansson's responsibilities in Halmstad and report to me,' Bergström said. 'Karla, you're going to stay on this case and partner with Olofsson. Is that all right with you?'

Karla and Hector both agreed.

'Right, Hansen. Let's go and pay a visit to the lady of the lake now, shall we?' the commissioner concluded.

BERGSTRÖM PULLED OFF his sunglasses, folded them into their case and stepped out of the car, followed by Karla Hansen.

They had first driven detective Nyman back to the police station in Halmstad, and stayed a lot longer than they had expected. Bergström had introduced himself to the team and explained the provisional changes in the chain of command until Kommissionär Johansson's return: Hector Nyman was now in charge, and would then be reporting to Bergström; the Torvsjön murder case would be based in Falkenberg, but run by Karla Hansen. Bergström had then weighed in on some other ongoing cases, sorted out a few organisational matters and even managed to resolve some internal rivalry.

Johansson would be away for at least a month, Møller had explained. 'At least' was the last straw for Bergström. The prosecutor was counting on him to hold the fort, and God only knew how long it would take till the old man was back at his age-defying thrill-seeking. He had stomached the news about as well as a glass of sour rosé.

All this meant that, for the first time in twenty-two years, Bergström would not be spending his summer in Skärhamn. Normally, around mid-July, the whole family retreated to their quaint little house nestled between two enormous rock formations in a village on the west coast, two hours by car from Falkenberg, for a breath of fresh air. They had been fixing the place up for years. It was a little gem in a string of fishermen's cabins on the water, and even boasted its own tiny beach, where the commissioner's sons had learned to swim and fish for crabs.

And so, Bergström had left Halmstad in a red fog of frustration, with not a single ounce of sympathy for the daredevil colleague who had ruined his holiday.

To cap it all, they still hadn't had time to visit the crime scene. He and Hansen had gone straight to the morgue where Nicholas Nordin, the new medical examiner, had been waiting for them for some time.

During the hour and a half it took them to get there, Karla Hansen had outlined what few details she had about the case for now: essentially, that they had found a body, and the victim had not yet been identified. Her explanations had been continually interrupted by a good half a dozen calls from Hector Nyman, who was already completely swamped by the task of running the Halmstad police station.

Oh, joy! Bergström thought.

◆◆◆◆◆

Bergström dragged his feet reluctantly into the morgue, right behind a tireless Karla Hansen: despite having been on her feet since daybreak, somehow the mother of two was managing to power on through.

A long-limbed man with slicked-back blond hair and a permanent frown was there to greet them. He nodded a brief hello to Karla and shook Bergström's hand. 'Nicholas-Nordin-Medical-Examiner,' he ventured.

Bergström introduced himself just as curtly, before *Nicholas-Nordin-Medical-Examiner* led the way to the autopsy lab, where he proceeded to flick on a series of light switches. The fluorescent tubes hummed briefly, as if in protest, then bathed the vast room in stark light. Four tables, each two metres apart, stood at the centre of the white-tiled room. Only one was occupied.

Bergström and Hansen followed Nordin, whose orthopaedic soles squeaked every step of the way across the garish green floor.

The medical examiner rested his hands on the edge of the stain-less-steel table to give the commissioner and the detective a moment to dab a touch of camphorated cream around their nostrils.

The sight of the crude Y-shaped incision always made Bergström's stomach lurch. The body emptied of its substance, cut, dissected and approximately reassembled. This time, though, it wasn't the swollen edges of the cuts running from the shoulders to the pubis that elic-ited a grimace. Rather, it was the extent of the mutilation to which the young woman's body had been subjected. Under the harsh over-head lights, the pallor of her skin took on the same bilious shade of yellow as her hair.

'Female, twenty-eight, perhaps thirty years old. Never carried a child,' Nordin began without further ado. 'One metre sixty tall, fifty-four kilos – no, probably fifty-six, considering the flesh missing from the breasts, hips, buttocks and thighs.' He gestured to the different parts of the body with his index and middle fingers. *Like a weather reporter*, thought Karla. *Sunny in Stockholm and Gothenburg. Flesh carved out of the hips and thighs.*

'She's been dead seventy-two hours.'

'How was the flesh cut out?' Karla asked, slipping a couple of mints into her mouth to keep the pungent odour of death at bay.

'I'm coming to that,' Nordin calmly answered. 'Death was by strangulation. With some kind of soft ligature. Her assailant was standing in front of her, as evidenced by the width and the depth of the mark left by the ligature here on the throat.' He pointed to two areas on either side of the victim's throat where the purplish bruising was darker.

Bergström leaned over for a closer look. The sour, rancid stench of decomposition gases mingling with detergent made him step back again.

'No evidence of sexual violence. The chunks of flesh were cut out *post mortem* with a kitchen knife; sharp blade about fifteen centime-tres long. There are deep abrasions to the left ankle from something resembling heavy chain links.'

'Are those marks recent?' the commissioner asked.

'Yes.'

'How long before the time of death?'

'Seventy-two hours at most.'

'She was held captive,' Hansen mused as she gulped down another mint.

'Her stomach was practically empty,' the medical examiner continued. 'I only found traces of lemon, ginger and honey.'

'Experimenting herbal teas on her, was he?' Karla muttered.

'Any birthmarks, scars, tattoos, that kind of thing?' Bergström asked.

'All three. A birthmark on the back of the knee, a scar under the chin, a very old one, and a four-leaf clover tattooed at the base of the neck.'

Hansen made a note of the particulars on her mobile.

'Anything else?' the commissioner asked.

'Yes. I found a black feather inserted into each ear canal.'

Julianne Bell ties her wild tawny mane into a messy bun, slips on a shower cap and steps into the shower.

It's an early start to her day, but it won't be a long one: after she puts in an appearance on the BBC's morning show, she has nothing else on the agenda.

Nothing at all.

Hard to believe, isn't it?

A small miracle, in fact.

A full five hours, just for her. An ellipsis to savour. Or rather a parenthesis, to let her imagination run wild.

All she has on, really, is a lunch at noon with Adrian, a stone's throw from the studio. He'll have just landed after a three-week trip to Bulgaria – a week longer than planned – scouting out locations for his next feature film.

Julianne steps out of the shower, quickly towels herself dry and moves to the walk-in wardrobe, organised with military precision. She catches her reflection in the mirror wedged between two rows of shelves holding towering heels and sensible ballet flats. The woman looking back at her makes for a disappointing, dare she say tragic, reflection. Crow's feet, frown lines ... nature taking its toll on her face. And her breasts ... in ten years, they've gone from pert and sassy to sorry and saggy. The ravages of time...

Julianne turns her back on the mirror. No need to rub her nose in it any more than necessary; the TV make-up artists will soon smooth away the years. She slips on linen trousers, a Tussar silk blouse and a pair of stripy trainers, then selects a blue silk Paul Smith dress, a pair of nude heels and a Van Cleef necklace – a sublime ode to summer and the perfect outfit for this morning's broadcast.

She's packing the lot into a large canvas tote when she remembers she has to wear the McQueen tailleur for the interview. She clicks her tongue against the roof of her mouth in irritation. Reluctantly, she hangs the dress back up again and retrieves the suit from her wardrobe, grabs her purse, her phone and her keys and stuffs them all into the pocket of her bag. She pulls on a baseball cap that stands no chance of taming her wild curls, and leaves the house.

Staring down at her feet, she walks to her Tesla, parked a few doors down the street, thinking of nothing but her afternoon.

Oh, to wander aimlessly around London. Perhaps she'll go to a museum. Visit an art gallery. See a film. Or get her rocks off. In the cinema. What a thrill that would be, to come in a darkened cinema… She sighs loudly in a bid to quell the surge of desire warming her crotch like a lover's moist palm.

Wrong metaphor. Her mind wanders away from palm to … fingers. Fingers that…

Good God…

She sits behind the wheel, her mouth dry as she tosses her bag over to the passenger seat.

Suddenly, she freezes. Her body stiffens with guilt; she clenches her jaw.

She's left the house without kissing her girls goodbye.

She's daydreaming about a fuck in a public place, oh yes, but she's forgetting how to be a mother.

How significant this is. In eight years, she's sometimes had to kiss the twins over the phone, but she's never forgotten their morning rendezvous. She thinks of it like reconnecting the umbilical cord for a second or two, a vital link that keeps the joy alive and her feet on the ground.

She sighs, tiring of her straying already.

She has to go back. In seven minutes, tops, she'll be back behind the wheel.

Julianne dips her hand into her bag to feel for her house keys when a terrible burning sensation spreads across her midriff. A deep, searing pain. She starts to tremble like a dead leaf caught up in a squall. And then the agonising surge of pain splits her skull in two.

FREDA'S DELICATE, WHITE FINGERS touched the withered and stained hand of the older chambermaid in the middle of the bed as they both leaned forward to smooth out the sheet with practised assurance. They fluffed the two pillows and carefully placed them at the head of the four-poster bed.

'Did you know her, that Annie Chapman woman?' the older chambermaid asked.

The grey scourge that had battered and bruised her body had spared her voice, making her sound curiously young and sprightly.

Freda shook her head as she turned down the bedspread. She was tired of all the questions about the Whitechapel crimes. She didn't like to be reminded of where she had to live.

Crossing London to go to work made her so happy; she loved nothing more than leaving her filth-encrusted slum behind for the opulent luxury of Kensington. The aromas of his Lordship and her Ladyship's residence were as pleasing to her as a compliment from a good-looking young man. Her Ladyship's lemony perfume and the buttery, sugary smells rising from the kitchen helped to lighten the burden of her fourteen hours of daily toil.

Today, the cook had even held on to a slice of brioche for her. A bit dry after a night in the pantry, but it had melted in her mouth like altar bread in church. 'God Almighty!' she had exclaimed, her mouth full of the delicious treat. She was still salivating at the thought.

Freda had always had the feeling she was born in the wrong place.

It was like a shadow looming over her. The first time she had set eyes on her employer's luxurious home, she had felt as if she had finally found her true place in the world, her country, her city. Her lowly birth had deprived her of the comfort her beauty might otherwise have afforded her. But she would still meet a man, no matter what age, and he would help her climb the social ladder; she had no doubt about it. If God had made such a terrible mistake, he would surely give her the means to put it right.

'Freda?'

She turned around to see the chambermaid looking at her through age-clouded eyes. Freda had completely lost the thread of their conversation.

'Yes, sorry, I...'

'I was asking if you were afraid to walk home. You do know what state they found that Annie Chapman woman in, don't you? Her throat slit and gutted like a pig, her guts cut to pieces and draped around her shoulders like a scarf. Jesus, Mary and Joseph, I still can't believe what I'm saying. I overheard her Ladyship say to his Lordship this morning that every piece of Annie Chapman that made her a woman had been cut right out from inside her and stolen away by that monster. That's why some are saying he might be a doctor.'

'You don't have to be a doctor to slit someone's belly open.'

'Indeed, that's true,' the chambermaid conceded, stuffing dirty sheets into the laundry basket with a grimace.

'Give that here, I'll do it,' Freda suggested, taking the rest of the laundry out of her arms.

'You know what gives me the shivers? It's that in all this butchery, he took care to lift everything the wretched woman had in her pockets and place it all at her feet. That kind of man can only be a degenerate, can't he? But apparently there's been a man in a leather apron going around the area threatening prostitutes for months. You heard about that?'

Freda nodded.

'They say he walks around with a knife threatening to slit open every woman of ill repute. One witness who saw him swears the man had dark skin. Must be an immigrant: there's no self-respecting Englishman who'd be capable of such barbaric acts. Ah, if only we hadn't taken all these people in and piled them up in the East End! It's a blight on our country and our reputation—'

'I'm sure the police will catch him and throw him in prison,' Freda interjected, saying the first thing that came to mind to stop the old woman going on about it, while wondering whether she should remind her colleague she was, in fact, Swedish.

'The police! But the police don't give a damn about the working people, Freda.' The older woman drew nearer and whispered to Freda: 'Did you hear what the London police chief went and did?'

Freda shook her head and kept on dusting the chest of drawers.

'Sir Charles Warren. A friend of his Lordship's. In November last year, Sir Charles chased a bunch of homeless people out of Trafalgar Square as if they were rabid dogs, effing and blinding and beating them with sticks. Hundreds of men, women and children were hurt, and two of them were killed.'

The chambermaid got down on all fours to check nothing had slipped under the bed.

'Ah, I tell you, if a bunch of fancy ladies had been massacred in the heart of Kensington, believe me, the culprit would already be behind bars,' she said, standing back up with difficulty. 'But, you see, it's the common women who are persecuted. So, if you think they're going to going to waste any time on a murdered whore in an area even the Queen is ashamed of, you've got another think coming.'

Freda threw some soiled towels smeared with menstrual blood into the laundry basket. 'What if all this palaver turns out to be abortions that have gone wrong?' she ventured.

'Don't tell me you believe that!' her colleague sniggered.

No. To be honest, Freda didn't believe that. Only one thing was beyond any doubt: the women of Whitechapel were living with Death on their doorstep.

EMILY ROY PULLED OFF her trainers, leggings and running T-shirt the moment the door slammed behind her. She strode her way up the stairs and along the hallway to the bathroom alongside her bedroom with all the grace, stealth and agility of a lioness. Mechanically, she wiped a bead of sweat from her patched-up breast, where the nipple had been sliced off by a madman and later sewn roughly back into place, and stepped into the shower.

She emerged a full ten minutes later, a towel wrapped under her arms. She dressed in jeans and a tank top, both black, and tied her wet hair back into a ponytail. Then she fetched a suitcase from the storage room adjoining her office down the hallway, set it down on the bed and unzipped it to reveal a hungry, carnivorous set of jaws. She banished the image from her mind with a wave of her hand.

Even without getting caught up in elementary psychology, she knew all too well that the very idea of this journey had been eating away at her for weeks. She desperately needed to collect her thoughts over her son's grave, but it was the rest of the trip that worried her.

She quickly filled and closed the suitcase, gathered her last few things, and stepped out onto Flask Walk.

As she was climbing into the back of a black cab, lugging her suitcase behind her, her mobile vibrated inside her backpack.

'BIA Roy?' a smooth voice enquired.

Emily responded with a curt 'yes' and was promptly asked to hold the line.

BIA. Behavioural Investigative Advisor. Back in her native Canada, they called them 'profilers' these days, but here in the UK, the pompous term persisted tenaciously.

'Miss Roy…'

She immediately recognised the polished English pronunciation of the person on the other end of the line.

Inside one set of gaping jaws was another voracious beast just waiting to emerge.

14 Green Street, Mayfair, London, home of the Bell family
Friday, 17 July 2015, 10 am

LELAND HARTGROVE WASN'T IN UNIFORM. He hadn't come here as head of the Metropolitan Police; he was here to help his friends. Just a shoulder to cry on, really. No, not to cry on, because surely there was no reason for tears yet, was there?

Leland Hartgrove was here to reassure them.

He was taking advantage of his position to do them a favour. He didn't like doing that kind of thing, but this was a choice he had made in all good conscience.

Adrian Bell was perched on the edge of the beige leather sofa, his back straight, fingers intertwined, hands on his thighs; the polite posture of a guest looking for the right moment to stand up and leave. His brother-in-law, Raymond, in contrast, was pacing up and down the cavernous living room with the nervous impatience of a man who was waiting for a job interview. Every so often, he would pause for a moment, always at the very same spot, right in the middle of the bay window formed by three sashes looking onto Green Street.

Leland had 'a bad feeling in his gut', as his wife liked to say; a sense of anxiety that clung to the tongue before surging downwards to churn his stomach.

The doorbell rang. Adrian froze. Raymond stopped his frantic pacing. Hartgrove recognised the edge in the voice identifying its owner to the constable posted at the door.

'One of mine,' he explained. 'I'll be back in a minute.'

Emily Roy stood calmly in the entrance hall alongside the

policeman on duty, the straps of her backpack concealing those of her tank top. Her outfit revealed a slender, fit body that lent her an authoritative presence in spite of her short stature.

'Thank you for coming, Miss Roy…'

The profiler heartily shook the hand extended by her superior. Hartgrove cast his eyes down to the chequered floor tiles.

'I'm listening.'

Startled by the curt tone of his subordinate, London's commissioner of police blinked. He swallowed, then carried on.

'Julianne Bell, forty-three years of age, was expected at the BBC television studios this morning at six for an appearance on the morning show. She never arrived.'

'Her occupation?'

The profiler's question came as no surprise to Hartgrove. Emily was not the sort to watch TV. Nor to spend time in a darkened cinema.

'She's an actress. Quite a famous one.'

'Family background?'

'Married. Has been for ten or twelve years or so, to Adrian Bell. He's a film director. They have eight-year-old twin girls. My wife and I are their godparents.'

'When was she last seen?'

'Around eight last night. The nanny, Antonia, caught a glimpse of Julianne as she was going back to her room after putting the girls to bed. This morning, at around five o'clock, she heard the shower in Julianne's bathroom and then, about twenty minutes later, the sound of the front door closing. Julianne's car, a black Tesla with tinted windows, was parked in the street last night, but it isn't there any more. Again, according to the nanny.'

'Where was the husband?'

'Adrian got back this morning from a business trip to Bulgaria. He'd been away for a few weeks and landed at Heathrow at eighty-thirty to be greeted with a flurry of panicked texts from Raymond, Julianne's brother, a theatrical agent. Adrian called me straight away.

I rang Detective Chief Superintendent Pearce, who suggested I contact you as the two of you had—'

'Has anyone else been here since yesterday evening, either during the night or early this morning, besides Julianne, the nanny and the twins?'

Hartgrove didn't take offence at her abrupt manner and curtailed his explanations.

'No.'

'They have a live-in nanny?'

'Yes.'

'How long has she worked for the Bells?'

'Since the twins were born.'

'Is it usual for Julianne Bell to drive her own car around London?'

'Yes, according to Adrian.'

'Is this the first time she's gone missing?'

'Yes.'

'Any mental-health issues, depression, scandals, extra-marital affairs, fans stalking her?'

'No, no, nothing of the sort.'

'Any quarrels with the husband?'

'Not according to Adrian. They were supposed to have lunch together today.'

'What about disagreements with the brother?'

'Apparently not.'

'Where was Julianne's car parked?'

'A few doors down, in front of number 18.'

'Registration?'

'LA13 SUV.'

Emily turned on her heels and opened the door before the policeman on duty could do it for her.

Taken by surprise, Leland Hartgrove stood rooted to the spot for a second. 'But ... Miss Roy ... don't you even want to see a photo of Julianne?' he asked in a high-pitched voice.

'I have everything I need.'

'And don't you want to meet the family?'
'Later,' she barked, and disappeared into the street.

Friday, 17 July 2015

Julianne is woken by a shooting pain. A deep, searing sensation spreading up from her kidneys to the top of her head. She blinks, and then quickly surrenders to the heaviness of her eyelids and closes her eyes again.

She massages her temples; with every movement she can feel the bones of her skull beneath her fingers. Her stiff muscles slowly return to life, one after another, each complaining in turn.

When she finally opens her numb eyes, she realises a wrinkled sheet has been pulled over her face. She folds it back and sees four bare, yellow walls around her. She also notices a toilet bowl, a washbasin and a door with a glass panel crisscrossed with iron bars. She casts her eyes down to the sheet covering her body. Blue daisies dancing across a white background.

Fear crushes her chest.

Taking care not to uncover herself, Julianne swings her feet over the edge of the mattress to the floor and hears a metallic clinking. She freezes, pulls away the sheet with a trembling hand. A heavy chain is attached to her left ankle; it snakes around her feet and disappears beneath the mattress.

In spite of her weary body's protests, Julianne stands up and lifts one corner of the foam rectangle. The chain is fixed to an iron ring screwed to the floor. Her eyes scan the narrow room once more in panic.

My girls … my girls … my girls…

A terrible feeling of hopelessness, emptiness, rises within her, making her nauseous. Bitter tears fall and shock waves shoot through her chest, burning the walls of her throat. She cries out in a vain attempt to make them go away. All she wants is to be with her daughters, the three of them intertwined like the strands of a braid. To savour that eternal spring-like smell she notices every time she puts them to bed. That fleeting moment of peace and quiet she always wishes could last for ever.

Julianne latches onto that thought. To keep the fear at bay. To ward off the evil. The evil that lies beyond the chain digging in to her ankle.

EMILY ROY WAS STANDING motionless on the pavement with her mobile glued to her ear and her sights set on a gleaming Porsche Panamera.

Julianne Bell had showered at five in the morning before hurriedly leaving home twenty minutes later, no doubt with the intention of driving to the BBC television studios in her black Tesla with tinted windows, registration LA13 SUV. That was according to the nanny, who had apparently been home at the time.

And so, Emily began her investigation at the front door of the Bell family residence at 14 Green Street, aided by at least 400,000 CCTV cameras in the English capital.

'Here you go, Em, I've got them all,' the profiler heard on the other end of the line. 'I'm emailing you the videos,' her colleague at the Met continued.

'How many angles?'

'Two, since there were only two cams covering the area in question. One on the northwest corner of Green Street and Park Street and the other on the southeast corner of Green Street and North Audley Street.'

Emily spotted the first camera, but couldn't see the second, which was situated at the end of the road, 150 metres away.

'Can you tell me where the Tesla was parked this morning, in relation to the Porsche Panamera that's in front of number 18 now?'

'Hang on a sec.' The sound of fingers racing across the keyboard was loud enough to cover the background noise from the street.

'Here we are … say "cheese" for the camera, Miss Roy! So … yeah, the Porsche is in the very same spot where your misper's Tesla was parked. The two vehicles either side of the Porsche, the Maserati and the … what sort of car is that other one?'

'A McLaren,' Emily said.

'So the Maserati and the McLaren were already parked where they are now when the Tesla was there. Tell me something though, Em, are there any cars in that posh street that cost less than a hundred grand? Because, right now, I can't see a single one! That said, all that bling on wheels doesn't make me the slightest bit envious. I'd take my '98 vintage old banger any day over one of those. At least my kids can smear their greasy McDonald's fingers all over my ride to their hearts' content. Anyway, you should have got the email by now. Have a look, and I'll stay on the line.'

Emily checked her smartphone and opened the first video. She saw a woman wearing a baseball cap, carrying a large handbag, walk down the steps of 14 Green Street. The profiler recognised Julianne Bell from the photos hanging in the hallway of the family residence. Julianne swiftly got into the black Tesla parked in front of number 18. Two minutes later, the door on the driver's side was half-opened for about three seconds, then closed again, and the car drove off towards Park Street. The second recording offered a wider angle of the same scene, though it wasn't as clear and showed a view from behind, from much further away.

Emily glued her mobile back to her ear.

'Are you able to zoom in with the North Audley Street camera?' she asked her colleague.

'Nope. It's zoomed in as far as it'll go already. The quality's crap. The cam's too far away.'

'I'll call you back.'

Emily crouched down and looked underneath the Porsche. Her eyes scanned the tarmac and found a ziplock freezer bag lying in the road by the front right tyre. She held up the torch on her smartphone to shed light on the bag and its contents.

Emily rose to her feet and punched in a different number.

'Hello!' Detective Chief Superintendent Jack Pearce mumbled with his mouth full. 'I'm sorry I had to nix your holiday plans—'

'Meet me as soon as you can at 18 Green Street in Mayfair.'

'Em—'

But Emily had already hung up.

COMMISSIONER LELAND HARTGROVE STRODE into the living room, followed by Emily and DCS Jack Pearce.

Adrian and Raymond Bell were perched on an imposing sofa, cramping the style of an artfully arranged assortment of bright orange velvet cushions completed with a matching Hermès throw. In front of them was a white marble coffee table, on which a number of books on the art of cinema were carefully positioned. The mere presence of the two men set the harmony of the meticulously laid-out room off balance. Like a twig caught in a fancy hairdo, Pearce thought.

The man with dark hair and the charcoal suit stood and shook Emily and Jack firmly by the hand.

'I'm Raymond Bell, Julianne's brother.'

'DCS Pearce. My colleague, Emily Roy.'

'This is my brother-in-law, Adrian; Julianne's husband.'

A few days' stubble cast Adrian's tanned cheeks in shadow. He hadn't thought to take off his leather jacket and linen scarf. He nodded to them in greeting, but didn't get up.

'Do sit down, please,' Raymond invited, gesturing to the four armchairs set in pairs, one on either side of the low-slung coffee table.

Emily sat down next to Hartgrove, then turned to her hosts, a look of motherly compassion spreading across her face.

'Mr Bell—'

'Both of us answer to that name,' Julianne's husband interjected, politely yet unequivocally. 'Do call me Adrian, it will avoid any confusion.'

Jack Pearce glanced knowingly at Emily. It was only their first interview with the Bells, but he could tell she was already starting to whittle away at the cracks in the family.

'Adrian,' the profiler corrected herself, with a warmth to her voice that surprised Hartgrove. 'Who lives here, other than the four of you and the nanny?'

'No one.'

'Do you have any other staff?'

'A housekeeper. She's here Monday to Friday, from noon to four.'

Twenty hours of cleaning duties, Pearce noted. The 'housekeeper' must spend her time cleaning every nook and cranny with a tooth-brush. He wondered whether the twins were even allowed to set foot in this room; by all appearances they and their Barbie dolls never stepped outside the perimeter of their room – if kids these days still played with Barbie dolls.

'Can you tell me about the last contact you had with Julianne?' Emily continued, still in the voice bathed in empathy she reserved for interviews like this.

Adrian Bell glanced down at the Persian carpet, and then up to a trio of chrome vases lined up on the chimney mantle.

'Seven-thirty last night. We checked the exact time in my call history. The girls were getting into their pyjamas and Julianne had just spoken to Raymond. She was looking forward to being back in the studio at the BBC. To talk about the film. Nothing too…'

He shook his head and fell into silence. A heavy silence no one dared to interrupt. As if the slightest word would dig them in deeper.

'I mean … she seemed … fine,' he finally added.

'I had Julianne on the phone around seven,' added Raymond Bell, 'while the girls were in the bath. I reminded her what she had to wear for the interview the next morning.'

'And what was that?' Emily asked.

'A blue pin-striped linen tailleur. McQueen. Supplied by the label for her TV appearance.'

Emily frowned for a second. 'Do you think she would already have been wearing that particular outfit this morning when she left for the studio?'

'No. Julianne…' Raymond took a deep breath. 'Julianne always changes into her work outfit when she gets there. She wears something more comfortable to travel.'

'What did she sound like when you spoke last night?'

'Perfectly fine. She was in the bathroom with the girls. She was laughing. All three of them were laughing.'

His eyes swept across the orange patterns in the carpet.

'Did either of you share any messages with Julianne – texts or emails – following your conversations with her last night?'

They shook their heads in unison.

Emily shifted and leaned back in the armchair. She gestured to Pearce for him to take over.

'Would either of you be in a position, if you looked through her wardrobe, to say what she was probably wearing this morning?' the DCS asked.

Adrian gestured a no and turned towards his brother-in-law.

'Julianne has a sizeable wardrobe,' Raymond explained. 'But I'm quite certain she would have been wearing a pair of trousers with a T-shirt or a blouse and a baseball cap. And trainers.'

'Can you tell me her height, weight, clothing and shoe size, if you know them?'

'Five-one, seven stone three. Size six clothes and size three shoes,' Raymond recited by heart.

'Raymond, you're Julianne's agent. How's her career going?'

'Well. Very well, in fact.'

'Any problems, conflicts, disagreements with other actors? Directors? Producers? Or threats from fans?'

'Yes, but nothing sig—'

'I gather there must be nearly half a million CCTV cameras in London; surely some of them must have picked Julianne up, don't you think?' Adrian interjected, fixing the DCS with a steely stare.

'Of course,' Pearce responded impassively. 'But we lost all trace of the Tesla as soon as it hit the M25.'

Raymond Bell sighed heavily.

'Julianne hasn't just left,' Adrian insisted. 'She hasn't run away. She would never abandon the girls.' He shook his head at the thought of it, drawing his lips in a betrayal of his fear and pain.

Pearce only nodded. He couldn't tell the man he was right, that his wife hadn't left him, hadn't flown the coop, hadn't abandoned them. Although, they might soon be wishing that were the case.

Buck's Row, Whitechapel, London
Saturday, 29 September 1888, 5 pm

FREDA AND LIZ HURRIEDLY WRAPPED their leftover fish and chips in a sheet of newspaper and rushed out of Freda's room as fast as their skirts would allow.

The vile odour in the street hit them like a ton of bricks, seeping into their every pore, sickening them to their stomachs. They held their noses in vain, but the stench was so fetid it lingered on the tongue, coating the palate with a layer of filth.

'Good God! Oh, for the love of God!' Liz cried out as they hurried towards Hanbury Street. 'Must be the septic tank in your building overflowing again. Though who are we to be blaming the Lord when we know what a cesspool we live in!'

Freda slowed her pace to step around a scattering of oyster shells strewn across the slippery pavement. She was beginning to wonder whether they'd done the right thing leaving her room: the stench of excrement was now blending in with the acrid smell of blood from the slaughterhouse. The rain might well wash away some of Whitechapel's filth, but it would do nothing to curb the unholy stink it released from the cobblestones.

'Dear God! It reeks out here tonight. Have they been emptying the latrines, or something?'

'I reckon it must be the sewers overflowing.'

'At least it's not raining too hard now. It was pissing it down today.'

A group of young sailors crossed their path. Liz greeted them with a caress of her bosom.

'How about three for the price of two, boys? Can I tickle your fancy?'

'Ask us again when you've found your missing teeth, princess,' the swarthier one quipped.

Liz gave them the middle finger, waving it in front of her face until they turned away.

'You should come and sleep at my place, Liz,' said Freda. 'With all that's happening, it might be safer if—'

'And let myself be looked after by a girl young enough to be my daughter? Not on your nelly, Freda, love. Don't you fret, I've already done the housekeeping at 32 Flower and Dean Street today and got sixpence out of it. Doesn't matter if I get any work tonight or not.'

'Hey, Long Liz, how are you, my darling?'

A woman as thin as a rake in a brown straw hat stopped to bend Liz's ear for a moment. Freda smiled at her, and then tuned out of the conversation. She couldn't take her eyes off the woman's face. It was so deformed, it was barely human, peppered with monstrous red and purple blisters that puffed her lower lip down as far as her chin and a hole in her right cheek like a window into her mouth filled with yellowed, porous gums and a greyish tongue.

'God, did you catch a sight of that one?' Liz whispered after the wretched soul had gone on her way. 'Phossy jaw. She used to make matches at the Bryant and May factory around here. Once upon a time, she was nearly as pretty as you, love, I kid you not! And women like her are a penny a dozen, Freda. That's why I keep telling you, don't ever go to work in that factory! Those men are killers. If anyone should have died instead of Mary Ann Nichols – our Polly – and Annie Chapman, it's them, Freda: William Bryant and Francis May.'

Liz kept her eyes glued to the cobblestones caked in filth and rotting vegetables as she spoke. 'If only you'd seen them protesting this summer, those poor women, it would have turned your stomach. To see them all marching along, cripples of all ages they were, each and every one of them with their skin eaten away by the phosphorus in those damned matches. And as if it weren't enough to make them ill and disfigured, those bastards pay them in rotten bloody food too – when they actually pay them, that is!'

Liz led the way in to the Queen's Head on Commercial Street and leaned against the bar. 'William Bryant and Francis May are no better than the Whitechapel Ripper, I'm telling you. But the difference is, the killing they do is perfectly legal.'

A BARRAGE OF CLOUDS had suddenly blown in front of the sun like a massive steel door slamming right in summer's face. Heavy raindrops now poured from the leaden sky, pummelling the windscreen relentlessly.

The rear door of the Vauxhall was yanked open, and Commissioner Hartgrove ducked into the back seat, his pale blue shirt saturated. 'What's happening?' he asked, wiping his dripping face with the back of his sleeve, scratching his cufflink across his cheek in the process.

'Emily found something just before we met up with you at the Bells', sir,' Pearce explained as he pulled away from the kerb.

Emily adjusted her seat belt, making sure it nestled between her breasts and wouldn't rub against her scar. 'I found the trainers Julianne was wearing this morning, inside a ziplock freezer bag underneath a car, right where the Tesla had been parked.'

Hartgrove gestured impatiently for Emily to continue.

'Back in 2004 and 2005, six women were abducted over a twelve-month period. And every time, the shoes they'd been wearing were found inside a plastic freezer bag at the scene of the abduction.'

The commissioner pinched the ridge of his nose between his thumb and index finger.

'Their bodies were later found in London, in the Tower Hamlets area.'

Hartgrove looked up sharply. 'The Tower Hamlets murders? But wasn't the killer apprehended at the time?'

'Yes,' said Pearce, more curtly than he meant to. The DCS cleared his throat, trying to quell the sense of dread surging within him.

'At each of the abduction scenes,' Emily continued, 'the killer also left a pair of socks inside the victim's left shoe. This morning, I came across a pair of socks, folded and tucked inside Julianne Bell's left shoe in a similar fashion.'

Hartgrove clenched his teeth so hard, it made his jaw creak.

'Do you think we have a copycat at work?' he croaked.

'If we are dealing with a copycat, then he's very well informed,' Emily answered flatly.

'Don't breathe a word of this to my wife,' Hartgrove warned, nipping the conversation in the bud.

The rest of the drive to Hartgrove's home in Putney, southwest of the city, unfolded to the sound of Pearce's voice and the sheets of rain teeming down as the DCS made a series of calls to colleagues at the Met to organise the investigation into Julianne Bell's disappearance.

The sky cleared as they approached Gwendolen Avenue, where the Hartgroves owned one of the regal brick houses lining the well-heeled street.

A severe-looking woman in a scarlet suit and bare feet opened the door to them. 'Any news?' she asked, without a word of greeting.

The commissioner shook his head. She sighed, then flashed the obligatory courtesy smile at Emily and Pearce. 'I'm sorry,' she apologised. 'I'm Florence Hartgrove. Do come in, I've made tea and sandwiches. Leland, please,' she said, before disappearing into the kitchen.

The commissioner led his colleagues into a cosy country-style living room with a bay window looking out onto a long, narrow garden. Emily and Pearce sat down in two overstuffed white armchairs, leaving the sofa to their hosts.

'Here we are,' Florence Hartgrove announced, setting a tray of sandwiches down on the coffee table. She poured tea for everyone before sitting next to her husband, interlacing her fingers and placing her hands sagely on her knee. The commissioner placed a protective hand over his wife's.

'How can I help you?' she asked, brushing the sole of one bare foot against the edge of the rug.

'We need information about Julianne that only you might be able to give us,' Emily said, without further ado.

Florence made an *o* shape with her mouth, suspending the letter between her lips. Eventually, she nodded in agreement, never taking her eyes off Emily.

'Your husband told us the two of you are very close friends,' the profiler continued. 'Do you really know Julianne inside out, or is that just how your husband sees it?'

Emily didn't give a damn about the rules of decorum and nurtured little respect for hierarchy or any other social codes, though she knew when and when not to go along with them.

Pearce threw a worried glance at his superior. The commissioner seemed to have abdicated his seniority: he barely raised an eyebrow at Emily's straight-talking.

'That's right, we are very close,' Florence replied, without batting an eye. 'We met about ten years ago. She was going to play a City trader on the big screen and got in touch with HSBC, the bank I was working for at the time, because she wanted to talk to someone who could tell her about the job, and shadow them for a few days.'

'How well do the Bells get on?'

'Which ones?' Florence replied sardonically.

The commissioner glanced at his wife in surprise. Emily gave his wife a complicit smile.

'I suppose I should start with the husband,' Florence continued, with the same blatant sarcasm. 'Adrian and Julianne are a steadfast, loving couple. I'm not embellishing things here; they really do have a strong marriage. They're equally supportive of each other's careers, even though Julianne happens to be more successful than Adrian.'

'He's a film director,' the commissioner chipped in. 'He took his wife's surname when they married.'

'Julianne's career is the family's priority. Everything revolves around her professional commitments: film shoots, plays, that kind of thing. Give and take, that's what being a couple is all about, isn't it? And Adrian's perfectly happy with the situation. And when the parents are happy, so are the children.'

'Any extra-marital relationships, on either side?'

'Julianne doesn't have a lover, no. Not that I'm aware of, at any rate. I'd be very surprised if she did. She talks to me quite openly about the passes some of her colleagues make at her, which she generally finds amusing. As far as Adrian is concerned, I don't know, but I doubt it. What do you think?' she asked, turning to her husband.

'It would surprise me,' Hartgrove said. 'The man only has eyes for his wife. And, anyway, he's not really the type.' He brushed the edge of his hand over his knee repeatedly, as if trying to sweep away some tenacious crumbs.

Florence looked away from her husband to a row of Japanese cherry trees down at the bottom of the garden.

'As for the other couple – Julianne and her brother, I mean,' she continued, still staring out at the trees, 'that's another story altogether…'

'How long has he been her agent?' Emily nudged.

'Essentially since the beginning of her career. Julianne was still very young when she was discovered, practically out of the blue. Raymond set himself up as her agent straight away, negotiating her contracts and crafting her image. In the first few years, he was juggling his own career too – in marketing, if I recall correctly – then he gave it up to be Julianne's agent full time.'

'What kind of relationship do they have?'

'He's very demanding and doesn't give her much room to breathe. I find him quite controlling…'

'I think you're a bit biased, Florence, because you've been there for some of their blow-ups,' her husband intervened. 'Raymond's just very protective of his sister. They lost their parents just as Julianne was getting into showbiz. As the older sibling, Raymond felt a certain responsibility to take her under his wing. Not to mention the fact that agents so often end up as nannies, nursemaids, confidants, secretaries and punching bags for actors. I'd say it's inevitable for there to be a certain amount of friction involved.'

'What sort of man is he?'

'A control freak. But very professional,' Florence conceded.

'A loving brother?'

'No shadow of a doubt.'

'A loner?'

'Not at all! He's a party animal, and he's always bedding one girl after another, if not two at the same time.'

Hartgrove shot a glance of disapproval at his wife, which she blatantly ignored.

Pearce couldn't help but conceal a smile. After all, the whole situation was a little absurd. It was an eye-opener to see London's highest-ranking police official taken down a peg by his wife.

'How did Adrian feel about their relationship?' Emily asked.

'He tolerated it…' Florence paused, her words hanging in midair, then wetted her lips before continuing, '…but Adrian was well aware that without Raymond, Julianne's career would have been short-lived. Raymond turned the crush people had on Julianne into an epic love story.'

Sitting on the mattress, her legs stretched out in front of her, Julianne Bell stares at her feet.

Her pedicured feet.

Her polished toenails.

The chain links throttling her ankle.

The nail polish looks so out of place.

Julianne is chained up in a windowless room.

There is only the door with bars over the glass. And a cat flap. But just like the other opening, the cat flap is blocked on the outside. No openings here at all. No window, no natural light, no way to keep track of time.

Her heart races. Its loud, heavy beating is all she can hear. That and the music stuck inside her head: the duet from Bizet's Pearl Hunters. *No, it was* The Pearl Fishers.

Her throat feels like it is lined with thorns. Her mouth is bone dry and her tongue unbearably heavy. Beads of sweat moisten the back of her neck, her armpits and her upper lip. As if there were a direct connection between the water deserting the inside of her mouth and the moisture pearling on the outside of her body.

Suddenly, she hears a sound. Something slamming; then something rubbing against something else. The cat flap opens. A bottle falls to the ground, rolls back and forth, as if it is unsure which way to go, and finally settles against the door. A bottle with no label, its contents opaque.

Julianne runs her tongue across her parched lips. She hasn't drunk anything since she ... woke up here. How long has it been? She has no idea and, anyway, it doesn't matter: she is thirsty. The tap in the washba-sin isn't working. The water at the bottom of the toilet bowl is dark blue.

She recalls the rule of three. A human being cannot survive for three minutes without air, three days without water or three weeks without food.

Three days? Bullshit.

She crawls off the mattress, reaches forward and snatches the bottle. She unscrews the cap and brings her nose to its neck. A heady aroma of lemon and ginger wafts into her nostrils. What else? Honey ... Lemon. Ginger. Honey.

Julianne swallows a small mouthful. Just enough to wet her lips and quell the fire burning in her throat for a couple of seconds. The thirst that immediately follows is even more unbearable. Hastily, she screws the cap back on to avoid temptation, and rolls the bottle across to the other side of the room. Its drunken, zigzagging path ends at the foot of the toilet bowl.

Julianne lies down on the mattress and pulls the sheet over herself. She closes her eyes and listens; listens to her body. She'll know soon enough whether there was anything else in the drink.

SITTING IN THE CONFERENCE ROOM, a little more upright than usual, Pearce's officers were eager to find out why the Big Boss had scrambled this briefing.

Hartgrove took a seat in the front row and felt a dozen pairs of eyes burning into the back of his neck. Pearce remained standing in front of his audience with a remote control in each hand. He pressed a button on one, and a photo of Julianne Bell appeared on the big screen on the wall.

'The actress Julianne Bell went missing this morning,' the DCS began. 'She was last seen at 5.22 am getting into her car, a black Tesla with tinted windows, registration LA13 SUV, which was parked on Green Street in Mayfair, in front of number 18, a few doors down from her home at number 14. The CCTV cameras lost track of the Tesla on the M25, somewhere between junctions 9 and 10, about fifteen minutes later.'

Pearce pressed a button on the other remote control and the black-and-white security video Emily had watched earlier began playing. It showed a woman with long curly hair under a baseball cap, wearing trousers, a blouse and striped trainers and carrying a large shoulder bag, exiting number 14 Green Street.

'That's Julianne Bell leaving her home and getting into her car,' Jack Pearce said. 'She sits in the Tesla for one minute and forty-eight seconds before the driver's door opens a crack and closes again three seconds later. Then, as you can see, the car drives off.'

A second clip followed in quick succession, this time showing the whole scene filmed from the opposite angle, and from further away.

'The trainers Julianne Bell was wearing when she left home were found by BIA Roy, precisely where the Tesla had been parked.'

All eyes in the audience looked around for the profiler, but Emily wasn't at the emergency meeting. A heavy cloak of silence fell over the room.

Pearce pressed a button on the remote again. This time the recording showed Green Street in the dead of at night, at 3.18 am, according to the time displayed in the bottom right corner of the screen. The video showed an individual whose features were concealed by a hood and a cap, kneeling beside the Tesla by the driver's door handle. A minute or so later, the individual managed to open the door, climb into the car and pull the door closed.

Pearce rewound the video and played the first scene again. He froze the image at the precise moment the driver's door opened a crack before the car drove off.

'Julianne Bell's abductor managed to crack the vehicle's electronic code and get inside, where he waited for her for the next two hours. He must have immobilised her – possibly with a Taser, which would explain how it all happened so quickly – and then taken off her shoes, zipped them up in a freezer bag and, as you can see here, opened the door to throw the bag out of the car before driving off. All in less than two minutes.'

The DCS wore a tight-lipped expression. 'Between October 2004 and September 2005, six women – Jeanine Sanderson, Diana Lantar, Katie Atkins, Chloe Blomer, Sylvia George and Clara Sandro – were all abducted a few weeks apart. A ziplock freezer bag containing their shoes was found at the scene of the abduction in each case. Their bodies were later discovered in the Tower Hamlets area.'

A chorus of whispers and sighs rippled through the audience.

'The bodies were dumped in the Tower Hamlets area,' he continued in the same steady voice, 'with the breasts and buttocks removed and masses of flesh cut out of the hips and thighs. Richard Hemfield was arrested on the second of April 2006 for these crimes. He's currently serving his sentence in Broadmoor.'

Pearce paused for a second and swallowed, to stem the bitterness rising in his throat. The buzz in the room grew louder.

'There were two unique elements to Richard Hemfield's modus operandi. First of all, a pair of socks was tucked into each victim's left shoe—'

'When you say "a pair of socks", Guv, do you mean the socks didn't actually belong to the victim?' a thin man with a long face asked.

'Hold your horses. The second element was that all the victims had a black feather inserted into each ear.'

The DCS looked down briefly at the beige lino, which bore many a scar from shifting chairs.

'Emily found a pair of socks folded in a similar manner inside Julianne Bell's left shoe.'

'Fuck … What the hell, Pearce?' a craggy-faced woman said.

'I want you all to go over the details of the Hemfield case with a fine-toothed comb,' he continued. 'I want to know if those socks were ever mentioned anywhere and, if so, who would have had access to that information. Go through the transcripts from the trial, court reports, news articles, TV and radio coverage, Web pages, you name it, to see if we let anything slip at the time and someone was able to get hold of the information and leak it. We will also be following up on some leads Julianne Bell's brother gave us. Apparently, she's had run-ins with a producer and a scriptwriter, and there might be some crazy fans in the picture.'

'Given how high-profile she is, we'll soon have the media on our backs. What do you want us to say to them, Guv?' asked a man whose T-shirt read 'I love animals, especially on my plate'.

'Just ignore them for now. The Bell family will do the same. Not a word about the Tower Hamlets case. Same goes for the socks.'

'Sir…' The DCS's secretary was standing insistently in the doorway in a navy blue trouser suit.

'Later, Kate.'

'I'm sorry, sir, but Kommissionär Bergström is on the phone—'

'I'll call him back after the meeting,' Pearce snapped.

'I'm sorry to insist, sir, but it's urgent. Kommissionär Bergström has some info for you about the Tower Hamlets murders.'

ALEXIS CASTELLS PULLED the plastic lid off her cup and licked a bit of milky foam speckled with brown sugar.

From the top of Primrose Hill, the whole of London lay at her feet. She could see from Pentonville Prison, where both George Michael and Oscar Wilde had resided, all the way to the historic heart of Westminster and the skyscrapers that loomed over the City. Her eyes lingered on the Shard, that needle of glass towering proudly over the London skyline, as she swallowed a mouthful of her latte, or rather, her *lah-tay*, as the English pronounced it.

She had initially planned to treat herself to a fancy lunch on her own to celebrate her momentous morning, but had instead jumped into a black cab and headed to this little hillock by Regent's Park in the northwest of the city, settling for a fresh-air-and-coffee break instead.

That morning, she had walked into the offices of Panderman Editions, her heart swelling with all the passion of a Verdi opera as her heels clicked away to keep pace. The famous publishing house had approached her a few weeks earlier and asked her to write a book about the Ebner case. In French, of course; they would take care of the translation. They wanted to handle all the subsidiary rights themselves. They were already anticipating a twelve-part TV adaptation by the BBC. Alexis had been all smiles ever since, to the point that her sister teased she must have a coat hanger stuck in her mouth. And so, Alexis had signed the contract over a celebratory breakfast with coffee, croissants and *pains au chocolat*, as the publishers and her editor wanted to greet their 'new French author' in suitable style.

Alexis drew her legs in closer to the park bench to give a breathless mum pushing a double buggy room to squeeze past. The painter William Blake had once proclaimed that he had 'conversed with the Spiritual Sun' up on Primrose Hill, the quote being engraved on an etching at the top of the hill. That may well have been the case in the eighteenth century, but today the spot was swarming with tourists and Londoners alike and was anything but a spiritual experience. That was the price to pay for sitting on the rooftop of London, she supposed.

As she finished her coffee, she thought about what she would rustle up to eat when she got home. She was still feeling lazy, so she hailed another cab, which dropped her off in front of her Hampstead flat less than ten minutes later.

Alexis was greedily tucking into a Brie sandwich when a sliver of her mother's face flashed up on her iPad screen.

'Ah! Let me have a look at you! You never do anything but text me these days! What are you eating?'

'Cheese,' she mumbled between two bites of her sandwich.

'Oh, did you buy it at the little market stand by your flat? The woman who runs it comes from Brittany. Do you remember that lovely Fourme d'Ambert we had? Well, that's where I bought it. Let me see what you're wearing.'

Still chewing away, Alexis tilted her iPad.

'That's the blouse I bought you,' her mother noted, with a quiver of delight in her voice.

Alexis nodded with her mouth full.

'Oh, darling, that makes me so happy! I never thought you would actually wear it.'

'Why do you say that, Mum?'

'Because you never wear what I buy you any more!'

Alexis drank a mouthful of water and said nothing. Maybe that way she could avoid the whole charade about the angora cardigan. One ... two ... thr...

'Remember that white angora cardigan?' her mother prompted, with more than a hint of bitterness.

The *white* angora cardigan.

'It was too small for me, Mum. I told you I couldn't button it up!'

'Well, all right then, if you say so ... You do always come up with an excuse, though. So, how did it go?'

'Very well indeed.'

'Oh, for goodness' sake, Alexis, how would anyone ever know you get paid to tell stories! Tell your mother more, won't you? Who was there to greet you? What did you talk about? Did they offer you something to drink at least? Was your editor there?'

Alexis nodded as she savoured the last mouthful of her sandwich. 'There's only one problem, though,' she said. 'The book has to be ready in time for Christmas. This coming Christmas.'

'Oh my goodness, darling! That's no time at all! However will you manage? You'll be glued to your desk again from morning to night!'

Alexis burst out laughing. She was in a good mood today.

The doorbell rang. *Saved by the bell.* She made the most of the opportunity to hang up on her mother, who was in the process of peeling onions and carrots in a renewed bid to teach her daughter how to properly prepare a beef casserole.

She blew a series of kisses at the screen and went to open the door to Emily.

‒‒‒‒

Alexis had met Emily Roy some four years earlier, when she was researching material for a book about the Scottish serial killer Johnny Burnett. The Ebner case had then brought them closer. But the two women hadn't seen each other since February 2014, the day when Alexis had dropped a convalescent Emily off at home after the prison in Kumla.

Alexis had tried on several occasions to build on the connection they had made during the course of the investigation, leaving long messages on Emily's voicemail, to which the profiler had responded with short, to-the-point text messages. Alexis hadn't been able to resist the urge to tell Emily about the book she had been commissioned to write for Panderman. She had received a brief 'Congratulations' in return, which in Emily's language was the equivalent of a Formula One driver popping the cork off a bottle of Champagne and spraying the crowd with it.

⸎

Emily greeted Alexis with a nod and dropped her backpack on the floor. She ignored the sofa covered in pages of scribbles and sat herself down on a pouf. Alexis did the same, joining her friend at the round Moroccan coffee table.

'We're reopening the Tower Hamlets investigation.'

Emily's bombshell hit Alexis like a blow to the solar plexus, knocking the wind right out of her. She opened her mouth, gasping for air. Just a mouthful, as her lungs seemed to have given up on her and sealed themselves closed.

Emily took Alexis's hand in hers.

'I didn't want you to have to read about it in the papers.'

All the joy Alexis had savoured that day vanished without a trace, leaving only a nasty taste in her mouth. A taste of bile; a taste of the past.

HER LADYSHIP AND HER FRIENDS were sitting on a pair of luxuriously upholstered mahogany sofas across from one another, flanked by an assortment of armchairs: the ladies were enjoying afternoon tea.

'Do come over here, Freda,' her Ladyship implored, delicately setting her fine porcelain cup and saucer down on the table.

Freda entered the opulent room and timidly made her way across the enormous rug she had brushed clean that very morning.

On her way up the staircase leading to the great room, she had wondered why her Ladyship wanted to see her. Had she made a mistake … some terrible, clumsy mistake? Perhaps her Ladyship had found out that the cook sometimes saved a few kitchen scraps for her? No doubt, she was going to tell her that her wages would be docked accordingly … Or perhaps she would dismiss her right there on the spot?

'This is Freda, one of our chambermaids.'

The ladies fluttered their eyelids in silence.

Freda curtseyed shyly, and held her arms behind her back.

'You live in Whitechapel, don't you?'

'Yes, milady.'

'Freda is Swedish,' her Ladyship explained, surely to account for her employee's foreign accent. 'Marjory, another of the chambermaids', she clarified for the benefit of her guests, 'was telling me that Mary Ann Nichols was murdered on your street?'

'Indeed, milady.'

The four women promptly dropped their currant scones onto their plates and stared at Freda as if they had just seen a ghost.

'Oh, how in-cre-di-ble!' the plumpest of the ladies exclaimed, raising her hand to ask for more tea. 'My dear, that's simply unbelievable!'

'And weren't you a friend of Lucky Liz's too?'

The question was like a slap in the face, catching Freda off guard like the blows her father used to dole out. She gritted her teeth and swallowed her pain, sorrow and suffering. *Lucky Liz*, the newspapers were calling her. *Lucky Liz*. What was so damned lucky about what happened to her?

'Yes, milady.'

'And so, did you see Liz Stride yesterday, the thirtieth of September, the day she died?'

Freda tried to hold back her tears, swallowing to keep them at bay.

She lowered her eyes towards the carpet these ladies had trampled all over with their heels.

'The day before, milady.'

'How incredible! Truly incredible, yes, truly,' exclaimed the youngest of the ladies, whose make-up barely concealed the pubescent blemishes dotting her spoiled little face. 'At which establishment did you dine together?'

Freda stared at her, lost for words.

'Where ... did ... you ... dine ... together?' the lady articulated, thinking the young Swedish woman didn't understand.

'What does that matter?' her Ladyship chimed in. 'What we all want to know is whether she saw Liz Stride's body!'

Freda felt sick to her stomach. They were all the same. Vultures drawn to the smell of blood. Only some of them wore lacy dresses and silk stockings.

'Did you see Lucky Liz's body then, Freda?'

'No, milady,' she whispered with downcast eyes.

'I heard she wasn't as badly cut up as the second victim of the night,' a lady with a hooked nose said.

The plumper lady widened her eyes in wonder. 'What? Were there two victims yesterday?'

Her three friends nodded in unison.

'Really, how could you not have heard?' said the pimply-faced one indignantly. 'It's all the newspapers are talking about! "Bloodthirsty maniac slaughters two for the price of one!" they're saying.'

'My dear, I think it's time you spent less time dining and more time reading…'

'We were up visiting family in Manchester,' she cried in her own defence, her reddening cheeks betraying her embarrassment.

'So you can't have heard what's even more intriguing than the double murder,' the hook-nosed woman chuckled, barely containing her excitement.

She left them hanging for a second, revelling in the power of anticipation.

'The killer has written a letter to the press.'

The rotund lady helped herself to a slice of lemon cake, but kept her eyes glued on her friend.

'A letter written in red ink, since he couldn't use his victim's blood. It thickened too quickly, like glue, apparently. I'm not making that up, that's what the letter said! Such bare-faced arrogance, I tell you. He goes on about how he'll cut off the ears of his next victim and will never rest from, and I quote, "ripping whores"' – the words were whispered and met with gasps of horror around the room – 'until the day they put him in handcuffs.'

The sparkle in the lady's eyes reminded Freda of the way the prostitutes in front of the Ten Bells looked at the drunken men they solicited.

'And, wait for this, my dear, that's not all! He signed his letter, "Yours truly, Jack the Ripper".' Her whole body rippled in trepidation.

Mesmerised by what she was hearing, the rotund lady was chewing her cake with her mouth wide open.

'So, to go back to the double murder,' her Ladyship continued, 'the first one happened around one in the morning, and that was

Elizabeth, or Liz, Stride. She only had her throat slit, hence the newspapers nicknaming her 'Lucky Liz'. A Jewish travelling salesman came across the body as he was passing by, and it seems he may have interrupted the deadly deed. Then there was Catherine Eddies—'

'Eddowes,' the hook-nosed lady corrected, folding her idle, pale hands in her lap.

'Yes, sorry. Then there was Catherine Eddowes, who was killed just half an hour later. She was completely ripped apart.'

Silence. A pause intended to heighten the anticipation. To make a stronger impact. Clearly, the Ripper was providing endless entertainment, Freda reflected, her heart in her mouth.

'Catherine Eddowes's throat was slit all the way to the bone, and then she was disembowelled, like "a pig to the slaughter". Those are not my words, but the policeman's who discovered the body.'

A somewhat bovine lady opened her icing-sugar-coated lips wide and shook her head in disbelief, making her cheeks wobble like jelly.

'What's more, Jack the Ripper cut Catherine Eddowes's guts right out of her and draped some of them over her right shoulder and the rest across her left side.'

'Dear God,' the plump woman stammered through lips caked in crumbs, clearly transfixed.

'But at the same time, what can you do about it?' the hook-nosed woman chimed in. 'They say Whitechapel is a den of depravity. Just the other day the Archbishop was telling me there were more than sixty brothels and twelve hundred prostitutes in the area, can you imagine? Twelve hundred, that's the population of a whole village! And we all know, don't we, that it's only a short step from perversion to murder.'

'As long as they only kill each other, it doesn't bother me,' said the pimply young lady. 'It just rids the city of vermin,' she continued, eliciting a series of contented nods.

Her Ladyship turned to Freda, her lips now drawn into a wide smile.

'Thank you, Freda, that will be all.'

WITH HER HAND LUGGAGE slung across her shoulder, Alexis Castells strolled down the corridors in the terminal without a single glance at the signs. She'd walked this way dozens of times in the past eighteen months, to the extent that she was beginning to feel 'Swedified', as Stellan put it.

Eighteen months, that was how long she had been coming and going between her flat in London and Stellan's house in Falkenberg. Their relationship was everything that Alexis was not: simple and spontaneous. Eighteen months free of endless questions and existential dilemmas. Those rare moments of anxiety she had experienced were all her mother's doing: she lived in fear of her daughter falling for a man from the far *Norrrrrth* – she liked to emphasise the neverending *rrrrr* of his strong Nordic accent – and settling up there for good in what she considered a wilderness. Not wanting to be coloured by her mother's judgment, Alexis had developed a habit of quickly changing the topic or, when her patience was stretched too far, simply hanging up on her.

Alexis retrieved her suitcase from the carousel and pulled it behind her as she headed for the exit. The image that crossed her mind brought a wry smile to her lips. It was a poor choice of metaphor that couldn't have been more ironic, or hard to swallow. The thought that she was dragging her own baggage – her suitcase and her past – along with her.

Emily's words were still racing through her mind and getting under her skin. The news had hung in mid-air for a moment, a millisecond of incomprehension and doubt when reality only existed in words, as if it were gearing up to hit you where it hurts. Then she had felt an overwhelming sadness, with residual grief surging from within.

⤙⤛⤜

Stellan was waiting for her by the exit gate. He was gazing with intent at all the arriving passengers with the naïve pride and air of contentment of a youthful lover yet to be confronted by the hard truth of compromise.

But his smile faded as soon as he noticed Alexis.

Is it really so obvious? she thought as she gave him a quick peck on the lips.

'What's wrong?' he asked, his voice full of concern.

She hadn't said anything to him yet. Hadn't thought to, to be honest. She'd been so preoccupied with the unruly mob of questions, fears and what-ifs crowding her mind, she'd forgotten all about telling Stellan.

'Alexis?'

She opened her mouth, hesitated and closed it again. She had no idea where to begin.

He guided her to one of the tables dotted around a coffee stand by the arrivals gate. He pulled up a chair, the anxiety on his face clear to see. Alexis sat across from him.

'Emily came to see me at home a few hours ago, right before I left for Heathrow. They're reopening the Tower Hamlets case. Apparently, there's new evidence that's casting some doubt on Richard Hemfield's guilt.'

Alexis's throat was bone dry, and she had raced through the words, but she hadn't skipped a beat.

Stellan looked at her, but said nothing.

He's worried I'm going to collapse on the spot, Alexis thought. *I must look like a complete mess.*

Stellan Eklund had only been sharing his life with Alexis for the past eighteen months, but she had told him all about Richard Hemfield. Not because Stellan was an ex-cop, but because she knew she couldn't fully open up to him if she didn't lay bare the scars of her past.

Not only had Richard Hemfield abducted, held captive, murdered and mutilated six women, but nine years earlier he had also killed Alexis's partner. Richard Hemfield had destroyed Alexis's future as she had seen it back then and, ironically, played a decisive role in what her life would later become.

You can't put your foot down on the accelerator and keep your eyes glued to the rear-view mirror at the same time, she had been told. *Unless you have a death wish. The pain of the past is like quicksand: as soon as you set foot there, you just have to accept the situation, keep calm and avoid struggling, or you'll sink even faster. Your mind has to be in the right place before you can embrace the saving grace of resilience with open arms, and you have to get to a place of acceptance before you can even think of bouncing back.*

Resilience. What a stupid theory that was, especially if you were familiar with the Latin origins of the word and knew that it had once meant 'to recoil'. A far cry from bouncing back, wasn't it?

Stellan sighed before he replied. 'That doesn't change the fact that Hemfield was definitely guilty of killing Samuel.'

The very sound of his name was like a punch in her gut. Alexis swallowed. Stellan had never uttered Samuel's name before. To hear the name on his lips made Samuel's existence, and absence, suddenly feel real again. As if he were now standing between them.

––––•••••––––

An ominous silence hung over them all the way to Falkenberg, as they were both lost in their own thoughts and hiding behind their fears. All Alexis could think about was getting back down to work. Opening the travel bag she had brought along as hand luggage, pulling out all the Tower Hamlets case files and going through them with a fine-toothed comb. For the umpteenth time.

As the car turned onto the dirt track leading to Stellan's house, Alexis turned her gaze to the neighbouring house that had belonged to her friend Linnéa, who had died the previous year. A couple of pensioners had moved in a few months ago. The tragic death of the previous owner had not deterred them as they were all too used to living with ghosts at their age, and one more didn't scare them in the slightest.

Alexis suddenly remembered she hadn't told her parents she'd arrived. She dug into her bag to retrieve her mobile, switched off airplane mode, typed a quick SMS to set her mother's mind at rest and then saw she had a voice message. Probably her mother, going on again about her daughter's callous detachment.

But it was Emily's abrupt tone of voice she found bouncing off her ear. The profiler was on her way to Sweden tonight as well, and she would be landing soon.

EMILY ROY HAULED HER SUITCASE onto the luggage rack beside the pale wood chest of drawers. She pulled off her high-top trainers, socks and jeans, and draped them over the back of the armchair which sat by the desk. She then extracted three folders and a bottle of sparkling water from her backpack and carried them over to the bed.

Jack Pearce had called when she was at Alexis's flat the previous afternoon. She had been so absorbed in her friend's silence, it had taken her a while to register that her mobile was ringing. Being there, it had felt like they were wrapped in cotton wool, as if they were pulling the covers over their heads to drown out the sound of the alarm clock. Emily had left Alexis alone with her grief and returned the DCS's call once she was back on the street outside. Pearce had told her that a body bearing the same hallmarks as the Tower Hamlets victims had been found in Halmstad, on the west coast of Sweden, and had dispatched her there that same evening.

Emily drank a swig of water and opened the first file. She smoothed the duvet cover down and spread out four documents on the bed.

Richard Hemfield. Convicted of the abduction, confinement and murder of all six Tower Hamlets victims who disappeared between October 2004 and September 2005. Serving his sentence since 2006 in the maximum-security wing at Broadmoor psychiatric hospital in England.

That was the year Emily had left Canada, in August, to join the ranks of Scotland Yard. Richard Hemfield had been behind bars for four months and Pearce and his officers were still talking about the case. The mutilated bodies dumped in the middle of London; the socks carefully folded and placed inside each left shoe; the black feathers inserted into the victims' ear canals; the sixteen months of fear, frustration, anger and panic; and Hemfield's eventual capture.

The photograph of a pair of gold-coloured ballet flats sealed inside a freezer bag had been pinned to the evidence wall of the big incident room at the Yard for a long time. The shoes had been left on the front steps of the first victim's home. Emily vividly remembered the image. The bag abandoned on the wet, muddy steps. The weeds growing in between the gaps in the stone. The glittery shine of the imitation leather shoes through the plastic. Tiny, almost child-like.

The golden slippers had belonged to Jeanine Sanderson.

On Friday, 29 October 2004, at around eight pm, Jeanine left work at the Boots pharmacy on Oxford Street. She had stopped for a quick bite of sushi not far away, on Regent Street. She had then spent the evening with colleagues in a pub on Great Marlborough Street, until ten or eleven pm; none of the witnesses was sure of the exact time.

Nineteen days later, Jeanine was found in east London, in the Tower Hamlets area. She was naked, sitting on a mound of cigarette butts, with her back to a red-brick wall. She had been strangled. Her breasts sliced off. Flesh had also been carved out of her hips, buttocks and thighs.

Jeanine would have celebrated her twenty-fourth birthday four days later. She was petite, single and had shoulder-length blonde hair. She was unlike any of Hemfield's other victims. Diana Lantar, Katie Atkins, Chloe Blomer, Sylvia George, Clara Sandro. None of them looked like her.

Going through the reports, Emily realised none of the victims had anything in common, other than their gender and the colour of their skin. Some were brunettes; others were blondes. Chloe Blomer was a redhead. Some were slim; some had an athletic build; some were overweight. Some were single; others married with children. They lived and worked in different areas and were from varying social backgrounds. The age spread was also broad, from twenty-four to forty-two years old. That made it challenging for Emily to determine Hemfield's victimology. Usually it was fairly straightforward to pinpoint what the victims might have in common and establish a pattern. It was all a question of perspective: examine the facts with sufficient detachment and then look at them through the eyes of the killer.

Emily combed through the pile of documents to find the autopsy reports.

According to the medical examiner, the killer had kept his victims alive for eleven to nineteen days before strangling them. The periods of confinement varied: Jeanine, the first victim, had been held captive for nineteen days; Diana, the second, for thirteen; Katie, the third, for eighteen … None presented any evidence of sexual abuse, nor *ante mortem* ill-treatment. All the mutilation took place *post mortem*. What the hell did he do with them all that time?

The face of Julianne Bell drifted across Emily's mind. 'A red-haired Audrey Hepburn', was how her husband had described her with a smile full of pain.

What must Julianne be going through right now?

Emily closed her eyes.

Was Richard Hemfield really innocent? And, if so, why had the Tower Hamlets killer been out of action for almost ten years? Did Hemfield have an accomplice? And what if Julianne had been abducted by a copycat?

Perhaps science would be able to lend a helping hand: in 2004, the DNA collected from the inside of the socks found in Jeanine Sanderson's ballet flats had not been hers and had never been identified. With every successive victim, however, the DNA collected from the socks had belonged to the previous victim. If they were now dealing with the same killer, there was every chance the same pattern would manifest itself. The M.O. was much too specific for him to deviate from it entirely, despite how much time had elapsed since his last murder. Logically, they should find another woman's DNA on the white-trimmed socks inside Julianne Bell's shoes: either that of the victim just discovered in Sweden, or the unidentified DNA from the earlier crime.

Emily opened her eyes again and scanned through the photographs from all six crime scenes once more.

The flesh had been carved out from parts of the body that signified femininity: breasts, hips, thighs and buttocks. What was the symbolism of the shoes? And the socks? The black feathers? The initial investigation had not turned up any answers to these questions and Hemfield's arrest had been the end of the discussion.

Emily shook her head slowly. There were too many unknowns at this stage for her to be able to outline any sort of profile.

She picked out six photographs showing the respective victims naked on the autopsy table. No sooner had she lined them all up, than an image appeared in her mind. An image she hadn't been expecting. A surprising one.

Torvsjön, Halmstad
Saturday, 18 July 2015, 8.30 am

EMILY ROY HAD BEEN UP SINCE FIVE, by which time the sun was already easing its way into the mottled sky. She had jogged the four kilometres from the hotel to the beach at a brisk pace and then swum until her calves seized with cramp. She had then made it back in time for a shower and a quick breakfast before she set off for Halmstad.

Kommissionär Bergström had collected her from the Grand Hotel in Falkenberg half an hour earlier. Failing to pick up on her reluctance, he had greeted the profiler with a hug. Just a brief Scandinavian embrace, which Emily had resigned herself to going along with. 'It's been a year and a half,' he said, before he got to the point and started to explain about the case.

Just before they had driven off, he had handed her an envelope containing the crime-scene photographs. Emily had spent the whole journey scrutinising them from every angle.

'We're almost there, E-mily.' Bergström pronounced her name the Scandinavian way, lending it a hint of poetry with a melodic diphthong on the *e*.

He followed the instructions the satnav gave him and pulled over on the hard shoulder. The road was awash with greenery on both sides; a mix of dense low bushes and frail birch trees reaching for the sky with leafy fingers.

The commissioner unfolded a map over the bonnet of the car. 'This is where we are,' he pointed. 'The path there, just a few metres away from here, is the shortest way from the road to where the body was left. We found evidence that someone had been there, but there was no way we could lift any prints. Heavy rain on Wednesday that only let up on Thursday morning didn't help. Anyway, that could have been anybody, not necessarily the killer.'

Bergström ran his index finger along the yellow line that zigzagged its way across the map.

'The SKL and the police followed that path to get to the body. There are two spots where you can park, there and there.'

One was situated approximately 200 metres to the east, and the other fifty metres to the west. Emily turned around, taking in her surroundings.

'He could have parked behind the birch trees without being seen from the road,' Bergström answered the profiler's silent question. 'The vegetation's the same all around the lake. Shall we go, then?'

Emily nodded, glanced at her watch and followed the commissioner down the path. Even though it was the shortest way to the lake from the road, the path couldn't have been used very often. Some of the grass was knee-high. But it was a convenient route. Isolated and quiet, ideal for the killer's ends.

According to Bergström, the sky had been overcast on the night of Wednesday the fifteenth. For freedom of movement and to carry the body without great difficulty, the killer must have been wearing a head torch.

They weaved their way between the birch trees until they reached the shore of Torvsjön lake, through a silence disturbed only by the rustling of the long grass. Emily stopped in front of the dead tree trunk where the victim's body had been found, checked the time and took a few steps back. She opened the envelope Bergström had given her in the car and pulled out the set of photographs. She examined these one after the other, pausing from time to time to turn her gaze to the forlorn tree trunk and its gnarled roots.

The young woman had been seated facing west, parallel to the shoreline. Head slumped against her chest, hair dirty but brushed.

Back straight against the tree trunk, palms turned to the sky, legs extended. Other than the buttocks, the mutilation had been put on display with ostentatious pride. The body had been carefully arranged to be looked at and admired.

'What are your thoughts?' the commissioner asked, following twenty whole minutes of silence.

Emily didn't answer. She was wondering what Torvsjön represented for the killer. The English victims had also all been found near water, by St Katharine Docks, in the east end of the city. The similarities between the Tower Hamlets murders and this one did not end there. In addition to that symbolism, there was the positioning of the bodies, the death by strangulation, the very particular mutilation and the feathers in the ear canals – all elements that led her to believe these were two investigations rolled into one.

'Nothing, for now,' she eventually said.

Emily was unwilling to speculate until this victim had been identified and her shoes found. Before drawing any conclusions, she had to look at the big picture. Observe every aspect with her usual patience and minute attention to detail. Only then would she know if this fitted the pattern.

Dorset Street, Whitechapel, London
Friday, 9 November 1888, 10.45 am

FREDA TURNED UP THE COLLAR of her overcoat for protection from the frigid wind that was whipping the back of her neck, sending shivers down her spine. London could hold its own with the Swedish coast in that regard: the wind here could be just as bitter, clawing its way through hats, shawls, scarves and dresses.

It had been six weeks since Liz's death. The woman the newspapers were making out to be a bad sort had been a good friend to Freda, making her road to misery more bearable. Elizabeth Stride had been a rock for her in the East End; God, how she missed her.

Six weeks too since Jack the Ripper's last murder. But every single night was haunted by the fear he would strike again, especially for the poor unfortunates working the very Whitechapel alleys the murderer had made his hunting ground.

For the past two months, theories about the identity of the killer had abounded; even Queen Victoria had her opinion. Her Royal Highness had remarked that all the murders had been committed on weekends, so she had ordered that all sailors on leave be interrogated. But the police were floundering and none of their efforts brought them any closer to the Ripper. Not an inch.

So the devil took advantage of the fact to make further contact.

This time, he had confided in George Lusk, the chairman of the Whitechapel Vigilance Committee – one of the rare people who gave a damn about the area, whatever his motivation might turn out to be. The infamous Jack had sent him a letter 'from hell', taunting

'Catch me when you can Mischter Lusk'. The Ripper was having fun, thumbing his nose at the police, the Queen and the press. Scoffing at the investigators' powerlessness and the people's terror. The newspapers had printed the vile letter, and her Ladyship had been outraged to see how many of the words were misspelled. Jack the Ripper had described how he had fried and tasted one of the victim's kidneys. And, as if his words weren't enough in themselves, he had also sent a parcel: a small cardboard box wrapped in brown paper, in which he had deposited what was left of the organ. Likely Catherine Eddowes's, which he had cut out and made off with before abandoning the poor woman's body on the filthy cobbled ground in Mitre Square.

Six weeks since Liz's death…

Freda hastened her pace, shivering as she pushed open the door to 27 Dorset Street. The damp cold was rising through the soles of her shoes, penetrating her clothing like cold, clammy fingers clutching at the skin beneath her corset and petticoat.

Her Ladyship and his Lordship were away for a week with the children at his Lordship's sister's in Hampshire, so Freda had taken a day off. Along with some other girls from the Swedish church, she had planned to go to St Paul's to enjoy the Lord Mayor's Show. The new mayor of the city would be parading the streets in all his finery, and Freda was longing to see such a fancy horse and carriage. There was very little joy, music, singing or reason to celebrate in her life, nothing to lift the doom and gloom smothering her like an extra overcoat.

'Hello, Freda!' John McCarthy smoothed his moustache as he greeted her from behind his counter.

'Good day, Mister McCarthy.'

'What do you need, love?'

'Some sugar, matches, candles and Keating's powder, if you please.'

'How are things going for you, over there in Kensington Park Gardens?' the shopkeeper asked as he picked the various items off the shelves behind the counter.

'Well, Mister McCarthy, it's another world altogether…'

'Of course it is, love, a world with a lot less filth!'

'Sir…'

Freda and John McCarthy turned around. The deafening din in the street had blocked out the footsteps of Thomas Bowyer, the grocer's clerk. He stared at his boss with the haggard look of a young soldier suddenly confronted with the horrors of war.

'Sir, I went there, like you asked, to 13 Miller's Court, to pick up the twenty-nine…'

He paused and took off his hat. Used the back of his sleeve to wipe away the beads of sweat dripping into his eyes in spite of the cold.

'The twenty-nine shillings Mary Kelly owed you … I … She didn't answer the door, and it was locked … So, I went around to have a look through the window. She'd broken it, you see, during an argument with her husband, and…'

'Spit it out, Thomas! Did she give you the money or am I going to have to deal with this myself?' McCarthy was losing his patience.

'She's … she's dead, sir. She's … she's … Oh, almighty God…'

Bowyer clenched his jaw and his lower lip began to quiver.

'What are you talking about?'

McCarthy pulled on his overcoat, donned his hat and hurried out of the shop with Thomas in tow.

Freda followed in their footsteps. She knew Mary Kelly. Mary *Jeanette* Kelly, as she insisted on being called. Going on for twenty-five years old, pretty as a picture, but with a fiery temper and a voice as smooth as silk. Freda had seen her no end of times in front of the Ten Bells, getting her knickers in a twist with any woman foolish enough to solicit on her patch. What could have happened to the poor girl, she dreaded to think.

They turned into the narrow alley alongside the shop that led to Miller's Court. McCarthy walked past the front door of number 13 and made his way straight to one of the two ground-floor windows. Cautiously, he reached his hand through the broken window and pulled the threadbare curtain aside.

Freda stepped closer. The tiny courtyard was still shrouded in shadow despite the time of day and the room was dark. It took a few seconds for her eyes to adjust to the low light.

'God almighty!' she muttered, gawping at the body on the bed.

The dead woman's head was turned facing the window, as if the poor soul was desperate for someone to look at her one last time. Freda was unable to say whether it was really Mary Kelly lying there, on a bed dripping with blood, since her face was mangled beyond recognition. Shreds of her forehead and chin were all that was left, together with a few teeth poking through the bloody mess. A pool of blood had seeped through the mattress and spread like a dark rug beside it. By the window, on the bedside table, where others might have kept their Bible, the killer had abandoned a mass of bloody flesh.

'God almighty!' Freda said again, unable to tear her eyes away from the bed.

The woman was lying on her back with her legs apart and heels together like a baby. Her thighs looked like they had been gnawed to the bone, and her genitals had been reduced to a bloody pulp, as if a rabid dog had been set loose to devour her. Her left arm, closest to the window, was slashed deep and folded back across her body. Her hand rested on her gaping stomach, below the two dark red indentations where her breasts had once been.

ALIÉNOR LINDBERGH PUSHED OPEN the swing doors to the con-ference room. She glanced at the twelve hefty case files and sat down in a chair that was equidistant from the door and the evidence wall. She wanted to make sure she wasn't caught off guard, keep her facial muscles from sending any mixed signals. From here, she would have a clear view of the wall where the crime-scene photographs would be displayed.

Eleven-fifty: ten minutes before the others were due to arrive. She pulled a ziplock freezer bag from her backpack, took out four cheese and green pepper sandwiches and made a start on her lunch.

She checked her watch as she chewed the last mouthful of her *tunnbröd*. It was five past twelve and no one had turned up yet. She opened the file she had brought along and flicked through it again to busy her mind, so she could think about something other than her colleagues being late.

One of the doors suddenly swung open, and Karla Hansen and Kristian Olofsson walked into the room.

'*Hej*, Aliénor,' Karla greeted her.

'It's nearly ten past twelve. Kommissionär Bergström asked us to be here at noon. You're late.'

'Jeez, don't bite our heads off for being ten minutes late, will you?' Olofsson grumbled as he slumped into one of the chairs.

Aliénor opened her eyes wide as the detective's metaphor took shape in her mind. She shook her head to get rid of the image.

'Be nice to her, Olofsson,' Karla intervened.

'I know she's just a kid, but we shouldn't have to treat her with kid gloves!'

'Hello, everyone,' Kommissionär Bergström cut in, as he walked briskly into the room.

A woman with a long dark ponytail was right behind him.

'Emily Roy!' Olofsson roared, throwing his arms up in the air like a football fan celebrating a goal.

Aliénor looked the profiler up and down.

'It looks like Kristian here has made a head start on the intro-ductions,' Bergström said, placing a file on the table. 'Emily, this is detective Karla Hansen, from Halmstad, and this is Aliénor Lind-bergh, who's going to be helping us out for a few months. Emily is the profiler from Scotland Yard who worked on the Ebner case with us last year.'

Emily nodded to them, and Karla returned the gesture. Aliénor was transfixed. The commissioner continued: 'We've just returned from the crime scene and—'

'I'd like to see the video,' Emily cut in.

Karla Hansen wrinkled her brow in surprise. Beside her, Olofsson stifled a laugh, puffing out his cheeks and keeping his mouth tightly shut. He glanced at the commissioner, who cocked his head to the side with a half smile. It didn't appear to bother him in the slightest how Emily Roy was taking charge. He motioned to Karla for her to play the video.

The footage began with a close-up of a pair of rain boots, then went on to show a police officer in uniform walking down a path lined with birch trees. The screen flashed white for a second as the bright light bathing the Torvsjön shoreline flooded through the trees, contrasting with the dim glow in the underbrush. Next, the camera lingered on the unsteady tree trunk against which the naked young woman was propped up. The sound of throats clearing, then Karla's voice reproaching the officer for neglecting to bring along a plastic bag.

The camera zoomed in on the victim again. When it stopped, there was the sound of Karla swearing repeatedly. *Helvete*. It was an appropriate choice of word, as the scene was decidedly hellish. The camera panned around the body, then zoomed in on each of the wounds. The screen went black.

As soon as the video ended, Emily asked, 'Is that beach on Torvsjön lake very popular?'

'That's tautologous, you know, because *sjö* means "lake" in Swedish,' Aliénor butted in. 'So you should say "that beach on Torvsjön", not "on Torvsjön lake".'

Emily stared at Aliénor.

Kristian sat up straight, eager to see the two women face off.

'Aliénor's the one who figured out the connection between Tower Hamlets and our victim,' Bergström pointed out, in defence of his new recruit.

Emily nodded, keeping her eyes locked on Aliénor.

Aliénor experienced the uneasy feeling that the profiler was expecting her to say something. Apologise, perhaps? Or explain herself? 'I've been tracking all the serial murders across Europe for the last sixteen years,' she said. 'Including the Tower Hamlets killings. Strangulation, mutilation and body positioning were common factors between that case and this one, so the connection was obvious.'

Olofsson whistled. 'For sixteen years? Were you reading about serial killers when you were still in nappies, then?'

'I was born in 1987. Sixteen years ago, I was twelve. When you're twelve, you don't wear nappies any more.'

'You don't waste any time, do you? I bet you don't mess around when it comes to foreplay either!'

'Kristian!' Bergström roared.

'I don't think foreplay's something to mess around with,' Aliénor replied, without batting an eye.

Karla had to bite her lip.

'Well, anyway, what you're saying doesn't make sense,' Olofsson carried on, keen to change the subject. 'This guy suddenly stops killing, then one day, out of the blue, when he's out doing his shop-ping, he says to himself, "Hmmm, maybe I should start up again?"'

'There are four reasons why a serial killer would interrupt his crime spree,' Aliénor explained in the same calm, didactic tone. 'Either he's dead – which is not the case, here, as the killer has begun to kill again; or he's ill and out of action, so he can't do any harm; or he's in prison for other crimes he may have committed; or he's moved away and has started killing somewhere else.'

Her explanation met with a dumbfounded silence.

'So does that mean Jack Pearce locked up the wrong guy?' Olofsson asked. 'Hell, he can't be sleeping well these days.'

'Before we go on,' Bergström said, 'there's something else you should know about Hemfield.'

The commissioner was interrupted by his phone ringing. He accepted the call.

It was Nicholas Nordin, the medical examiner: he had just identi-fied the victim.

Julianne is woken by a wave of cramps barrelling through her stomach.

Through her half-closed eyes, she can make out the three permanently lit spotlights set into the middle of the ceiling. She knows no night or day any more. No telling how long she's been sleeping. A few minutes? Several hours?

She rolls onto her side and hugs her knees to her chest in an attempt to ease the pain shooting through her stomach. The clink of the chain around her ankle echoes her every movement.

Why am I tied down if there is no way for me to get out of this room?

This time, fear howls louder than pain. Her heart races; sending shockwaves all the way to her ears.

Are the girls managing to sleep? Are they eating properly? Are they OK?

Terrible images scroll across her retinas, parching her throat even more.

Maybe Adrian and Raymond haven't even told them what's happened yet?

Julianne had failed to arrive for her appearance at the BBC, so the news of her abduction would be all over the TV, radio and newspapers. All the other parents and children would have heard, too.

The twins mustn't find out. Adrian, please, don't send them to school…

A clicking sound reverberates off the yellow walls. The cat flap. Now she recognises the sound, it doesn't make her jump. The flap opens.

Another bottle rolls across the floor, the fourth since her arrival. Water, lemon, ginger and honey. Still nothing to eat.

Adrian and the girls at the fair, enjoying the bumper cars. She had never heard him laugh so much.

Nothing to eat. Only this turbid water to temper the pangs of hunger tying her stomach in knots.

Where am I? *she wonders.* What am I doing here? Who abducted me? Why? Was I kidnapped for a ransom?

She cries out. The sound drowns inside her throat. Like a candle being snuffed out. A stream of urine flows down her legs.

Is he going to rape me?

She squeezes her thighs together. Rape was a death you had to live with. A fate worse than death…

Is he going to kill me?

A ROUND OF APPLAUSE and cheering drew Jakob Paulsson from his sleep. He sat up on the sofa, ran his pasty tongue across his dry lips and listlessly took in his surroundings, as if he were anywhere but his own home. He reached over to the coffee table and took a swig from a bottle of Ramlösa sparkling water, then stretched back out on the sofa.

Remote control in hand, he was zapping through the channels, not taking anything in, when the doorbell rang. Three times.

'Jakob! Can you get that, please? My hands are covered in flour!'

Saga was home. He couldn't recall having seen her or even heard her come in, though.

The bell rang again.

'Jakob, are you awake?'

'I'm going!' he shouted out, his voice hoarse.

Jakob rose and crossed the hallway with languid steps, his eyes glued to the floor to avoid Maria's gaze, which peered at him from every one of the dozen or so photographs hanging on the wall.

He opened the door to find two women standing on the front steps.

'Jakob Paulsson?' asked the tallest.

Jakob's heart pounded, drowning out every other sound. He nodded. Swallowed hard.

'Good afternoon, my name is Karla Hansen, with the Halmstad police, and this is Emily Roy. Can we come in?'

'Jakob, who is it?' his sister called out.

A woman with a mass of blow-dried locks cascading over her tanned shoulders joined them on the doorstep. 'I'm Saga, Jakob's sister,' she introduced herself.

'It's the … police…' Jakob mumbled, stumbling over every word.

A wave of grief suddenly washed over Saga's face, her eyes heavy with the question she didn't dare ask.

Emily and Karla glanced briefly at each other.

'I'm sorry,' the detective said.

Paulsson's shoulders began shaking with barely perceptible tremors. Bowing his head and rubbing his eyes, he allowed the tears to flow.

Saga stroked his cheek and took his hands in hers. 'Come, Jakob, come…'

She guided him back inside and motioned for Karla and Emily to follow them. They sat in the living room.

Emily had asked Karla to conduct the conversation in Swedish; the profiler would only intervene when the time was right. To be precise, Emily hadn't suggested it; rather, she had dictated that approach. Karla hadn't even felt the need to bite her tongue, and had gone along with the whole idea surprisingly easily.

'How … What's happened to Maria?' Jakob Paulsson asked, wiping his eyes with the back of his hand.

Karla wrapped the news in cotton wool. 'She was found at Torvsjön.'

'Who found her?'

'Two teenage boys.'

'Torvsjön? Did she … drown?' he asked, his face contorted by pain.

'No. We found her on the lake's shore.'

There were no words to make it any easier. Might as well get it over with. Like ripping off a sticking plaster, as her eldest daughter put it.

'Maria was murdered. I'm truly sorry, Jakob.'

Jakob Paulsson's face melted into a bottomless pool of grief and held-back tears.

'I don't understand,' Saga said. 'When did she die? She ... disappeared over nine days ago...' Her voice was barely audible.

'She died on Monday.'

'But ... before ... she ... I don't understand...'

Karla felt a lump in her throat; Jakob and Saga's grief was starting to get to her too.

'We believe she must have been abducted during her night out in Halmstad, or on her way home.'

Saga froze. 'Was she ... raped?'

'No, she wasn't raped.'

Jakob gripped his knees in his hands.

'How did she die?'

'She was strangled,' Karla replied, biting her lower lip.

Jakob Paulsson flinched with another surge of anguish.

'C-can I see her?' he spluttered.

'She's in Gothenburg, for now.'

'Gothenburg?'

'At the forensic laboratory, Jakob,' his sister pointed out.

Jakob turned towards her, as if he'd only just noticed she was there.

Saga gave him a sad smile. 'Do you know who...' she asked, letting the end of her sentence hang in mid-air.

'Not yet, no.' Karla paused for a moment, sizing up Maria's partner. Emily seemed to read her mind and gave her a discreet nod.

Karla began: 'Would you be willing to answer some questions, Mr Paulsson, to help with our enquiries?'

He nodded, his face still stricken with pain.

'Very well ... thank you. How long had you known Maria?'

'Eight years ... well, nearly eight years.'

Suddenly he bent over and brought his hand to his mouth, overcome by nausea. He felt like he was going to throw up.

'I'm sorry. I think I'd better lie down,' he said, rising to his feet.

'Of course, Mr Paulsson.'

His sister also stood up.

'I'd rather be alone, Saga.' He turned his back on them and exited the living room.

His steps echoed down the hallway, and the three women heard him walk up the stairs.

Saga sat down again and stared at her fingers caked in flour. 'Maria and Jakob ... were together for eight years. Maria worked at a hair salon in the town centre. The night she disappeared, nine days ago, she was out celebrating one of her friend's birthdays at a bar in Halmstad, the ... I can't recall the name ... but I'm sure you have all that information already...'

'Did the three of you live here together?'

'Good God, no! I have my own apartment a five-minute walk away. I pop in from time to time to cook for Jakob and make sure...'

Saga began to scratch at some of the clumps of flour stuck to her wrist and under her fingernails.

Emily's hand brushed against Karla's as she leaned forward, placing her elbows on her thighs with a compassionate smile.

'Saga, would you mind if we continued the conversation in English? I'm working with the Swedish police, but I don't speak your language very well yet.'

Jakob's sister nodded in agreement.

'Saga, could you tell me what sort of person Maria, your sister-in-law, really was?'

Saga drew her lips together with a hint of scorn. She brushed her skirt with the back of her hand as she scoffed with barely concealed bitterness.

'Maria was a...' She closed her mouth and sighed.

'Maria was always cheating on him, and she never hid it. She slept with ... But Jakob always forgave her. That stupid brother of mine forgives too easily.' She cupped her face in her hands and shook her head, as if she were the one in the firing line.

'I could never understand...' she continued, tears choking her words. 'I could never understand why he stayed with her. And now, this…'

She clenched her jaw and closed her eyes. 'He'll never get over this.'

'Did she have a regular lover?'

'No. Well, I don't think so. She was more the type to screw a stranger she'd met in a bar in the back seat of a car.'

'Do you know whether she'd had any bad arguments with any of those men?'

'No, nothing at all. You know, she didn't do it to find a replacement for Jakob. I think it was all about the sex.'

Saga spat the word out with disgust and wiped the corner of her lips.

'Might your brother have come across a pair of shoes belonging to Maria anywhere near the house, on the day she disappeared?'

Saga's eyes widened in surprise.

'How did you know that? Yes, we did find her fancy heels by the letterbox, inside a plastic bag! What the hell was that all about? As if all Jakob and I had to do was pick up her mess! The bag had been left outside in the rain, but I just stuffed it in her wardrobe as it was, on top of a pile of clothes. So she'd get the message I wasn't there to wait on her hand and foot. And so she'd know I knew very well where she'd spent the night.'

KARLA WIPED THE KITCHEN TABLE and worktop clean and turned the dishwasher on.

The girls had insisted on having home-made pizza for dinner. So the three of them had slaved in the kitchen for hours and, after only a few brief squabbles, two exquisite pizzas had emerged from the oven. One 'with everything' and another with goat's cheese and mint, which, according to her youngest, looked more like a pie.

Dan Hansen walked into the kitchen laughing.

'What is it?' Karla asked her husband as he pulled a tub of ice cream out of the freezer.

'Listen to this: your older daughter wants you to know she's managed to get a job at the vet's for the rest of the summer; she's found her calling in life and can therefore no longer take her classes in Spanish because – she said all hoity-toity – "animals don't speak foreign languages anyway"! Then the little one, who'd been hanging on her every word, butted in and said, "But Pia, you're forgetting the most important thing: the vet is Tomas's dad and you really want to kiss Tomas, don't you? With tongues too, I heard you say to Alessia." At which point our eldest turned beet-red, pulled the bed covers over her head and ordered me out of the room!'

'And you're laughing about that? She's only eleven! When I was that age, I didn't even know you could use your tongue!'

'You didn't know you could use your tongue where?'

Karla shook her head, restraining a smile. 'Anyway, one thing's for sure,' she said. 'Pia's going to want a room of her own now. You'll have to give up your study, darling. Poor you,' she teased.

Dan bit into a strawberry and spooned vanilla ice cream into two bowls. He drizzled caramel sauce on the top and handed one of the bowls to his wife.

'Tell me, how did your book signings go? How many bras did you autograph this time?' Karla asked, savouring her dessert.

'There are plenty of men who read my books too, you know.'

'How many pairs of boxer shorts, then?'

Dan sprinkled some chocolate shavings over his ice cream. 'It would have been nice if you and the girls could have been there.'

'To help you autograph underwear?'

'Because you're missing out on some of the good stuff. There was one teenage boy who burst into tears when I was signing his book. He told me that Silylan, you know, the warrior in volume IV of *The Battle of Enguessan*, had given him the courage to stand up to the kids who were bullying him at school.'

Karla blew him a kiss. 'That's wonderful. I'm so happy for you, darling.'

'And how's your investigation going?'

'You really don't want to know.'

'Tell me about your new colleagues.'

Karla recalled the unwarranted anger that had taken hold of her before the meeting with Bergström. Now the very thought of it made her want to hide under the table.

'Well, it turns out Bergström isn't as full of himself as I thought he was. I thought he was going to sideline me completely, but he hasn't. He's very professional, he's a good listener and he's all about teamwork.'

Her husband gave her a quizzical look. 'And … you're OK with that?'

'Oh, come on! Of course I'm a team player! As long as everyone on the team is up to the task and you can delegate things down to them, it's all fine. And that's certainly the case here, thank goodness.

Even the detective who works for him, Kristian Olofsson – who must spend as much on hair gel as we do on food – seems quite competent, as long as he's given clear instructions. Oh, and the prosecutor's young trainee has just started with Bergström. Aliénor Lindbergh. She's fascinating. Actually, she's not that young, she just turned twenty-eight. She's finishing her doctorate in criminology. She's autistic. Asperger's.'

'I'm sure she's thrilled to be on the case. What about the English profiler?'

'She's Canadian. But she's working at Scotland Yard. She's a hell of a woman: trained at Quantico, now the leading profiler in the UK. An impressive strike rate. And quite the personality.'

'Pleasant?'

'No. Abrupt. Borderline rude and disagreeable. But with that brain of hers, I'll forgive all her sins.'

'Look at you, going all feminist on me!'

'Listen, I'm a big-breasted blonde in a man's world, so I have no choice but to be a feminist,' Karla said between two mouthfuls of ice cream.

'Ah…' said Dan, with a twinkle in his eye.

'What?'

'What do you mean, "What"? Have you seen yourself, licking your spoon and going on about your breasts?'

'I've been licking my spoon for some time.'

'And I've been licking mine too.'

'But you don't have a pair like I do, so it doesn't have quite the same effect.'

'So it seems…'

Dan set his bowl down and walked around to her side of the table. Karla cast a nervous glance down the hallway.

'They're asleep,' he reassured her, pushing the kitchen door closed.

He kissed her. Hot lips. Frozen tongues.

Karla slipped off her jeans. Dan pulled down her panties. Karla lifted herself up onto the table and wrapped her thighs around her husband. Dan pulled Karla's tank top over her head and freed her heavy breasts from her bra, pinching her hardening nipples between his fingers. She sighed, moaning as he licked them with his cool tongue.

'I see Detective Hansen had something particular in mind when she started talking about feminism,' Dan teased as he unbuttoned his trousers.

'Oh, I had plenty in mind…' she whispered, as she pulled him inside her.

EMILY LOOKED FROM ONE PHOTOGRAPH to another. From one body to another. She had moved the images from the magnetic board to the wall, knowing she'd need a larger canvas to give the victims space to tell her their stories, and to ensure she could piece everything together in the right sequence.

Standing in front of this patchwork of pinned-up lives and deaths, the profiler revisited all seven crime scenes, looking for similarities, trying to understand the logic of the landscape the serial killer – or killers, she couldn't be sure yet – had left behind. Here was a case that had been closed for nearly ten years, now reopened thanks to an abduction and a murder in two different countries. She had to go back to square one and painstakingly re-examine everything.

The double doors swung open with a long hiss, followed by a groaning of hinges.

Emily turned around. Aliénor was standing in the doorway as straight as a ruler, in spite of the hefty backpack weighing down her slender frame.

Bergström had filled her in about Aliénor after their midday meeting. Hansen and Olofsson had been forewarned, not that this had prevented Kristian from acting with his usual lack of manners, patience or tact.

Emily looked the new recruit up and down. Aliénor's posture had something of a ballet dancer's, her head held high, chin forward and shoulders lowered. She also seemed to have all the right qualities for a dancer: discipline, tenacity and determination.

'Do you have Asperger's too?' the young woman abruptly asked her.

Emily shook her head.

'But you act like an Aspie.'

Emily found this amusing.

'What are you working on?' Aliénor continued.

'The reports about the victims.'

'You're establishing the victimology.'

Emily nodded.

'Let me know how I can help,' Aliénor said, taking a seat. She swiftly took a notebook out of her backpack and slipped a pen from its leather loop. She clearly hadn't considered that Emily might prefer to work alone.

Emily didn't take umbrage.

'We have to do a fifteen-point analysis for each victim,' the profiler explained, clenching her fists on the table. 'For each of the eight victims – the six found in London, Julianne Bell and the Swedish one – I'll need a physical description, including the clothes she was wearing; a list of her current and previous occupations; where she lived, as well as any past addresses; her marital status and family background; her level of education; her reputation at work and in her social environment; whether she used drugs or alcohol; her hobbies; her friends and enemies; recent changes in lifestyle and, finally, whether she had a criminal record.'

Aliénor finished noting all of that down and stood up, pen still in hand. She jammed one of the swing doors open with a wedge of wood, then opened one of the triple-glazed windows. 'It smells in here,' she said, sitting down again.

They were working diligently to the sound of nothing but rustling papers, when they heard hurried footsteps in the corridor outside. A few seconds later, Alexis entered the conference room with a messenger bag slung across her shoulder.

Emily's call, the previous evening, had pushed her over the edge. A murder similar to the Tower Hamlets killings had been uncovered in Halmstad. The profiler had said she would be arriving in Falkenberg and had asked her to come by the police station around eight the next evening as there was something connected to the investigation she wanted to discuss.

Alexis had spent all that day in the company of ghosts. She had taken all the ten-year-old case files apart and scrutinised every last detail of the previous investigation. She had gone over the minutes of the trial again, as well as the witness statements and news articles, all the while struggling with memories still so bitter it made her grit her teeth.

Alexis now pulled a stack of files out of her bag and set them down on the table. Only then did she look Emily in the eye.

'This contains all the things you won't read about in the official records: my own investigation into the case.'

The waif-like young woman sitting a few chairs away from Emily was glaring at her questioningly. Alexis wondered for a second whether she had, perhaps, forgotten to take off her shower cap or had only applied mascara to one eye. Stellan had had to go to Stockholm for the day for an appointment, and she had been doing silly things since he left, such as dipping her morning toast into her orange juice or trying to reheat her coffee in the fridge rather than the microwave.

'Sorry, I should have introduced myself. I'm Alexis Castells.'

'Aliénor Lindbergh. Pleased to meet you,' the young woman said, with an exaggerated smile. 'You were the partner of Samuel Garel, the French police officer killed by Richard Hemfield at the time of his arrest.'

The words felt like a slap in the face. Alexis went as white as a sheet, and lowered her eyes.

Aliénor could see the shock on Alexis's face, but couldn't fathom why she had reacted that way. All she had done was state what they all knew – especially Alexis since she was the one most directly concerned. But she had seemed surprised, as if it was the first she had heard of the death of her erstwhile partner.

'Stellan's not back from Stockholm yet?' Emily suddenly asked.

Still reeling from the shock, Alexis turned to her friend.

'Er, he should be back in two, three hours' time, I think,' she mumbled.

Alexis turned her thoughts to Stellan. They'd been apart for almost two weeks but after meeting up again yesterday, they hadn't made love. If was as if Samuel had been lying in bed between them.

With the back of her hand, Alexis swept away a lock of hair that had slipped free of her loose ponytail.

'You said there was something you wanted to talk about, Emily?'

'There's one element you're not aware of in the investigation. Something that was kept under wraps. As you know, the shoes the victims were wearing at the time of their abduction were all found inside freezer bags near their homes. Inside each left shoe was a pair of socks. Anyway, in the case of the first Tower Hamlets murder, the DNA gathered from those socks was never identified, whereas in each of the subsequent ones it belonged to the previous victim.'

Alexis fumbled discreetly for something to hang onto. Her hands found a chair and she gripped it for support, fearing she might collapse otherwise.

'We're still waiting for the results of the DNA tests on the socks found in the abductions of Julianne Bell and Maria Paulsson, the victim in Halmstad. One other thing: a black feather was found in each of Maria Paulsson's ears, as it was in all of the murders attributed to Richard Hemfield.'

Alexis widened her eyes in surprise. It was hard for her to register the information. She didn't want to think about what that meant. She just couldn't.

She drew a deep breath to regain her composure. The air caught in her nose, so she opened her mouth wide to take in more, but it snagged on the thorns lining her throat.

'I spent all day going over my files,' she blurted after a few seconds. 'Richard Hemfield is definitely guilty, Emily. He's guilty.'

'You might not be in the best position to draw that kind of conclusion.'

'What?' Alexis spat.

'It is a capital mistake to theorise before one has data. Insensibly one begins to twist facts to suit theories, instead of theories to suit facts.'

'Arthur Conan Doyle,' Aliénor murmured. 'Sherlock Holmes in *A Scandal in Bohemia*.'

'Your mind is made up that Richard Hemfield is the guilty party,' Emily calmly continued.

'Bloody hell, though, Emily. He *is* guilty! He was convicted, wasn't he?'

'In light of these new aspects – in other words, the disappearance of Julianne Bell and the murder of Maria Paulsson – the only certainty now is that Hemfield killed Samuel. As for the rest, we have to keep on looking.'

Alexis threw daggers at Emily with her eyes. Then, picking up her files, she rushed out of the room.

FREDA TURNED AROUND and rested her forehead against the damp wall.

Twelve years. Twelve years she had devoted to serving her Ladyship.

Her beauty had not withered, and people still thought she was no more than in her early twenties. She had her high cheekbones to thank for saving her face from the ravages of age. Only her rough, yellowed hands betrayed the long years of hard work spent washing laundry in icy water.

Following the death of Freda's older colleague in the winter of 1889, her Ladyship had asked her to take over as head chambermaid. And so, Freda had left the East End for Kensington. God knows how happy she had been. Only a tiny room under the eaves, riddled with mice, but no real vermin. What was more, for the past three years she had been maid to her Ladyship's eldest daughter. The pesky girl was as ugly as her father, but Freda was such a talented hair stylist and make-up artist, she had managed to make her look presentable enough to find a husband. The young heiress had married the previous summer.

Freda pressed her cheek against the cool brickwork to relax her neck. Suddenly, she blinked and cried out in surprise. Without realising it, she had wandered back to the narrow alley leading to Miller's Court. She had not returned to that forlorn courtyard since the morning of 9 November 1888, when she had clapped eyes on the body of Mary Kelly, torn to shreds, slaughtered by Jack the Ripper.

She could still picture the woman's thighs and hips carved through to the bone, her guts spilled across the mattress and the bedside table. She shuddered at the memory of the woman's severed breast placed beneath her head like a cushion. The thought of it all sent shivers down her spine. Jack the Ripper had disappeared, it seemed, following the murder of Mary *Jeanette* Kelly. There had been much speculation in the press, as if his desertion of the Whitechapel streets was a matter for regret, but the Ripper had never surfaced again.

Freda grimaced: her spells of nausea had returned. What a nightmare ... what a nightmare this wretched life was. She had managed to steer clear of alcoholism and prostitution for twelve years, but nevertheless, her body had still betrayed her. As Liz had once told her, one wrong choice was enough to set you on the path to hell.

Still, she had waited. Oh, how patient she had been, waiting for the right man to fall into her lap. She had allowed herself to be courted, found love letters slipped under her door, enjoyed the occasional secret rendezvous full of chaste kisses and promises of eternal love. Eight long months it had taken for her amorous suitor to ask for her hand in marriage. And that was when she had made her fateful mistake. She had offered herself to him, taking all the precautions Liz had told her about, of course, but God had punished her nonetheless. How could she have been so foolish as to think she was above the divine laws? When the bastard found out she was pregnant, he had panicked, wanting nothing more to do with her.

Freda had kept on working as the error of her ways grew inside her belly, along with the sickening feeling that she had lost all power over her own body to something that was now firmly in control. No one had told her that pregnancy was such a terrible thing: the overwhelming fatigue, the pain in her breasts and the lead weight in her legs. Surviving her fourteen daily hours of domestic duty had proven a challenge. Until the day she had fainted in the living room out of sheer fatigue, sending a row of priceless vases crashing to the floor as she fell. Her Ladyship had dismissed her with the same wry smile as when she had quizzed Freda about Liz Stride's dead body. The witch had thrown her out, never knowing that Freda was carrying her own noble descendant in her belly.

Freda had then returned to Whitechapel, inhabited by a child that was taking everything she had; a monster devouring her from the inside out.

Freda suddenly felt as if she had a slug stuck to her buttock, by the back of her thigh. She pulled down her skirt and petticoat and turned to smile at the man who'd done his business. He'd paid her well and might even come back for more in the future, you never knew. An unpleasant wet-dog smell wafted under her nose as the man leaned in to pinch her dark nipple. Very soon, Freda thought, a tiny mouth would be latching on there like a leech to suck her dry.

'ALEXIS, DARLING, prepare the French dressing, would you?'

The sharp tone of her mother's voice brought Alexis to her senses. Since the previous evening, she had been unable to let go of what Emily had said. In her mind, she kept going over how matter-of-factly the profiler had expressed her doubts about Hemfield's guilt, trampling all over her grief and suffering with an indifference as surprising as it was hurtful. Alexis felt as if she had been left alone to defend a deserted fortress. Alone against Hemfield.

'You've forgotten the herbs and the pepper,' her mother nagged, putting the seasonings on the worktop for her to use.

Since her arrival two hours earlier, Mado Castells had been cracking the whip in the kitchen. Her husband, Norbert, Stellan and Bergström were pandering to her every need: laying the table, cutting the gingerbread, slicing the foie gras, keeping an eye on the cannelloni with goat's cheese browning in the oven, making room in the fridge for the *crema catalanas* … Everyone had a job to do.

Because Alexis's father had refused to travel with six kilos of ingredients, Mado had given her daughter a shopping list worthy of a Christmas dinner. All she had brought over from France – behind her husband's back, of course – were two whole foies gras.

Her parents' visit to Falkenberg had been planned for close to three months, and Alexis hadn't had the heart to put it off. That said, with the imminent reopening of the Tower Hamlets investigation, she knew she really didn't have the energy for this kind of meet-the-parents get together. Stellan was officially the first man she had gone out with since Samuel's death; her parents naturally knew nothing about her one-night stands, although her sister did. As a result, Papa and Maman Castells had been keen to meet Stellan as soon as they heard he was in the picture, to make sure he wouldn't cause further harm to their already damaged daughter. Alexis had dug her heels in at first, but had given up after six months.

To her great surprise, her mother had wanted to come to Sweden and 'observe him in his natural habitat', as she had put it. As if Herr Stellan Eklund was soon to become an extinct species.

'What else can I do now, Maman?' Alexis asked, as she put some dirty utensils in the dishwasher.

'The wine, please.'

'Perhaps I should leave that to Stellan?'

'Stellan is in charge of the foie gras and the bread. Open the Sauternes, darling,' her mother insisted, while sautéeing some fresh figs in a frying pan bubbling with butter.

Alexis smiled at Stellan and mimed a thank you. If his mother had taken over *her* kitchen, she would have lost her rag completely.

'We were thinking of taking you to visit Båstad,' Alexis said as she uncorked the first bottle. 'That's where Stellan used to spend his summers as a child.'

'Båstad, what an excellent idea,' Bergström remarked, in Spanish.

This is going to be an interesting meal, Alexis thought. What with her and Stellan speaking to each other in English, her and her parents speaking French, Stellan and Bergström conversing in Swedish and Bergström using his Spanish to communicate with her parents, it was like the Eurovision song contest.

'I'd rather do some shopping in Falkenberg this afternoon,' her mother said, taking off her apron.

'What for, Mado?' Alexis's father asked. 'You already came here with a case full to bursting!'

'I'd like to visit the town, pick up two or three little souvenirs for the little ones, get a sense of how people live here, you know.'

How people live here. *In wooden huts, mum, and they wash themselves in the mountain streams like true Vikings*, Alexis thought to herself, heavy on the irony.

'That won't be possible, Mado,' her husband replied, his face a mask.

'Ah, of course, it's Sunday, I'd forgotten.'

'No, that's not the problem. The shops here are only open one day a week. On Tuesdays, when new supplies come in.'

Mado's face froze. Her eyes nearly popped out of their sockets at the thought of the living hell her darling daughter might be moving to.

Norbert suddenly burst out laughing; Alexis translated for Stellan and Bergström, who hadn't understood enough to follow the conversation. The laughter spread contagiously through the room.

'I'll take you into town this afternoon, Maman, if you like,' Alexis intervened, stroking her mother's cheek.

'Thank you, darling,' Mado replied, casting a victorious glance at her husband. 'Well, everything seems to be ready. Shall we sit down to eat?'

✦✦✦✦✦

They savoured the first few mouthfuls of foie gras with slices of delicious homemade gingerbread in the silence such a gourmet experience commanded.

'It's such a pity, Stellan, that your father couldn't join us,' Mado remarked, helping herself to another slice. 'We had so been looking forward to meeting him.'

Like any self-respecting Swede, Eklund senior was a huge fan of the greens. Invited by one of his clients to play golf in Florida, he had jetted off to Palm Beach without a second thought.

'Yes, it is a pity. Next time…' Stellan said, captivated by the exquisite delights on his plate.

'So, Leonardo,' Mado began, getting up from the table to refill the bread basket.

'It's Lennart, Maman.'

If you say so, darling. I do believe Lennart is Leonardo in Spanish and Léonard in French, though.'

'Perhaps I should tell him to call you Magda, then?'

Scandinavian names didn't seem to roll off her mother's tongue very easily. With her French accent, she was having trouble pronouncing the final *n* on Stellan's name, making it sound more like a popular beer. Ah, being Swedish was such a perilous thing when the elder Castells were around.

'So, Leh-nart-euh, how are your wife and sons? Are the boys happy in Madrid?'

'Very much so … I don't think they'll ever come back! Lena was so sorry she couldn't be here, but as we had to cancel our summer holiday, she made the most of the opportunity to go down and visit them for a few days.'

'Why did you have to cancel your summer holiday?' Alexis's father asked, pouring another round of Sauternes. 'Is it really so busy at the police station? Isn't summer normally pretty calm in Sweden? Don't tell me there's another serial killer on the loose?' he laughed.

The joke was met with dead silence.

Bergström, Stellan and Alexis exchanged glances that spoke louder than words.

Mado came over and sat next to Alexis, concern written all over her face. She looked her daughter in the eye inquisitively. 'Alexis, what's going on?'

ALIÉNOR PULLED THE THERMOS flask from her backpack and set it down on the conference-room table.

Something vitally important had occurred on Saturday night. She hadn't realised it until she woke up this morning and meticulously went over every aspect of the day ahead in her mind. She had planned to arrive at 14 Arvidstorpsvägen by 6.50 am, secure her bike to the post at the foot of the front steps, enter the police station and walk through the open-plan area and down the narrow corridor, then push open the swing doors to the conference room Olofsson affectionately referred to as the 'conf', sit down in the chair that was precisely equidistant from the door and the evidence wall…

There.

It was at that point in her mental rehearsal that she had paused. She was planning to work in the 'conf'. Not in the tiny corner Bergström had allowed her to colonise in the open-plan area, but in the vast conference room.

It had taken her parents years to understand why they would find her sleeping with clenched fists inside the cubbyhole at the back of the kitchen, where her mother kept the dog baskets. They had actually forbidden her to go there whenever they had guests over. On those occasions, she would retreat to her room, spread her duvet out under the bed and jam sheets and blankets between the mattress and the box spring so they would hang down to the floor. She would spend the night inside this improvised tent, even though it was so much less comfortable than the baskets their maid used to clean incessantly. Dear old Gerda, who couldn't help sneezing at the very sight of a furry animal.

Aliénor was twelve years old when her history teacher, Owe Edwardson, helped her attain a certain normality and sense of belonging. He had called her parents into the school on Saint John's Eve to tell them he had found the Rosetta Stone that would help them speak their daughter's language. That was the first they had heard about autism and Asperger's syndrome.

Six full months of agonising appointments with ever more serious specialists had ensued, not to mention a series of unpleasant and anxiety-inducing tests that all pointed to the same conclusion.

From that moment on, the way her family regarded her changed. Gone were the rejection, exasperation, sadness, lack of understanding and anger, to be replaced by a sense of curiosity and a growing acceptance. Aliénor finally felt she could be herself. They still didn't quite understand her, but at least she was now respected and included as part of the family equation. Now she was only rarely accused of being unstable, moody, fussy or 'spoiled'. Aliénor had always found it strange to be called those kinds of names. True, she still lived with her parents, but at her mother's request. Her salary, though, was now sufficient to cover her basic needs: food, laundry, toiletries (toilet paper, toothbrush, toothpaste, soap, shampoo, deodorant and sanitary towels), books and a computer with Internet access. Clothing accounted for just a small part of her budget: she owned very few clothes and only replaced them when they wore out.

Aliénor poured some coffee into the plastic cup that came with her Thermos flask. She took a few small sips, then brought out the list Emily Roy had dictated to her at 2.20 am on Sunday morning, just before she had left the police station.

Aliénor had waited seven hours before calling Lennart Bergström to ask whether she could help by gathering all the information the profiler had requested about the Halmstad murder. The commissioner had replied that he'd be eternally grateful if she would.

Aliénor reread the list she had carefully written in her spiral notebook:

1. The preliminary investigation report (including evidence gathered by forensics, the circumstances in which the body was discovered and interviews with witnesses and neighbours).
2. The autopsy report (including toxicology tests, photographs of the wounds once they had been cleaned up and the medical examiner's remarks, not just his final assessment).
3. Aerial photographs of the area where the victim was found.
4. A scale map of the surrounding area with all houses, apartment buildings, schools, petrol stations, supermarkets and shops clearly marked.
5. Socioeconomic data about the place where the body was discovered (i.e. what segment of the population tended to live there or frequent the area).

Aliénor would go one step further, she decided: she would develop a theory and put it to Miss Roy. And Kommissionär Bergström.

She took a swig of coffee, inched her chair in until her body was jammed tight between the backrest and the edge of the table and got down to work.

JENNY SILENCED THE ALARM as quickly as she could, so as not to wake Mother up, since she had only returned home two hours ago and had gone straight to bed in her clothes that reeked of beer and the remnants of her night's work.

'Bloody alarm clock!' Freda groaned, wiping her sperm-encrusted thighs with the frill of her dress. She opened her eyes reluctantly and turned to Jenny, who was sitting on the edge of the bed, stifling a yawn as she took off her nightgown. Freda's eyes lingered on her daughter's curvy buttocks that formed a heart-shaped hollow in the straw mattress, and her round, shapely breasts. She rolled over towards her and suddenly punched her hard in her right breast. Jenny shrieked.

'Hussy!' Freda wailed. 'Aren't you ashamed to be parading your wares around like that in front of your own mother?'

Jenny leaped out of bed, pulled her clothes from the chair by the chimney and dressed in a hurry. She was all too familiar with the way these blow-ups ended.

It took Freda three tries to sit up in bed.

'Hey, what are you after, shoving your pert little tits and arse in my face like that that? Trying to remind me mine are all saggy now, are you? If it's anyone's fault I look like that, it's yours! It's all your fault! You're the one who made your father run a mile and stole away my youth! If it weren't for you, I'd still be in Kensington with a hat collection as big as Queen Mary's. Do you want to see what my tits look like now, do you? As soon as your teeth came in, you used to bite me until they bled, nasty little runt that you were! As if I enjoyed stuffing them inside your ungrateful mouth to feed you! I'd rather have fed you meat to fatten you up, believe me.'

Still under the influence of alcohol, Freda was alternating between English and Swedish.

'Come here,' she ordered.

Jenny was standing by the door, braiding her hair with trembling hands.

'Come here, I tell you!'

Jenny approached the bed. Her mother grabbed her skirt and yanked her closer. The young woman's knees cracked against the bed frame.

'I don't want to see you anywhere near my patch, do you understand? Any more and you'll be snatching the bread out of my mouth! Where is it you work, again?'

'Mayfair, mother.'

'Oh, of course. Mayfair. Mopping up rich people's filth. Just like me! That's exactly what I used to do before you came along.'

Freda's laughter was strained. Her breath reeked.

Jenny didn't dare look at her mother; it would only give her another reason to slap or spank her. She kept her head down and her eyes glued to the chapped fingers tugging at her skirt. Rough hands with fingernails yellowed by ill health. Mother was dying, Jenny was sure of it. Her stomach pains made her scream in agony and Jenny had seen the blood in her chamber pot. But she wasn't about to look after her. The witch would perish alone.

'You'll end up the same way as me, my girl. You'll get yourself knocked up by the boss's son and she'll throw you out, and you'll find yourself spreading your legs for all the working men in the East End.'

Even though she had been approached many a time by ladies in fancy perfumed clothes, Jenny had always refused to work in their brothels, with no regrets as to the fortune she might have earned.

She had grown up watching her mother spreading her legs for all those writing pigs, and she swore she would never stoop to such horrors. She knew all too well that the unsavoury characters who came to polish their whistle weren't exactly clean as a new penny. She would far rather be crushed by her domestic duties than a stranger's filthy, sweaty body.

'Are you going to give me an answer, or what?'

Her mother pinched her arm, only adding to the bruises she already had.

'Where did you put the money you brought home yesterday?'

'I wasn't given any money yesterday, Mother. I get my wages on Saturday night.'

'What day is it today?'

'Tuesday, Mother.'

Freda let go of her skirt. Jenny hurried back towards the door, pulled on her overcoat, put on her shoes and left the room.

The smog hung so thickly over the streets of Whitechapel, you could almost believe you still had your head under the bedcovers.

Jenny slipped her hand into her shopping bag and pulled out the wooden crucifix the pastor had given her on her eighteenth birthday. It came in very handy on public transport and on smoggy days for keeping pickpockets and wandering hands at bay.

Three weeks, she mused, as she jiggled the crucifix around her dress. Only three more weeks in this hellhole, having to listen to, smell, bear the burden of Mother and sleep at her side.

Three. Short. Weeks.

OLOFSSON GROANED AS HE STEPPED out of the car. Bergström had dispatched Hansen and him to the salon where Maria Paulsson had worked, to get a better picture than the less-than-flattering portrait the victim's sister-in-law had painted. The traffic had been hellish; Olofsson had spent most of the journey shouting and swearing at other drivers, much to his colleague's amusement.

The detective pointed with his chin to the front window of the hair salon. Karla looked up at the traditional but elegant neon sign: two black 'L's with rounded edges, separated by a dot.

'Can you smell it?' he asked Karla as they walked into the hairdressers'.

'Smell what?'

'The delicious aroma of dough, my dear.'

Karla nodded in agreement. It was the sort of place that would set you back at least 700 kroner – 70 euros! – for a blow dry. A hairdryer would be a much better investment, she thought.

'Good morning, madam – sir – and welcome to L.L. I'm Mia. Are we looking to make an appointment for madam, or sir? Or both of you, perhaps?' enquired a young woman standing behind a tempered-glass counter.

Olofsson's gaze took her in, from her dark hair and hazel eyes to her non-existent breasts, before lingering on her generous glossy-red lips.

Karla was admiring the French braid curling around the woman's neck like a pendant. If only she knew how to do her own girls' hair properly… All she could ever manage were ponytails, which invariably turned out less tidy than she hoped.

Karla self-consciously ran her fingers through her own hair. One finger snagged on a plastic hair clip that she must have forgotten to take out after her shower earlier. That meant she hadn't even brushed her hair.

'Good morning, Mia,' she replied, a little more snidely than she should have. 'We're the police; we have an appointment with Leah Lager.'

The young woman's smile widened, as if the word 'police' had gone over her head entirely.

You, sweetie, are going to have lipstick all over your teeth before you know it, Karla thought.

'Isn't it fabulous?' the receptionist said cheerily, stroking her braid. 'It only took Leah five minutes to do it. She's incredible, I just love her! She's expecting you. First door on the right,' she added, still so brimming with enthusiasm it was almost endearing.

Almost.

The two detectives made their way through the salon. Olofsson was ruminating on the brunette's disappointingly flat chest, though fortunately it was offset by that exquisite fleshy mouth of hers. He would have loved to have seen what she could do with it…

'Hungering after something, Olofsson?' Karla teased.

Kristian looked up at her with surprise. Not only could his colleague seemingly read his thoughts, but she was a far cry from those damned feminists who wore their wombs on their sleeves. She was easy on the eye and seemed easy to be with too. What a refreshing change from Bergström the killjoy.

'There's never a wrong time to have a little nibble,' he winked.

Karla chuckled as she knocked on the door.

It was opened by a woman in her forties, with strawberry blonde hair parted down the middle and just a judicious touch of make-up.

Leah Lager stretched out a manicured hand. Olofsson recognised the famous *H* stamped on the salon owner's bracelets. H for Hermès. H for Ha-sorry-way-too-expensive-for-you.

'Thank you for coming, detectives. Please sit down.'

The cramped office looked out onto a patio full of flowers. They sat on two dark wooden café chairs, which reminded Karla of those she had picked up at a Fjällbacka flea market some time ago for her kitchen. Only a touch more comfortable. *Well, much more comfortable, actually.*

'It's terrible, truly terrible, what's happened to Maria,' Leah Lager gushed, as she sat behind her desk. 'The whole team is in shock.'

Except for Mia, whose new hairstyle was enough to make her forget all about the violent death of her colleague. Karla made a mental note.

'I'm sorry, Leah,' the detective said, 'but I have to ask you some questions you probably already answered when Maria Paulsson went missing.'

'I understand. That's not a problem.'

'First of all, could you tell us how long you'd known Maria?'

'Oh, it must be almost ten years. I'd just got back from mat leave for my fourth, and was getting this place off the ground. My very first salon. Maria had just qualified as a colourist and was looking for a job. We've worked together ever since.'

'Can you tell me about the evening she disappeared?'

'We'd gone to Hemma, in Halmstad town centre, with three other girlfriends. We had a bite to eat, downed a few drinks and then, around eleven, those of us who weren't already married went ... "hunting".'

Leah drew air quotes around her last word. It wasn't exactly a bastion of the English language, but the hand gesture was everywhere these days, thanks to TV.

Karla had read all four friends' witness statements. So preoccupied were they by their 'hunt' (cue the air quotes), none of them had any idea what became of Maria.

'I left the bar at around eleven-thirty,' Leah went on. 'I'm up at five every morning, and I need a good four hours' sleep at least if I want to be able to function properly the next day.'

Karla was impressed. A business owner. Looking radiant in spite of burning the candle at both ends. In spite of her four kids. Four. Kids. The woman could create hairstyles to make any celebrity hairdresser green with envy. And she still found the time in her jam-packed day, to squeeze in a session of yoga, or Pilates, or meditation, as evidenced by the rolled-up mat leaning against the side of her desk. Karla had a vision of Leah at sunrise with an apron tied around her immaculate white trouser suit, kneading the dough for her home-made multigrain bread with one hand and flipping pancakes with the other. For goodness' sake. The kind of superwoman descended from Guanyin, the goddess of a thousand arms, who only existed in the books Karla's husband wrote. She was still scratching her head about one thing, though: when did the woman find the time to bathe in unicorn milk?

'And what did Maria do?' Olofsson asked, glaring impatiently at Karla, who was lost in her thoughts.

'Maria was an excellent colourist, as well as a great manager. She helped me develop the L.L brand; without her, I'd never have been able to open the eight salons in my little empire,' Leah laughed. 'She also helped me out with the kids from time to time when I had to travel, and my husband was away on business.'

She paused in a telling way.

'The more we know, Leah, the more likely we are to find the person who did this,' Olofsson assured her.

It was all Karla could do not to roll her eyes. In mercy. The detective's words were straight out of an episode of *CSI*. Still, they seemed to have the desired effect on the witness.

CSI: 1; Karla: 0.

'Maria wasn't suited to living with someone. She was very independent and enjoyed changing sexual partners. And she never hid it.'

'Did Jakob know about her affairs?'

'Yes, he knew, but he refused to leave her. Even though his sister, Saga, kept bending his ear about it.'

'Who told you that?'

'Maria.'

'How did she get on with her sister-in-law?'

'If it were me, I would have lost my rag years ago with that woman, but she didn't seem to bother Maria in the slightest. To give you an idea, one day Saga came over to their house unannounced, let herself in and caught them in the act. So, Maria strolled out of the bedroom stark naked and calmly asked her to wait outside until they were finished.'

'Do you know if Jakob was unfaithful too?'

'Not according to Maria. I even wonder whether he got a kick out of … Maria's extra-marital flings. You know what I mean … Maybe that's what kept the couple afloat?'

Olofsson shifted in his chair. He could never share his woman with another man. 'One saucer per cup' – that had always been his motto.

'Do you know if any of the wives or girlfriends of the men she slept with ever confronted her?' Karla asked. 'Or even some of the men themselves, if they took objection to being … used?'

'Not that I know of. But that kind of thing was bound to happen. Maria had a long string of conquests; much too long for her not to come across a bump in the road at some point.'

Here we go, the detective reflected, *we're back in cowboy land.*
CSI: 2; Karla: 0.

The body is hot, sweating, weighing heavy on top of Julianne. Powerful arms pin her down. She swallows her tears and the pain that wrenches her stomach. She turns her head to keep the man's hair from her mouth. So that she won't smell his foul breath in her face. He reeks of vinegar, urine, rancid butter. He…

She opens her eyes and sees the yellow wall. A lock of hair caught in her eyelashes. Julianne blinks. Swallows. She is lying on her stomach. The man is not there. She is alone. Alone with her nightmare. The thought of his greasy hair falling in her face. The acrid smell of his skin and his sex.

Julianne barely manages to turn her face away from the mattress before she throws up on the floor.

What's worse? My nightmare or … this hell on earth?

A shooting pain tears across her lower back. It takes her breath away. She pants, swallows and spits out strings of bile, then rests her forehead against the sheet.

My God, what's happening to me?

She waits for her breathing to steady, then shifts onto her left side as she groans to stem the pain. She grabs the sheet with the tips of her fingers and throws it off.

She is naked. She hadn't realised when she woke up, but she is naked. And there is a dressing on her right buttock. A large piece of gauze held in place with surgical tape.

Fear drowns out her pain and grabs her by the throat.

What … what has happened to me?

She reaches her arm down and feels for her buttock with her hand.

Have I…

She doesn't finish that thought. She begins to scratch at the sticky tape with the nail of her index finger. Frantically. As if it were a label. She unsticks the rest of the dressing and grits her teeth.

Oh, my…

Sheer horror ravages her face. Widens her eyes. Twists her mouth. She releases a primal scream. A howl that tears right through the stale air of the tiny room in which she is held captive.

Broadmoor Psychiatric Hospital
Crowthorne, Berkshire, England
Monday, 20 July 2015, 10 am

JACK PEARCE TOOK OFF his shoes and the jacket of his suit, surrendered his weapon, emptied the contents of his pockets and deposited the lot in a plastic tray, ready to go through the scanner. He stepped through the security gate, retrieved his things and flashed his Metropolitan Police badge together with the visitor's pass he had been given on arrival at the psychiatric hospital.

The guard asked him to wait for a few minutes and pointed to a row of four brown chairs screwed to the floor.

Pearce didn't have to wait for long. A heavy-set man with a crew cut and thick, black-framed glasses came to greet him, his steps punctuated by the clinking bunches of keys hanging from his belt. He adjusted his clip-on tie and extended a powerful hand towards his visitor.

'DCS Pearce?'

Pearce nodded, shaking the man's hand.

'Pat Viggel, Clinical Director. Follow me.'

They walked in silence down a corridor lined with a series of doors, one opposite the other. Each door had two separate openings: the first by the handle and the second, obscured by a small curtain, about sixty centimetres higher. Once they reached the end of the corridor, they made their way through an immense oval room filled with light-coloured wooden chairs, sofas and low tables, then set off down another corridor.

The director stopped in front of the second door on the right – the 'consulting room', according to the laminated sheet of A4 paper that was stuck to it at eye level.

He fumbled with two blue keys, inserted the second one into the lock and opened the door, as a shout rang out from the adjoining room. Something that ended with a 'go fuck yourself, arsehole'.

'They shouldn't be long,' the director said, raising his voice in an attempt to cover up the shouting from next door.

Pearce sat in a threadbare chair at a small square table.

The director remained standing by the door, which was still open, seemingly indifferent to the obscenities streaming in an endless loop from the person on the other side of the wall.

A few seconds later, escorted by two orderlies wearing latex gloves, each holding one of his shoulders and wrists, Richard Hemfield made an appearance. As soon as he recognised Pearce, his poorly trimmed moustache twitched as he smiled wryly.

If it were not for his grey hooded tracksuit, he would have had an air of the nineteenth century about him, thought Pearce – something of the Victorian artist, suddenly propelled into the present day. Perhaps the image had sprung to mind because Hemfield shared a first name, beard and moustache with Dadd, the famous schizophrenic Victorian artist who had been so obsessed by the supernatural and depictions of fairies, and who had also been incarcerated at Broadmoor.

Hemfield sat down across from the DCS, while both orderlies and the director stood right behind him, blocking the way to the door.

'Detective Chief Superintendent Jack Pearce,' Hemfield sneered, with the same wry smile.

His voice might have been higher-pitched, but he still spoke the way he had ten years earlier: slowly and didactically, with a curiously affable tone.

'I've put weight on. But you've gone greyer,' he said, with a twinkle in his eyes behind the small, round glasses. 'The pleasures of the flesh are few and far between here, Jack. Did you know that?

They make us paint. Sing. Bang a drum, or whatever else they can dream up. We even do drama. Therapy through art, you see. But genuine pleasures ... true pleasures ... I only have two of those left. Two and a half, in fact. The food, which for Broadmoor is more than half decent, and masturbation. Alas, my fantasies get poorer by the day. The medication is killing my libido. And it's making me fat. At least I'm not losing hair, from my head or anywhere else. I'm lucky about that.'

Pearce held him in his gaze.

'For the past ten years, I've been gathering my memories,' Hemfield continued. 'Putting them down on paper. My notebook is in my cell – sorry, my room,' he corrected, raising his hand in apology to the director. 'Shall we go and fetch it?'

Pearce shook his head.

'Anyway. I'm gathering my memories. To wrap my head around it all. Come to terms with why I'm here. And figure a way out.'

He paused, sweeping his gaze across the table. Then he clicked his tongue against the roof of his mouth and swallowed loudly.

'The medication ... heartburn. As I was saying ... Oh, yes. I'm gathering my memories. My criminal record has proven to be a great help, believe me.'

He raised his arms and let his hands fall slowly to his lap. His gestures were, as ever, carefully calibrated. Delivered in slow motion, just like his words.

'But what can a man do? I love women. I love to watch them go about their lives ... moving around, making love, pleasuring themselves ... I love women. I love their smell. I love to inhale their aroma, the scent of their skin and especially right behind their ear lobes ... between their thighs ... I love that particular aroma, don't you? They're all so wonderfully unique. I love picking out all the variations in those smells. Quite the bouquet of scents.'

He paused again, nodding with his chin.

'I started out by asking, you know ... When I was a child ... I must have been ten years old ... I asked a woman if I could smell her tights. When you think about it, tights are always in contact with a woman's most intimate parts.'

He twisted his lips into a pout.

'But she said no. So I got the message. I came to understand that some things are best left unsaid.'

Hemfield placed his hands down flat on the table, pointing long, dagger-like fingers at the DCS.

'You can help me, Jack. Samuel Garel. The French policeman I killed. His parents. They're dead. Of grief, no doubt. I would like to apologise to his partner … Alexis Castells … if she still goes by that name, that is. I've written letters to her. But I doubt the hospital authorities ever sent them. Ask her to come and see me, Jack.'

'I will not ask her to come and see you, Richard.'

'OK. OK.'

Hemfield sighed.

'All I did wrong was to be Jeanine Sanderson's neighbour and get myself caught masturbating inside her flat, with her tights in my hand. I also made the mistake of finding myself in the same place where Clara Sandro's body was found.'

Pearce clenched his jaw. Hemfield's eyes widened.

'So, you see! I've always known that was a mistake. But, after all these years, you begin to confuse reality and fantasy. It's not surprising. Look around us, Jack. Pat wears clip-on ties to avoid being strangled by his patients. Long sleeves and latex gloves to protect himself from being scratched and having urine, vomit and excrement thrown at him. It takes six of them to drag some patients back to their rooms. For ten years, I've been eating with plastic cutlery, every piece of which has to be inspected and accounted for after each meal. Do you know how much I'm costing the state? Three hundred thousand pounds a year. Three hundred thousand. Five times more than if I were incarcerated in a standard prison. Three hundred thousand pounds down the drain.'

Pearce adjusted his suit jacket. Hemfield pointed a finger at him.

'Look! I just saw it again. There, in your eyes.'

Hemfield smiled, his ruddy cheekbones grazing the frames of his glasses.

'You know I'm innocent. That's why you've come to visit me today. You want to see whether you still have that unsettling feeling, the feeling you were on the wrong track. You know it now, Jack. It wasn't me who killed those women.'

MERCEDES LANSLOW HURRIED towards the front door – or at any rate, as quickly as her arthritis would allow. Today, her left shoulder was screaming in pain. She had massaged it twice already that morning, before applying a patch her acupuncturist had given her. She had no idea what it contained – everything was written in Korean – but she wasn't bothered, as the pain eventually surrendered.

'Emily, darling!'

She shook the profiler's hand, overcoming the wave of protest surging through her elderly body; she resisted a grimace and brushed aside a stray strand of hair from her white chignon.

'Come, darling. I've made tea and scones.'

They walked through the narrow entryway littered with terracotta pots, gardening tools and bags of potting soil to a living room with bay windows overlooking a vegetable garden. The walls were covered with bookshelves from floor to ceiling.

'Charles is in his study. He's reading over a chapter of my next romance novel.'

Charles, Mercedes's husband was a well-known anthropologist and Emily's former professor. Late in the evening the previous Saturday, she had called him from her hotel room in Falkenberg requesting his assistance. He had suggested she come over once she was back in London.

'Did I tell you my publisher's been at it again? He wants me to reveal my identity. Really, darling, can you imagine me chatting idly about my adventures on a TV set? I'll let you pour, if you don't mind. Milk and sugar for me, please.'

'You *are* the one who writes the books, though,' Emily said, pouring the tea.

'Naturally. But it's so unusual for a woman of my age to write those sorts of things.'

A smile spread across the profiler's lips. 'Indeed.'

'Can you imagine me, all shrivelled like a walnut, my hands and legs crippled by arthritis, explaining to an interviewer who's absolutely mortified, perhaps even disgusted, by the thought of me doing such things? All that sagging flesh and friction. I'm seventy-nine years old and I still enjoy a good hard one, my dear. As far as I know, there's no best-before date when it comes to sex, is there?'

'Oh, I can just imagine!' Emily replied, amused at how odd those words sounded coming from her prim and proper English hostess.

'Are you there, darling?' called Mercedes's husband, his voice trailing off towards the end of his question.

'Yes, Charles, I'm with Emily.'

A short, rotund, bald man, wearing a crumpled linen suit and turquoise Moroccan leather slippers, tottered into the living room, clutching a stack of papers.

'Can you explain to me why you always give your protagonists' nether regions the Brazilian treatment?' he asked, with nary a glance at their guest.

Mercedes shrugged her right shoulder.

'I also found your metaphor about sand a bit too obvious. And you should give your breasts some thought. Some men prefer them small and perky, rather than heaving at the bra seams. That said, it's hot as hell, darling! Emily, do you want to come this way?'

Emily picked up her cup and followed her host upstairs.

The eminent professor's lair was as dusty as it was cluttered. Piles of books served as tables for old, dirty teacups; three waste-paper baskets overflowed with crumpled-up pages and a collection of bronze figurines were wedged up against a row of ancient spines crammed onto a mahogany bookshelf.

'Get rid of that beastly colonial brew and have a taste of my pine-nut mint tea,' he scoffed, sitting down at his desk. 'Just back from Sweden, then?'

'I flew in just before lunch,' Emily answered, pouring her dregs into a plant pot and helping herself to the professor's tea.

'So, what's this nightmare you have for me?'

The profiler pulled a series of photographs from her backpack: shots of all seven victims on the autopsy tables. She spread them out across the mess of handwritten notes and newspaper clippings littering the desk.

The anthropologist peered intently at the photographs. 'What made you think of cannibalism, Emily?' he asked, never taking his eyes off the photographs.

'What you told us all in Montreal, in one of your lectures: "thighs, buttocks, breasts: those are the best bits".'

'The Iroquois actually preferred the neck. But generally, yes, that's accurate. Thighs, buttocks and "maidens' nipples", as Saint Jerome might have put it, are the morsels of choice for cannibals. Do you remember Voltaire's *Candide*, when the good lady folk think of cutting off a buttock to enjoy a rare feast? Many Amerindian tribes preferred eating men though, particularly young ones, because the abundance of muscles made for tastier meat, it seems. Is your insane killer in the habit of fattening up his victims?'

'Apparently not. But he does seem to purge them clean: all their stomachs and intestines were empty when they died.'

'Perhaps to prevent them from defecating at the time of death. Also, to add flavour and make the meat more tender. Think of it like a marinade.'

Lanslow looked up at the profiler.

'I agree with your theory, Emily: I'd say you're dealing with a cannibal serial killer.'

He downed the rest of his tea, and refilled his cup.

'Do you know what the connoisseurs say? That once you've tasted human flesh, you can't live without it. The Marquis de Sade went on about that in *Juliette*, through the voice of Minski the giant. Have you read Sade's work?'

Emily shook her head.

'Ah, but you should! It's fascinating. Absolutely fascinating. What was I saying? Oh, yes ... that you can't live without the taste of human flesh once you've partaken. That was the case with the Beanes. They were an incestuous cannibal family living in a cave in Scotland towards the end of the sixteenth century. For over forty years, Sawney Beane and his swarm of children and grandchildren feasted exclusively on human flesh. According to the elegant expression of a forgotten French diplomat, the gastronomic qualities of our own meat is capable of "awakening the tired palates of the rich". There are even recipes out there, believe it or not. Heaven knows what it tastes like. No one seems to agree on that point; some compare it to pork, others to venison or even tuna. Personally, I've never been tempted, so I can't enlighten you with my own opinion.'

The elderly professor opened the drawers of his desk one after the other, closing each of them following a summary inspection.

'I thought I had some fig rolls in here. I'm not sure where I put them ... Anyway, cannibalism runs all the way through the history of Western civilisation,' he continued, still searching for the biscuits. '"I am the living bread that came down from heaven",' he cried out dramatically. '"Whoever eats this bread will live for ever. This bread is my flesh, which I will give for the life of the world", or again, "Jesus took bread, and when he had given thanks, he broke it and gave it to his disciples, saying, 'Take it; this is my body'". There are certain cannibalistic connotations to the Eucharist, don't you think?'

He finally pulled out a bag of crumbling coconut macaroons and popped one into his mouth.

'And there are even some nursery rhymes with cannibalistic allusions. Ever heard the French one, *Il était un petit navire*? Well, it tells the tale of a young shipmate who ends up being eaten by the crew of a boat whose provisions have run out. Charming, isn't it? Anyway, psychologists have come up with all kinds of far-fetched theories about cannibalism in a vain attempt to reinvent the Oedipus complex. But they're all a bunch of damned quacks, if you ask me.'

'What sort of theories?'

'I was thinking of one in which breastfeeding is seen as the origin of cannibalism. Hogswash.'

Emily's scar twinged, and she touched a hand fleetingly to her breast.

'In the end, cannibalism is the ultimate form of possession. The other becomes a part of you and is yours for ever. Chewing and swallowing become a sexual act, or "cannibalistic intercourse", according to some. Do you know what the infamous serial killer Andrei Chikatilo admitted at his trial?'

Charles licked some coconut crumbs from his fingers.

'That when he cut off the tongues of his victims and swallowed them, he had an orgasm.'

Falkenberg
Wednesday, 14 December 1921, 10 am

JENNY'S TRAIN HAD REACHED Falkenberg the previous day, in the middle of the afternoon. Though she had left England several days before, London lingered around her, breezing over her skin like the scent of a man after making love. Her head was spinning with the din of the city, its omnipresent wall of voices, as if the capital lived with its mouth wide open. Jenny still felt as if she were on the Tube, wedged up against other passengers in their threadbare coats, her nose assaulted by whiffs of vinegar and urine that would make you want to retch.

In the city, nothing ever seemed to stop. The crowds, the noise, the work; nothing could slow stubborn Lady London's pace – not the rain, nor the smog, nor even the night. In her wake trailed all the wretched souls who were desperate to make it, but died trying. Why were they there? They themselves didn't know. They had forgotten why they worked sixteen hours a day and had no idea what life elsewhere might be like.

Jenny had finally managed to rid herself of that terrible feeling of being no one, of being invisible. That feeling had held her in its grip, tighter and tighter every day, until she had felt she was being strangled. All it had taken was a good look inside her purse once she had paid for her room for ten nights. She had enough savings to live decently for a solid month, without any pressure, if she made the right choices.

The cold took her breath away when she stepped out of the hotel.

It was like walking naked into an ice box. The manager had given her the name of a shop further along the high street where she might find herself some warmer clothes and shoes.

Falkenberg's main shopping street was clean, with no rubbish littering the pavements and no stench in the air. Most of all, though, the street was empty and eerily silent. Jenny even retraced her steps a few times, unsure whether she was in the right place. When she finally came across the shop, she burst into uncontrollable laughter. She recalled all her painful treks to Selfridges on Oxford Street, where the purchase of a pair of gloves or a bottle of perfume for her Ladyship would take hours and consume so much energy. Things here seemed remarkably simple.

What a good idea it had been for her to save shilling after shilling for her departure! Everything was now unfolding so much better than she could have imagined. Who cared if her life was now sprinkled with snow and ice, and daylight withered away in the winter? Forgoing the occasional ray of London sunlight was a small price to pay to be able to hear the wind whistling through the trees.

Jenny walked into the shop and bought what she needed. As she was trying on the shoes and coat, the shopkeeper offered to look after the rest of her shopping while Jenny had a walk around the town. Jenny looked at her suspiciously at first, but then she apologised and told the woman the same story she had given to the hotel manager the day before, and that very morning at the coffee shop: her mother was born here in Falkenberg, but she, Jenny, had grown up abroad, and all this was so new to her. Some still remembered pretty Freda; others had known her grandfather, old Wallin, who had owned a farm on land the town had since acquired. Jenny had then continued bending the truth, saying that her sweet, dear Mamma had died and that, not having any close family in London, she had wanted to return to her roots. The story immediately drew people's sympathy, and her new town opened its arms wide.

It was a human-sized town that could welcome you without swallowing you whole.

EMILY OPENED HER LITTLE black box and observed its contents at length. That evening, there was so much to see.

The doorbell rang twenty minutes later, quickly followed by the jingling of keys in all three locks. Jack Pearce walked in, carrying two cardboard boxes he set down by the front door before joining Emily in the living room. He found her sitting naked on a wooden stool with her legs parted; a relaxed posture she hoped would seem neither sexual nor provocative, although … He noticed the little black box on the side table. She had closed it again, but was still enthralled.

⁕

Pearce wets his lips. Relishes the pleasure of anticipation before the pleasures of the flesh. The time when the balance of power shifts in their relationship, when the spectator becomes the actor. When Emily hands all the power over to him and he is the one who makes the rules, for the next few minutes or hours. An interlude to be savoured.

Emily gazes at him in complete surrender.

Jack moves towards her, kneeling between her thighs and burying his face in her chest. Emily. Her scent of leather and honey. Delicately he caresses her damaged nipple, then turns his attention to the other, licking it as he kneads her small soft breasts in his hands. He brushes his fingers across her stomach, down towards the edge of her moist lips, cupping her crotch before sliding his fingers deep inside her. Emily's thighs shudder. She throws her head back in pleasure. He can feel the goosebumps on her skin under his tongue.

'Stand up,' he whispers. 'Turn around.'

She stands unsteadily; leans against the wall with outstretched arms.

He unzips, releasing his erection, and embraces her from behind. She moans. He wants to penetrate her right there and then. Feel the orgasm rippling through her body.

His hungry lips roam over the warm skin from the nape of her neck to her shoulder. He parts her legs and slips his hand between her thighs again. His fingers graze against her sparse pubic hair, tracing a slow line all the way back to her buttocks. He grabs her by the hips, pulls her towards him and enters her. Emily lets out a deep, throaty moan.

'Deeper, deeper,' she whispers, implores.

He slips out from inside her, lifts her light body and takes her in his arms. She coils her legs around his waist, searching for his mouth. Her tongue is on fire with the taste of sea and sex.

He climbs the stairs with the woman he loves huddled in his arms; Emily melts into his exquisite embrace. He lays her down on the bed. With the utmost care. His gaze lingering on this image of her: her long hair cascading around her face like a radiant sun, her firm body and defined muscles, the inner strength belied by the delicate shape of her breasts and the sheer contrast with her dark mound, her eyes, the glimmer of love concealed beneath her thirst for pleasure.

He bends her knees and lifts them in towards her stomach. Then he enters her again in one swift movement. She comes. He feels her clench tight around him, her whole body rippling beneath his fingers. He keeps going. Deeper, she begs him. Deeper…

◆◆◆◆

Pearce woke to a humming sound. The water heater and the pipes. They always hummed when someone was in the shower.

Emily stepped into the hallway, wearing an oversize black T-shirt. 'Em!'

She stopped in the doorway. She had pulled her wet hair into a ponytail. There were still beads of water on her face.

'How are you feeling?'

'Like I've had my fill.'

'I'm talking about your trip being cancelled.'

Emily looked away to her left.

'When will you be leaving?'

'As soon as the investigation is wrapped up.'

Pearce knew the rest of the conversation would be slippery, like trying to catch a fish in your bare hands.

'I want to come with you, Emily.'

'It's not your child who died.'

'Of course it is. Your child has become mine.'

Emily didn't move a muscle.

'I want to go and see our child. I want to mourn by his grave, at your side. And I want to come with you to see your sister.'

She folded her arms across her chest. Confirming she was still present.

'I'm coming with you to Montreal.'

'I'll be working.'

He knew when to drop it.

'All the files you asked me for are in the boxes downstairs,' he said, with an air of resignation.

'Come down with me. I've found something.'

The DCS got out of bed, pulled on his boxer shorts and followed Emily downstairs.

The exquisite interlude was over.

Tuesday, 21 July 2015

Julianne had started to count every time she woke up, every time she felt the stiffness of the early morning in her body. Then she stopped. When she realised he had taken a slice out of her buttock. She hasn't counted the days since.

Now she wakes with a scream every day. Every time. And when she feels the dry film on her tongue, she knows the last bottle of lemony water was drugged. And she knows he has taken another slice.

He has already helped himself to several slices of her buttocks. And her thighs. She sees a new piece of gauze about ten centimetres by three taped to the top of her leg.

Suddenly, she is overcome by tears and feels as if a scrunched-up ball of paper has been stuffed into her mouth. The tears come and go like that now. Without warning. She moans, and then stops, and then she moans again. Not unlike when she was pregnant and couldn't help herself from throwing up.

This morning … No, not this morning … Julianne has no idea if it is actually morning … but earlier on, she felt like dying. In her mind, she had begged the girls to let her go. But they had said no. Her daughters had said no.

'Mummy, Mummy, Mummy…'

That was their answer: 'Mummy, Mummy, Mummy…'

'Mummy is busy, my darlings.'

She had laughed. She had laughed so much, the bitter taste of her saliva had come up through her nose.

She moves an arm that is starting to go to sleep. Turns her head. Every movement of her body rubs salt in her wounds. The pain is like a fire burning on her skin.

'Mummy, Mummy, Mummy…'

'Yes, darlings…'

'Mummy, Mummy, Mum-my!'

'Shhh … Mummy is busy, my darlings. Mummy is at the butcher's.'

JACK PEARCE PLACED TWO MUGS of steaming coffee on the conference-room table, then sat down next to Emily in front of the big screen on the wall.

Bergström, Olofsson and Hansen appeared on the screen a few seconds later, each with a mug in their hands too.

Pearce took a swig of his bitter coffee before starting the meeting.

'I've just had a call from the lab. The DNA found in the socks stuffed into Maria Paulsson's shoes is identical to that found in Jeanine Sanderson's, the first Tower Hamlets victim. The same DNA was also found in the socks we pulled out of Julianne Bell's shoes. This confirms that all three cases are connected. The Tower Hamlets murders, Maria Paulsson's murder and Julianne Bell's abduction were all committed by the same individual.'

'Looks like the killer's beginning a new cycle,' Karla Hansen said between sips of coffee.

'And we don't know whose DNA it is?' the commissioner asked.

'That is unfortunately the case,' Pearce replied, turning to hand over to Emily.

'We're dealing with a cannibal serial killer who is very particular about his meat.' Emily cut right to the chase, leaving her audience dumbfounded. 'The wounds inflicted on the victims are very telling. First, the type of flesh being cut: buttocks, thighs, breasts and hips. These are all choice morsels. And then the time spent with the victims prior to any wounds being inflicted, other than the marks from the chain holding them captive. The flesh was removed *post mortem*. And then we have the ingestion of a mix of honey, lemon and ginger, and perhaps other spices that had already worked their way through the stomach and were not detected during the autopsy. That's the killer's way of tenderising his meat.'

'A bit like those blends of herbs you use to season poultry,' Olofsson chimed in cheerfully. 'You know, you sprinkle the sachet full of spices over your chicken, then you put it in the oven for thirty—'

'Olofsson!' Bergström cut him short, annoyed.

'What? That's essentially what our killer's doing, isn't it?' The detective shrugged as he grabbed a cinnamon bun from the basket of breakfast pastries. He wolfed the *kanelbulle* down in two bites, then helped himself to another one.

'This cannibal killer is a meticulous and well-organised man, as his careful planning demonstrates,' the profiler continued. 'He's highly intelligent—'

'That's according to a study that was done in the States in the mid-nineties.' Aliénor's voice sounded muted and distant. She must have been sitting at the other end of the room, deliberately out of the webcam's line of sight.

'Aliénor Lindbergh,' Emily scrawled on a notepad for Pearce's benefit. He nodded. She had told him all about Bergström's latest recruit.

'Cannibal killers fall into the thirty to thirty-five per cent of apprehended serial killers with a level of intelligence superior to the norm,' Aliénor continued.

'Their intelligence is what allows them to conceal their sociopathic tendencies,' said Emily. 'That's how they hide their true colours from the people who know them, as well as the experts. On the outside, our man will seem pleasant, helpful and amenable. He's socially integrated and has a profession. His expertise and experience lead me to assume he's between the ages of forty and fifty, as I can't imagine he would have been under thirty at the time of the Tower Hamlets murders. His victims are respectively quite different in appearance, but they are all white, which suggests that he is Caucasian.'

Silence greeted the end of Emily's presentation. Kommissionär Bergström was the one to break it.

'Ten years ago, during the Tower Hamlets investigation, was the possibility of a cannibal killer ever considered?'

Pearce clenched his jaw.

'No, it wasn't,' he admitted, looking down at the conference-room table.

'Emily, do you think there might be two of them?' Karla intervened. 'Given the challenges of the distances involved.'

'There is nothing to suggest there is more than one killer. Right now, the Tower Hamlets crimes and Maria Paulsson's are identical in every way. The same type of blade was used to cut out the flesh, and the same concoction was administered during their confinement. Only Julianne Bell's body will provide us with a definitive answer to that question.'

Karla froze for a second before she nodded. Sometimes, the profiler's answers made her feel like she was standing under a hot-and-cold shower.

'So, if I understand correctly, Richard Hemfield is no longer part of the equation?' Olofsson asked, picking the specks of sugar one by one off a third *kanelbulle* and popping them into his mouth.

'We still have a number of questions to resolve before we can speculate as to Hemfield's innocence,' the DCS said. 'For instance, whether there may be an accomplice or a copycat. We should know more tomorrow.'

He and Emily exchanged a quick glance.

'So, for now he's staying in the slammer, then?' Olofsson asked.

'Yes, but perhaps not for as long as we thought,' said Emily.

Pearce shifted in his chair.

'There is something else,' Emily added. 'Serial killers develop a form of signature as they progress through their crimes. However, from the first Tower Hamlets victim onwards to our latest victim in Torvsjön, this signature has remained the same. And there is a definite reason for that: he's been a master of his craft from the very beginning. Which means that before killing Jeanine Sanderson, the killer must have practised. He must have fashioned, polished and perfected his style already. That means we should look into all the crimes committed in England or Sweden with the slightest hint of this signature – just for starters, from 1994 to 2004, a full ten years before the first Tower Hamlets murder. And by that, I mean bodies found with a feather in the ear, missing women whose shoes were found near their home or workplace, you get the picture.'

Bergström nodded, then said: 'Is it possible that the killer might have slept with his victims?'

'Good point, Kommissionär!' Olofsson said.

'No,' Emily said sharply. 'The consuming of flesh replaces the act of intercourse. Cannibalism in itself is a sexual act. An even more powerful act, in fact; it's a form of communion between the killer and his victims, as if they keep on living inside him.'

'You've misinterpreted some crucial pieces of information.' Aliénor's voice emerged faintly from the back of the room.

'Could you elaborate on that, please, Aliénor?' Pearce asked, his interest piqued.

'You know my name?'

'Yes. Emily has told me about you.'

'OK. First, there's the evidence that the victims were all easy prey, flighty women, party girls; next, the fact that the initial series of crimes occurred in the Tower Hamlets area; and lastly, that Maria Paulsson lived in Torslanda.'

'And?' Olofsson was growing impatient.

'Well, Jack the Ripper's victims were all prostitutes, women of low virtue. He committed his crimes in Whitechapel, which is adjacent to Tower Hamlets. Jack the Ripper's third victim, Elizabeth Gustafsdotter, better known as Elizabeth or Liz Stride, was born in Torslanda.'

'Ha!' the detective scoffed. 'So now you're trying to tell us Jack the Ripper was a cannibal, are you?'

'Yes, that's precisely what I was about to say, Detective Olofsson. In one of the letters attributed to him, titled "From Hell" and addressed on the fifteenth of October 1888 to George Lusk, the chairman of the Whitechapel Vigilance Committee, Jack the Ripper claimed he had fried and eaten half of one of his victims' kidneys. He sent the other half in the same envelope.'

JENNY WAS JOLTED AWAKE by one of those damned hairpins digging into her scalp. She had been working hard to replicate an Ingrid Bergman hairdo, rinsing her hair with white vinegar every time she washed it to make it shine and impress her customers, and every night she carefully rolled her wet locks around the curlers to achieve the desired effect. The result was picture perfect. She had first come across the actress some ten years earlier in *Swedenhielms*. God, how beautiful she was! No wonder Hollywood had come calling. And then, for their wedding anniversary, Finn had taken her to see George Cukor's *Gaslight*. What a darling her Finn was.

Mother had missed out on so many things. In her flight from her violent father, she had found herself in a foreign city equally violent and cruel. A city that had ultimately killed her. Jenny, on the other hand, had chosen to return to the place where she should have been born. And God just kept reminding her how much he approved of the choice she had made, even if it had meant leaving Mother behind. Every battle mourns its victims.

It had been so easy for her to find a decent, even a pleasant, job. First, she had worked at a grocer's in the town centre for two years. Jenny had then found a job with Falkenberg's largest bakery. The owner's daughter-in-law had just died of pneumonia and they had been desperate for someone to replace the unfortunate woman.

Five years later, she had married the widower – a handsome, strapping lad with a heart as big as his sexual appetite. At the beginning of their marriage, catering to his urges had been no mean feat. She had suffered endlessly from what the doctor, with a sly smile, called 'honeymoon cystitis'.

Several years had gone by before Jenny fell pregnant, which didn't seem to bother Finn and was certainly all right by her. She had never dared to say it out loud, and always banished the thought from her mind whenever it came up, but Jenny had no desire to have children. They were an obstacle to happiness, as she could see all around her. But God had decided otherwise. She'd fallen pregnant shortly after her thirty-first birthday. And then got two for the price of one.

Sigvard and Hilda's first years had been hell. The twins demanded her undivided attention, and Jenny struggled to satisfy her husband. Things had begun to improve as they neared their third birthday; she no longer had to fill their baby bottles with beer to be able to enjoy a few hours of peace; the two little monsters slept together and appeased each other, were out of nappies and ate absolutely anything she put on their plates. She was far from rejoicing in a newfound happiness, but at least she had achieved some balance, which would allow her to step back into the role of Finn's wife. Life was changing for the better; the bakery her in-laws had bequeathed to them was doing good business and they lived very comfortably.

Jenny had made certain she would never fall pregnant again by settling the matter for once and for all behind Finn's back; he wasn't that thrilled to be a father, anyway. All her randy husband seemed interested in was work and sex, and neither the birth of their twins nor the passing years had changed that.

Ten years earlier, for the twins' fourth birthday, Finn had bought a magnificent farm, just a few minutes away by bike from the sea. Isolated from everything, in the middle of endless fields, the house felt like a small castle and, for Jenny, it was everything she had ever dreamed of. Finn had allowed her to decorate it according to her own tastes, and she'd ordered furniture and finery from the big city. They even had a bathroom with a bathtub and an indoor toilet. The days of sharing a bed with Mother's stinking body, in a room no larger than a broom cupboard, were truly a thing of the past.

Jenny pulled out the two hairpins that were digging into her scalp, inadvertently loosening a couple of curlers, which fell to the floor. She swore silently, swung her legs out of bed, slipped on her dressing gown with a shiver and shuffled off to the bathroom.

She was about to close the door to the twins' room when she noticed a faint light coming from inside. She stepped into the doorway.

Hilda was kneeling at the foot of her bed. One tiny breast had fallen out of her nightshirt and was peering from the middle of her chest like the eye of a cyclops. Her eyes were closed, her nipple intermittently grazing against the top of the thigh that stood in its way, her lips curled around a penis that should never have been in her mouth.

Jenny shoved the door open, slamming it against the wall. The erect penis sprang up, pointing towards her. Terrified, Hilda opened her eyes and buried her face in her hands.

Jenny ran across the bedroom, grabbed Hilda by the hair and dragged her out into the hallway. She pulled her down the stairs without a word, the only sound their heavy breathing and the banging of their knees, elbows and feet against the steps. Then she threw Hilda in the cellar.

Jenny locked the door behind her and struggled to catch her breath as she made her way back up to bed. Hilda was getting heavier.

She took off her dressing gown and got into bed next to Finn, who had slipped back into their bedroom.

'Didn't I tell you not to use her any more, Finn? Didn't I tell you…'

Her words were interrupted by her husband's tongue forcing its way into her mouth. He took her hand and guided it down to his still-erect penis.

'I'm sorry, *älskling*,' he whispered, directing her caresses. 'I'm sorry…'

EMILY STARTED THE CAR and motioned for Alexis to hurry as she lugged her suitcase into the boot. Alexis fell into the passenger seat with barely a word of greeting.

Emily had called Alexis the previous morning. She hadn't mentioned their falling-out at Falkenberg Police Station a few days earlier, but had made a proposal that had left Alexis lost for words.

The writer had immediately bought a ticket to London and told Stellan and her parents she was leaving, with no room for discussion. That hadn't prevented her mother from sharing her opinion at great length. This meet-the-parents visit had quickly taken on the air of a stage drama and Alexis had closed the door leaving three worried faces behind her. She had to resolve this whole affair once and for all. File it away. Bury the past that was weighing down her present.

She was on her way to meet Richard Hemfield at the Broadmoor high-security psychiatric hospital. He wanted to apologise. *Apologise.* An initiative that owed more to his sense of voyeurism than actual repentance, she reckoned. It didn't take a degree in psychology to figure that out. Still, the information she gleaned would allow Emily to fine-tune her profile and further the investigation, whichever direction it might lead them in. Even if they had conflicting opinions about Hemfield's guilt, Alexis had to play the game.

'We've got the lab results,' the profiler told her, without taking her eyes off the road. 'The DNA found in Maria Paulsson's and Julianne

Bell's socks is identical to that found in Jeanine Sanderson's, the first Tower Hamlets victim.'

I know who Jeanine Sanderson is, Emily. I know her height, her weight, her mother's maiden name and the shoes she was wearing when Hemfield took her. Gold faux-leather ballet flats.

Alexis swallowed her anger before she opened her mouth.

'You already suspect Hemfield wasn't responsible for the Tower Hamlets murders, don't you?'

'It appears he might not have been,' Emily replied.

'Don't you think he might have had an accomplice, at least?'

Alexis turned to look at the profiler, waving her hands in front of her face in line with her mounting anger.

'I just don't understand, Emily. I can't wrap my head around your reaction or the way you're going about this! I can't believe it … you're in complete denial. I just hope you're following your own rule of thumb that the theories should fit the facts, and not the other way around.'

The sound of Alexis's high-pitched voice filled the car like the kind of music you wished you could turn off.

Emily didn't react. Her body was relaxed, her movements fluid. She was cool and controlled, as if she hadn't heard a word Alexis had said.

'I'm considering and exploring every single possibility,' she finally said in a calm tone of voice, once Alexis had simmered down.

Alexis shook her head and twisted her lips in resentment. She was almost looking forward to getting to the psychiatric hospital.

••••••

A ruddy-cheeked man was waiting for them on the other side of the security gate. Pat Viggel, the clinical director at Broadmoor, gave them a weak smile and shook their hands quickly but firmly.

'The interview will take place in one of our group-therapy rooms,' he explained, leading the two women down a corridor. 'That way, we can film the session and you, Miss Roy, will be able to follow the conversation as it happens in our screening room. Two orderlies will be in there with you at all times, Miss Castells.'

The reality of what was about to happen hit Alexis like a slap in the face. She nodded, glancing down at the black marks on the floor and back up to the bars over a window set high in the wall.

'Have you prepared the documents on my list?' Emily abruptly asked.

Pat Viggel was unmoved. 'Yes, all of them: the mail received by Hemfield since his incarceration – none of which has been passed on to him, I must say, but which has all been X-rayed and opened by our staff – as well as all the letters he wanted to send, which were never relayed.'

'No contact with his lawyer since he was brought here?'

'No. He sacked him after the trial and never hired another.'

'Any visitors?'

'He's never agreed to any. Apart from DCS Jack Pearce, the day before yesterday, and you, today. No calls, either. He's usually pretty easy-going. None of the female staff work in his proximity as his hands have a tendency to wander, but aside from that and his compulsive masturbation, he's OK. He's not the worst of our patients, I can assure you.'

'Did you make a note of the people who requested visiting rights?'

'Yes, don't worry, I've given you all of that. We'll help you take the boxes to your car after your visit.'

After your *visit*.

Alexis felt a tightening in her throat. She discreetly wiped her sweaty palms on her trousers. Her anger was turning to fear. Or perhaps it had been fear all along.

THE HEAVY CLUNK of the lock no longer made her flinch. Hilda didn't mind being thrown in here, because it meant that her mother had stopped things from going any further.

She moved her joints: no sprains or breaks, at least. She stood slowly, nursing her sorry body, and switched the cellar light on. She used her fingers to brush her hair and sweep away the tufts her mother had pulled out, and looked down at her arms and legs. No wounds to speak of. She would only have some swelling and bruises, which were not hard to cover up in winter.

She always tried to keep pace with her mother's momentum, but seldom managed to walk or get back up quickly enough to avoid being dragged for a few metres. The two sets of stairs were the worst part: her knees always slammed against the edges of the steps and it took days for the swelling to go down.

The bolt slid back, and the door opened without creaking, revealing her brother. Sigvard closed it behind him carefully. He had oiled the hinges so as not to alert their parents. After punishing Hilda, they were usually otherwise occupied for a while, but Sigvard didn't want to take any risks.

When his father ordered him out of the room he shared with Hilda, the teenager always knew what was about to happen. He left the room with fire raging in his belly as he heard the rustling of his father's trousers and his groans of pleasure.

Once he had tried to intervene. Hilda had made him promise

not to do so ever again as she was the one their father had ended up punishing.

Sigvard set the pile of things down and pulled out the coat. With a look of deep concern for her, he helped his sister put it on. She reassured him with a shake of her head, avoiding his gaze. She leaned back so he could help her put on the woollen tights and a pair of worn corduroy trousers. He slipped the fur-lined slippers onto her feet and finished the job by putting a hat on her head.

When he sat up, he kissed her on the cheek and nose, before hurriedly unfolding both blankets. He had to be quick, since the temperature down here hovered around five degrees, and Hilda was already numb with cold. He spread one of the blankets on the floor, waited for his sister to lie down on it, and then covered her with the other. Hilda would have to hide the blankets on the bottom shelf in the morning, and he would come and spirit them away when Mother sent him down to the cellar to fetch provisions. He would do the same with the clothing he had brought.

He would leave the cellar as soon as his sister had fallen asleep. Mother had caught him once in the early hours of the morning, sleeping next to Hilda. The punishment he had been dealt still haunted him. Now they had to be extremely careful.

Sigvard stretched out alongside Hilda and stroked her cheek with his still-warm hand. She closed her eyes and swallowed a few times.

His throat was a knot of hate.

Hilda stretched, then snuggled against him. She wanted him to let go of his anger, he knew that.

He kissed his sister on the cheek again and buried his face in her hair.

'It's all going to be all right, my Hilda,' he whispered in the hollow of her neck. 'Now, go to sleep.'

THE DOOR TO THE GROUP-THERAPY room was ajar. A burst of laughter disturbed the silence.

'Hemfield, we're here,' Pat Viggel announced.

'And so are we, my dear Pat.'

Hemfield's sour tone and lingering delivery crawled all over Alexis like a sweaty, wandering palm.

The director gave the door a push until it nudged against the doorstop.

Hemfield came into view, a broad and tight-lipped smile inflating his ruddy cheeks. Alexis realised she had never seen him up close like this. The trial had been held in-camera and she had only ever caught a glimpse of him entering or leaving the court.

He was sitting facing the door, at one end of a rectangular table about two metres long. Alexis was out of reach; out of *his* reach. There was no Plexiglas screen, nor were there any bars, as Emily had warned her. The two orderlies Viggel had promised would be present were there, though. One on each side, flanking the patient. The remnants of their laughter a moment ago lingered in the corners of their mouths.

'For once, I'm not the one frightening people. These two latex-gloved brutes deliver all the dramatic tension by themselves,' Hemfield joked.

Viggel pulled out the chair at the other end of the table for Alexis. The one with its back to the door. Alexis sat down.

'Well, I'll leave you to it, then,' the director said. 'James and Albert are staying here with you.'

The two orderlies nodded.

Viggel smiled politely at his visitor before turning on his heels.

Alexis heard the door clunk into place behind her, followed by the double-click of the lock. Her heart was going berserk in her chest. As if it too was desperate to run for its life.

'Thank you for coming, Alexis.'

Hemfield pronounced her name with emphasis on every syllable, as if he were savouring each letter with the tip of his tongue.

'You never got my letters, did you?'

Alexis shook her head.

'That's what I thought. I suspect they're not forwarding anything.'

Suddenly, Hemfield looked up and stared at a point in mid-air just above Alexis's head, waving his finger rhythmically in front of his face. Instinctively, Alexis turned around. Hemfield was playing to the camera. She thought of Emily, who was watching them from the screening room. A secret presence she found reassuring, perhaps even more so than her two bodyguards.

'Pat, you could at least have told me,' Hemfield said, amused. 'I know, I know, you were more interested in what I was actually writing. Yes, I know, I know, Pat, that you were just following the rules and regulations. Yes, yes yes yes yes, I know, Pat. We're all under someone's thumb.'

He readjusted his small, round glasses on his nose.

'What about you, Alexis, whose thumb are you under?'

Alexis briefly opened her mouth, then closed it again.

'No need to beat around the bush. I don't take umbrage, you know. Knock yourself out, Alexis.'

She hesitated a second longer before taking the plunge.

'My past.'

'At least that's an honest answer, Alexis. But it's a pathetic one. There's nothing more pathetic than letting your past weigh you down.'

'But we're all in the same boat, Richard, don't you think?' she riposted, sweeping her gaze around the four walls of the room with the hint of a smirk.

'You're confusing two very different things, Alexis: paying for the errors of one's ways and suffering from them. One should be resilient, not relentless.'

'Relentless?'

'It's only by looking to our past that we can learn lessons for our present. Looking back, yes, but not in contemplation. Resilience is a recurring topic of discussion with my psychiatrist, as a matter of fact.'

Alexis swallowed, still in the grip of her fear.

'What do you look back to?' she forced herself to ask.

'To my mother, of course, Alexis – who else? My mother who caught me touching myself. I was only five years old at the time. Can you imagine? I didn't even know what I was doing. She told me that if she found me playing with myself again, she would cut it off. That sort of threat leaves a long-lasting mark, wouldn't you say, Alexis?'

Hemfield laid his hands flat on the table, one beside the other.

'I must really stop saying your name. I can see it's making you uncomfortable.'

Alexis's sorrow erupted into anger. A dark, primal anger that made her want to growl like an animal.

'You abducted, imprisoned, killed and cut up six women, Richard,' she hissed, her eyes, dripping with hate, boring into him. 'And you shattered Samuel's skull.'

'I did not kill those women,' he replied in the same equable tone of voice.

'The first blow knocked him to the ground,' she continued, breathlessly. 'Then you hit him two more times when he was down. You shattered his skull.'

The two orderlies shuffled closer to Hemfield. Alexis suddenly had the feeling they were there to protect him, the prisoner, rather than her, the victim.

Hemfield carefully plucked the glasses from the bridge of his nose, folded them and put them away in his shirt pocket. His face was blank.

'Do you know what I'm wondering?'

He closed his eyes and pinched the skin of his eyebrows.

'I'm wondering what your cunt smells like.'

Alexis froze. She could almost feel Hemfield's nose prodding its way between her thighs. She swallowed back the bile rising in her throat.

One of the orderlies shifted from one leg to the other with a sideways glance at his impassive colleague.

'It's nothing personal, you know. It's just the first thing that crosses my mind when I'm in the presence of a woman. The way you smell. Especially your cunt … And then the scent of your skin above your top lip and just behind your ear lobes. These thoughts of mine never cease, in spite of all the therapy and medical treatment. It's as if they're ingrained in me.'

His eyes were still closed.

Pale-faced and petrified, Alexis kept on staring at him.

'So, I start to follow you … watching your every move … at home … at the nursery where you take your children … at your work … at your gym … at your dance class … at the restaurant where you meet the girls for dinner. Then, when I feel confident enough, I'll start digging through your dustbins, looking for tampons or pads. The odour of a woman's menstrual flow can vary, you know. Depending on the woman, of course, but also when it blends with other secretions. When I know your routine well enough, I'll break into your home when you and your family are out, because I need time alone – some me time – in your space. I'll delve into your laundry basket, sniff around your bathroom, in search of your dirty laundry. Then I'll masturbate as I bury my nose in your underwear … and some of your clothes … the crotch of your trousers, for instance. Then I'll enter your bedroom, and I'll masturbate again, this time with your clean underwear … leaving my mark, like an animal defending its territory. And then I'll go home with dried sperm all over my hands, with a pair of your panties in my pocket. I'll use them as a napkin when I eat, for a few weeks … until I find another pair to replace them.'

EMILY LINED UP EIGHT women's photographs on the wooden surface of her kitchen table. Below all but one of the smiling head-shots she placed a photograph of the matching dead body.

Alexis had not said a single word when they left Broadmoor. No tears, nor heavy sighs. Nothing. As if she had left a part of herself back there with Hemfield. When Emily dropped her off at her flat a few hours earlier, Alexis had stepped out of the car, closed the door gently and lifted her suitcase out of the boot just as coolly.

Emily took a swig of her London Porter, staring at the empty space below the photograph of Julianne Bell. Richard Hemfield just did not fit the cannibal serial-killer profile she had established: his old-fashioned demeanour, his voyeurism, his compulsive masturba-tion and his frequent changes in employment all contradicted the profile at almost every level.

As he enlightened them about his deviances and explained how he was neither a kidnapper, nor a strangler, let alone a butcher, but rather 'simply' a voyeur, he had taken off his glasses and closed his eyes. To make doubly sure he wouldn't see Alexis's reaction while he laid bare his obsessions and fantasies. A serial killer who strangled his victims would take great pleasure in the power he wielded over them. Reading the fear in their faces would provoke an intense sexual excitement. Which was not the case when it came to Hemfield. His pupils had dilated only once: when Alexis had entered the room. He had sniffed her out at length as she sat down facing him, trying to inhale the womanly scent that fuelled his every fantasy. Hemfield was profoundly excited by a woman's proximity and, in that secure wing of Broadmoor, the so-called weaker sex were thin on the ground. However, he had never been arrested for rape, attempted or otherwise.

Emily grabbed a coaster and put it down on the table before resting her beer on it.

Hemfield was Jeanine Sanderson's neighbour. Several months before her death, she had caught him masturbating in her bedroom with her tights in his lap. She had not called the police, but had mentioned the fact to a female friend, telling her she thought Hemfield was 'harmless'.

When the police learned that on the night the body of Clara Sandro – the last victim – was found, Hemfield was drinking a beer alone in a pub just a street away, this had proven circumstantial enough to charge him with the Tower Hamlets murders. With a string of arrests for voyeurism, harassment and theft on his record, he was the ideal culprit in the eyes of the Metropolitan Police. But when the authorities knocked on Hemfield's door in January 2006, the man was nowhere to be found. For two whole weeks he managed to hide out in London.

On 2 February 2006, Detective Jeremy Priory of the Met and profiler Jon Pierland were on their way back from a crime scene in Stanmore, in the north end of the city. They were accompanied by Samuel Garel, aged thirty-eight, one of three French police officers seconded from the Quai des Orfèvres, selected by the Police Judiciaire to shadow British profilers on the job. Over the radio in the car, they heard that Richard Hemfield had been spotted three kilometres away, in Harrow, walking along Crundale Avenue. While they waited for back-up to arrive, the two police officers agreed to separate. Jon Pierland was to scour the area in the car with Samuel Garel, and Jeremy Priory, who was armed, would do the same on foot. Two minutes later, Samuel Garel noticed Hemfield turning into an alleyway. Pierland got out of the car, followed by Garel, and they started to chase Hemfield. But, Pierland, who was considerably older, was soon out of breath. Garel kept on running and caught up with Hemfield, who grabbed an iron bar that was lying on the ground beside a rubbish skip and hit Garel on the head. Pierland reached the end of the alley as Hemfield delivered two further blows to the fallen Garel's head. Hemfield immediately let go of the iron bar and kneeled by his victim, placing his right hand on the police officer's bleeding head and rocking himself back and forth. When Detective Jeremy Priory arrived at the scene three minutes later, Hemfield was still in the same position, clearly in shock. Garel died of his injuries on the way to the hospital. Hemfield was found guilty of the murders of the six women found in Tower Hamlets, as well as Samuel Garel's, and was incarcerated in Broadmoor.

Emily took another swig of her warming beer.

Could Hemfield have had an accomplice for the Tower Hamlets murders?

When one half of a serial-killer duo disappears, the victimology, modus operandi and/or characteristic signature all inevitably change. It would be like asking someone who writes with their right hand to switch to their left overnight. The handwriting is no longer the same; it becomes irregular, unbalanced. It may eventually regain its original style and form, but the words written by the left hand will never look identical to those written by the right. By the same token, if the Tower Hamlets murders had been committed by twin killers and the murder of Maria Paulsson was attributable to only one of the duo, there should have been clear divergences. But they were a match on every level. The accomplice theory didn't make sense.

Could Hemfield have met an accomplice during his time in Broadmoor? Someone he could have schooled and groomed to take over from him? It was possible, but how would he have communicated with them? There was certainly no Internet connection in the wing of the hospital reserved for dangerous criminals, almost all of whom were serial killers or mass murderers. Nor had Richard

Hemfield been able to send out letters, or, indeed, receive any. Could Hemfield have met another patient? Impossible: no prisoner from the secure wing had set foot outside Broadmoor in the last ten years. Could he have bribed someone? He had no money, and there was no one to send him any; and what else could he offer in exchange? What if such a hypothetical person committed the crime because he or she worshipped Hemfield? An orderly? A psychologist? All staff in high-security psychiatric hospitals underwent extensive criminal and psychiatric background checks. Not wanting to leave any stone unturned, though, the profiler had requested the hospital's personnel files.

Emily shook her head. None of this speculation would stand up. Anyway, there was nothing dominant or mentor-like about Hemfield's personality.

Perhaps the latest crimes were the work of a copycat? The DNA matches in the socks spanning all three investigations ruled out this possibility.

Suddenly, something Karla Hansen had said came to mind: 'like the killer's beginning a new cycle...' However, the killer wasn't initiating one new cycle, but two: one here in London and one in Halmstad, in Sweden. As if, following ten years of inactivity, he had suddenly gained confidence and arrogance.

Which only left one plausible option: Hemfield was not guilty.

Pearce would never get over it. Ever since she had shown him the plastic bag containing Julianne Bell's shoes, guilt had seemed to be written all over his face. The DCS had been praised so highly in the wake of Hemfield's arrest, but now grew defensive whenever he was asked to talk about the case. One thing was clear: something about the whole affair had always nagged at him. And the profile Emily had established was the last nail in the coffin. Pearce had never dreamed the killer might have been a cannibal, never in a million years.

Once again, the profiler looked at the faces of the eight women on the table: Jeanine Sanderson, Diana Lantar, Katie Atkins, Chloe

Blomer, Sylvia George, Clara Sandro, Maria Paulsson and Julianne Bell. Putting the wrong man behind bars didn't just destroy a career: it destroyed everything about you.

She put the kettle on, picked up a mug from the draining board and dropped a bag of green tea into it. She ran her index finger around the still-wet rim of the mug and wiped it on the tea-towel hanging from the oven-door handle.

Why had the killer stopped his work for a decade? As Aliénor had pointed out, there could be three reasons: either he was locked up in prison; or he was bedridden and out of action, unable to harm anyone; or he had killed somewhere else and the murders had not been associated with the Tower Hamlets case.

First of all, they would have to contact Interpol and disseminate the information they had on an international scale; then draw up a list of all known criminals who had been out of action or in prison between September 2005, when the initial murders had come to an end, and July 2015, when Maria Paulsson was abducted. With a fine-toothed comb, they would have to go through the letters sent to Hemfield that Viggel had given them, and check the backgrounds of the people who had written them, as the new killer might have attempted to contact Hemfield.

For her part, Emily would reread all the reports Aliénor had sent on Maria Paulsson's murder, to determine the connection between Halmstad and London. Why was the killer now using two geographically distant places as graveyards? He appeared to know the Halmstad area as well as Whitechapel and Mayfair in London. Did he live in Torslanda, where Maria Paulsson had resided? In Halmstad, where the young woman's body was found? Or in London, where the bodies of the Tower Hamlets victims had been found?

Emily stared in contemplation at the tea bag in her otherwise empty mug. She put the kettle back on to reheat the water.

The theory Aliénor had come up with seemed so far-fetched, she found it puzzling. Could the link between the London murders, the Halmstad killing and the abduction of Julianne Bell have anything to do with some morbid obsession about Elizabeth Stride, Jack the Ripper's Swedish victim?

She poured the boiling water into the mug and added a spoonful of thyme honey.

Why not? she thought.

Halmstad
Thursday, 23 July 2015, 7.45 am

THE TRAFFIC LIGHT turned red. Karla Hansen shifted the car into neutral, reached for one of the croissants she was taking to the police station and took a big bite out of it.

'Do you want one, sweetheart?' she asked Pia, her eldest daughter, who was sitting next to her.

'No. Absolutely not. I don't want to end up with a belly like yours,' the girl retorted, eyes glued to her smartphone.

Karla almost spat out her delicious, all-butter croissant. She glanced down at her waistline, compressed as it was by the seat belt. 'What's wrong with my stomach?'

'Your tummy isn't fat, Mum: it's flabby. Like pizza dough.'

Two honks of a car horn urged Karla to get moving.

'Let me remind you, this "pizza dough", as you call it, once served as your bedroom and your pantry! And you felt so comfortable in there we had to force you to leave the premises!'

'Yuck! You're gross, Mum,' Pia complained.

'Am I hearing you right? I'm the one being insulted, yet it's you who are finding me revolting?'

'Omigod! Mum!' her daughter shrieked.

'Pia, what is it? Are you OK?' Karla cried, pulling over at the side of the road in a flash. 'Are you OK?' she repeated, cupping a hand around her daughter's face in concern.

'Mum, why did you stop like that? You scared me! Of course, I'm OK. I just saw something amazing: she's on StarSpotter. Look!'

'What do you think you're doing, screaming like that, Pia?' Karla said, as annoyed as she was reassured. 'What got into you? We're in a car here, not a roller coaster.'

'Look, Mum, look! She's on StarSpotter!'

'What's StarStopper? And who are you talking about?'

'Not StarStopper! Star*Spotter*. It's an app, Mum. An ap-pli-ca-tion on my iPhone. It's not about stopping stars, but *spotting* them. You know, seeing where they are.'

'Thanks for the English lesson. How would I manage without you?'

'Stop talking and listen to what I'm saying: your actress is on StarSpotter.'

'What actress?'

'The one who was abducted. Julianne Bell.'

Karla grabbed the phone her daughter was holding out to her.

A minute later, she was on the phone to Bergström.

>>+++<<

Olofsson pushed a pile of folders aside and perched himself on the edge of Aliénor's desk, mug in hand.

'Hey, Lindbergh, even in the broom cupboard you'd have more space than you do here.'

'However, there are brooms in said cupboard,' Aliénor said, not even raising her eyes from the document she was highlighting.

'What are you doing?'

'I'm highlighting.'

'Did you know that Ronald Reagan was descended from a family of cannibals?'

'The fortieth president of the United States did not have cannibal ancestry. Two of his uncles ate their brother, who had died of his wounds, when they were stuck in a cave after a snowstorm, that's all.'

'Holy crap, Little Miss Google, what did you have for breakfast?'

Aliénor, wide-eyed, looked up at him.

'Whatever do you put in that Thermos flask of yours?'

'Just coffee,' she said calmly, returning to her highlighting.

'And she brings her own coffee … You know we have coffee in the kitchenette here? All part of our benefits in kind. That, and the *droit du seigneur*, naturally…'

Aliénor set down her orange Stabilo Boss, picked up a red ballpoint pen and wrote a series of letters in the margin of the document.

'If ever there was an antiquated *droit du seigneur* in our police force, Detective Olofsson, then Kommissionär Bergström would be the one to exercise it, as he outranks you. So, I would be engaging in sexual relations with him, not you.'

Olofsson grimaced. 'Sheesh, thanks a bunch! Now it'll take me all day to get rid of the image of that old fart on top of…'

'Olofsson! Lindbergh! In the conference room, now!' Bergström's shout made them both jump.

'I'll bet they've found Julianne Bell's body,' the detective suggested as they made their way towards the conference room.

HILDA CAME OUT of the pantry carrying pots of jam, caster sugar and tinned fruit.

'Switch the light off and close the door, please, *älskling*,' she asked the child who was following her.

She walked into the kitchen and set everything down on the table. Skorpan was coveting the pears in syrup with big, blue, overtired eyes.

'Are you still hungry?'

'Only for some cake ... Will you make one?'

Hilda smiled, running her fingers through the child's blonde hair. 'Sigvard will bring one back from the bakery: a *Prinsesstårta*.'

The child's greedy eyes sparkled with joy.

'So, what are you going to be making with all this?'

'Biscuits, my little angel. You'll get to taste them tomorrow.'

She stroked the child's cheek. It was as smooth as an apricot's. Skorpan pulled a face. The bruise was turning yellow, but it still hurt just as much. Hilda was sure nothing was broken, but Skorpan was suffering. Some parents were not deserving of the name.

She swept back the child's blonde fringe and kissed the delicate forehead beneath. 'Go play with the others, *älskling*; Sigvard will be home soon.'

With a resolute nod that bounced the child's pretty bowl haircut up and down, Skorpan ran out of the kitchen. Cries of joy greeted the child's return to the living room, where the others had begun a game of *Kubb*. Hilda had put a rug down for them to avoid damaging the tiles like they had the last time.

A snowstorm had been raging all morning and they were stuck in the house; even the barn was freezing. But Hilda wasn't too bothered about the state of their living room, as long as these poor kids were having fun.

She set the table for two. The little ones had already eaten, and this was always a special time of the day with her brother. Dining together was their chance to talk about their day with the children laughing and squabbling in the other room.

Twenty years earlier, they had lost both their parents in close succession. Jenny and Finn had not lived to a ripe old age. The bakery had been passed down to them, and Sigvard had taken care of it like a precious heirloom. His bread and his cakes outclassed his father's and business was booming. Hilda looked after the farm, and Sigvard, and all the orphans or mistreated children she fostered while they were waiting to be adopted.

Sigvard was not married, and neither was she. Her brother always played away from home and Hilda had never had any interest in '*it*', or in men, full stop. Her world was limited to her brother, and the children, and the bounds of their farm; that was it.

Hilda set down a steaming quiche made with *Västerbotten* cheese in the middle of the table.

The front door creaked open as she was taking the nettle soup off the stove.

Her brother walked into the kitchen with a cardboard box in his arms. '*Hej!*'

Hilda took the cake and kissed him on the cheek.

'Amazing!' he said, when he saw the quiche on the table.

He sat down right away; Hilda pulled her apron off, draped it over the back of her chair and sat across from her brother.

'I ran into our neighbour,' he said, between spoonfuls of soup.

Hilda didn't say anything. She wasn't overly fond of their neighbours.

'You took another little one in?'

'Yes…'

Sigvard served them each a thick slice of quiche.

'Oh Hilda, another one, really?'

She cut the crust off her own piece, put it on her brother's plate and dug into the quiche.

'It's not like we can't afford it, is it?' she finally said.

'How about a bit of peace and quiet, for once?'

'They're never in your way, so why does it matter? You've got the bakery and I have my kids. You fill bellies and I fill hearts.'

Sigvard's face took on a serious, almost absent look. Yes, Hilda thought, an air of absence. His thoughts seemed to have taken him far away from here. Far away from her.

'Come,' he murmured, pushing his chair out from the table.

Hilda pushed her own chair back in turn, the sound of one scraping across the floor an echo of the other. She moved around to the other side of the table and sat on her brother's knee.

She closed her eyes when his calloused hand stroked her face, cupping her cheek in his palm.

'I need to tell you something, my Hilda.'

'I'm not sure I want to hear what you're about to say,' she said, keeping her eyes closed.

'I've met someone.'

She blinked slowly, like a lizard lounging in the sun.

'I am aware of the fact that you meet a lot of … others,' she smiled, tenderly kissing his fingers.

'She's going to come here and live with me.'

Hilda stopped what she was doing and stared painfully at her brother.

'I won't have another woman here, Sigvard.'

He swept a stray lock of hair from her freckled forehead.

'I want her to be by my side. I really do.'

Hilda lowered her eyes. She brushed a few quiche crumbs off her brother's canvas trousers.

'I won't have another woman here.'

'Hilda. I want this woman to live with me, can't you understand?'

His sister's face crinkled with sadness for a moment.

'We'll move into the outbuilding, by the barn,' her brother continued.

Sniffing, she shook her head.

'I don't want you moving out of the house, Sigvard. It's out of the question.'

'I'll just be next door—'

'I. Said. No.' She spelled it out in a flat, calm voice.

Hilda stood up and went back to her chair.

'She'll move in with us, if you insist, but here with you, in your room. In our house. I won't have it any other way. Do I make myself clear?'

Sigvard looked down at his plate and nodded a yes.

'And I don't want to hear another word on the subject until we've finished our meal.'

JULIANNE BELL'S BROTHER GREETED Jack Pearce and Emily Roy with the same firm, determined handshake as the first time they had met almost a week earlier. He was dressed in an elegant midnight-blue suit and a white shirt with cufflinks, and wore an IWC Portugieser on his left wrist, but had no shoes on. Raymond Bell seemed naked, Pearce thought, and it wasn't just the socks. The man seemed like he'd lost his aura. Without his sister, Raymond Bell was nothing.

He led the DCS and Emily into a vast living room. In one corner stood a circular fireplace, an unexpected touch of minimalist design amid the bohemian clutter of the rest of the room. A huge sectional sofa formed by blocks of multicoloured foam cushions was surrounded by magazines, books, throws, trays and more cushions, strewn higgledy-piggledy across the improvised sofa – an invitation to idle relaxation.

'We've just found your sister's car close to Stansted Airport.' Emily cut to the chase.

Raymond Bell winced. 'Was she…'

'No,' Pearce reassured him, compassion oozing from his voice.

'A week … It's been nearly a week,' he murmured to himself.

'On the night prior to her disappearance, your sister was not at home,' Emily pressed, in the same surly tone.

Raymond Bell shook his head, frowning at the revelation.

'I don't … But … you told us she was seen leaving her home, the morning when … just before…'

'That's correct. But she didn't spend the night at home.'

'But ... you would have seen her leave, wouldn't you? Well, the CCTV cameras, I mean.'

'She was located by some fans, thanks to the StarSpotter application, in the early hours of the morning, a few streets away from her home.'

Raymond Bell's vacant gaze wandered around the room, bouncing off the walls and windows like a little, lost bird.

'CCTV footage shows your sister on North Audley Street at 10.16 pm and then again at 4.45 am,' the DCS explained. 'She left home and returned through the garden gate, no doubt to evade the paparazzi.'

'Your sister went to meet her lover, Raymond,' Emily carried on.

'A lov— No! My sister didn't have a lover!' he cried.

'You seem very sure of yourself.'

Raymond started to pace nervously up and down.

'Julianne lived for her career and her family. For her daughters.'

'I can't help but notice you mentioned her career before her family,' Emily calmly pointed out.

'*We* felt that her career was very important.'

'*We?*'

'Yes, *we*. I looked after my sister's career. My sister helped me earn a living,' he said.

'*Lived. Felt. Helped.* Have you already buried your sister?'

Raymond stormed across the room and came face to face with Emily. His lips twisted with anger as he raised a menacing finger to her. The profiler didn't move a muscle. Neither did Pearce.

'My sister's been missing for almost a week. A week! Do you really believe Julianne is still alive?'

Emily locked eyes with him. Kept on staring at him, waiting for him to be the one to back down. Raymond's body finally relaxed. He closed his eyes for a few seconds and sat down on the sofa.

'So, Julianne *lived* for her career and her daughters. Not for her husband?' Emily pressed.

'Of course, Julianne lived for her husband as much as her daughters, of course she did…'

Weariness weighed heavy in Raymond Bell's voice.

'But her family had to adapt to the needs of her career, that's what I meant to say. It wasn't difficult, it was just … a sort of family contract, a compromise if you will, but a gentle sort of compromise…'

He rubbed his forehead with his hand in a rough, almost primal way.

'But … where did she go, that night?'

'To a hotel. Forty-seven Park Street, to be precise.'

'A hotel? Why? With whom?'

'We were hoping you could answer these questions, Raymond.'

'But … doesn't the hotel have any security cameras?'

'Only on the outside, and most of the people coming and going wear hats and sunglasses, or even hold an umbrella, to remain incognito. Your sister is not the first celebrity to seek out a suitable place to meet up with a lover away from prying eyes.'

He shook his head.

'Do you think it's her … that this person abducted her?'

'That's what we hope to find out.'

Wandering aimlessly around London. Going to a museum. Visiting an art gallery. Or getting her rocks off in the cinema. Coming in a darkened room. That's what she'd been thinking about before she was brought here. She'd been planning her afternoon of freedom; a few delicious hours she had hoped to spend making love in a public place.

Thursday, 16 July was their three-month anniversary.

That night, she had waited until the girls were sound asleep. Until the nanny started snoring. And then she had slipped out. Leaving the key in the lock, so she might close the door in complete silence. Then she had walked down to the ground floor, down the hallway, through the garden gate that led onto North Audley Street, where no paparazzi were likely to be lingering.

That night, she had snuck out like a teenager.

A lovestruck teenager.

Just a few hours before she woke up here, she was still in her lover's arms, embracing the lie, wallowing in adultery. The relationship was so wrong, she knew it, could feel it, but still she kept it going, as every secret rendezvous erased the memory of the last.

Just a few hours before she woke up here, her body was still shuddering with the aftershocks of her orgasms. It had been a wild night. As crazy as all the bad choices she had once made. So wild, and so risky.

Just a few hours before she woke up here, for the umpteenth time in three months, she had trampled on all her good resolutions with the sheer impudence of youth.

A youth she thought she had lost so long ago.

ALEXIS CHECKED THE TIME and put her computer to sleep. She stared at the dark screen for a few seconds, picked up her handbag, which she had left on a stool beside her desk, and went out.

She bought a caramel macchiato from the new espresso bar that had recently opened inside an old red phone box on the corner of her street, and walked down Fitzjohn's Avenue sipping from her paper cup.

The kiss of the sun on her cheeks was much gentler than yesterday, no doubt thanks to the cotton-like streaks of clouds slicing through the summer sky. Alexis couldn't recall ever seeing clouds of that particular shape; it was as if someone had taken a brush and painted long white stripes on a deep-blue canvas.

Richard Hemfield. Hemfield.

He was everywhere, wherever she looked; like the face of a lover inviting himself into your bed. Their meeting at Broadmoor the previous day had set her back in the grieving process. Her obsession had been far from appeased; on the contrary, it was now feeding on her emotions. Steeped in hate and anger, Alexis had allowed the life to be sucked out of her and devoured by this man.

This had to stop. She had to take the upper hand and prevent her ghosts from leading her to the edge of the abyss. She would pick up the threads of Hemfield's biographical information, comb through his past and find the connection between the London murders, the killing in Sweden and Julianne Bell's abduction. Do something so she could be at peace. And if she didn't find anything? Well, if she didn't, at least she would finally move on.

Alexis arrived at the St John's Wood Willow Nursery ten minutes early. She waited in front of the school observing the frantic crowd of parents, nannies and grandparents hurrying their way in through the doors and coming out with their arms full of children.

'Miss Castells?' enquired a young woman with a cherubic face standing at the top of the steps. 'Mr Ackermann is expecting you.'

Alexis nodded and followed her inside the building. Not surprising she had been so easily identified, she mused: she was the only person waiting outside in the sun with a coffee in her hand, not running after a child.

Oliver Ackermann, head of St John's Wood Willow Nursery, was in his forties, well groomed, and had a thick, neatly trimmed moustache and beard. He rose and warmly shook her hand.

'Thank you for seeing me, Mr Ackermann,' Alexis began.

'You're welcome,' he said kindly.

Oliver Ackermann's was the first name to have emerged from the past. He had been called as a witness for the defence at Hemfield's trial.

Convincing him to meet had not proven easy. Alexis had had to tug at his heart strings, play up the death of her partner and tell him all about her personal quest. She had also promised their conversation would go no further; Ackermann had no desire to be associated any more with the Tower Hamlets business.

'Could you tell me how you first met Richard Hemfield?'

'Through a friend from uni, Tancredi Bertuzzi. An Italian, of course. We had rented an incredible flat along with another student, who ended up bailing on us and going back to Australia. We were desperate to find another flatmate, and Tancredi suggested Richard. He wasn't actually a student, but he was our age and worked at the student union café. He seemed quite reserved, not really the party type, which suited us well, and he'd been trying to find a shared flat for a few weeks already. Two days later, he moved in with us.'

'What year was that?'

'Let me see … The Maida Vale flat, that was in … 1991.'

'How long did you all live together?'

'Two years.'

'Does your Italian friend still live in London?'

'No; he moved back to Perugia after uni. He's been living there ever since.'

'Married?'

'With four children. All girls. According to some, you should eat a diet high in salt if you want to have a boy; well, that doesn't appear to have worked too well for his wife,' he joked, idly smoothing his full beard.

'What sort of man was Richard Hemfield?'

'Very reserved, like I said, but I wouldn't say he was antisocial. I mean, he wasn't always holed up in his room, but he wasn't that talkative either.'

'Did he go out with girls?'

Ackermann fidgeted in his chair.

'I think so, yes.'

'You're not certain?'

'He didn't have a steady girlfriend, at least not that I knew of. I saw him talking to a few women, here and there, at parties, but he never brought anyone home. On the other hand, I wouldn't say he was a prude. Quite the opposite, in fact…'

'What are you implying?' Alexis encouraged.

'The walls of the flat were thin,' Ackermann explained, avoiding Alexis's gaze, 'and the sound of some of the porn films he watched in his room was a giveaway. One night, when I came home late from my girlfriend's, I even caught him in the kitchen spying on Tancredi and his girlfriend. He was, er, pleasuring himself.'

Ackermann cleared his throat to conceal his embarrassment.

'Did he ever talk about his past, something that might be significant or that struck you as odd?'

He shook his head.

'Any big rows with you or Tancredi?'

'No, nothing at all.'

'Did he have any friends, mates, other than you and Tancredi?'

Ackermann's forehead creased and he religiously brushed his fingertips through his moustache as he struggled to recall.

'Well, there *was* this one guy…'

THINGS WERE GETTING BACK to normal.

The front door swished open just as she was taking the casserole out of the oven.

Her brother walked into the kitchen with a cardboard box in his arms.

'*Hej!*'

Hilda took the cake from him and kissed him on the cheek.

'Smells delicious!' he said, spying the steaming dish in the middle of the kitchen table.

Things were definitely getting back to normal.

Hilda smiled.

'It's coq au vin. The children devoured theirs.'

He sat down at the table; Hilda took off her apron, draped it over the back of her chair and sat down in turn, across from her brother.

Sigvard served generous portions for them both while Hilda buttered two slices of *knäckebröd*, placing a thin slice of cheese on each before putting one on the side of her plate, and one on her brother's.

Sigvard tucked into the wine-and-herb-infused meat without a word. The only sounds to escape his mouth were those of gastronomic pleasure. Occasionally, he paused to extract a morsel stuck between his teeth, before licking his fingers and resuming his meal, feasting his eyes on the plate with undisguised, childlike greed.

He suddenly looked up at his sister, who hadn't even touched her food yet.

'Aren't you eating?'

With her elbows on the table and her chin resting on her inter-laced fingers, Hilda couldn't help but relish the sight of him enjoying his dinner.

'Yes, of course. It's just such a pleasure to see you with such an appetite.'

'It's superb, Hilda, it really is. You've outdone yourself!' he exclaimed, grabbing the ladle sticking out of the pot. 'Can I help myself to seconds, or were you hoping to have leftovers for lunch tomorrow?'

With a broad, contented smile, she told him to go ahead, and tucked right into the tasty stew along with him.

As they cleared the table, they chatted about some new recipes for French pastries Sigvard was keen to try out. Then, true to habit, he hugged his sister, gave her a long, gentle kiss on the forehead and went up to his room.

As soon as the stairs creaked, Skorpan appeared in the kitchen, leaving a small group of playmates in the living room to enjoy the fascinating adventures of *Pippi Longstocking* on the television.

'Hilda! What are we making this evening?'

Skorpan's skinny legs quivered with impatience.

'What would you like us to make, *älskling*?'

'Hmm…'

The child tapped a little finger on hungry lips, eyes flitting from left to right, pretending to be deep in thought.

Hilda burst out laughing.

'*Kanelbullar!*'

'All right, *kanelbullar* it is. I'll go and fetch the ingredients.'

'I'll come with you.'

'Of course! Come, my *älskling*.'

Skorpan hung onto Hilda's slender waist and kissed her on the hip.

Hilda stroked the child's fair hair, observing the delicate curves of a nose as pert and round as a rosebud. In the distance, she heard the familiar hum of the television in Sigvard's room. Now that his girlfriend was out of the picture, the days of missed dinners and stifled orgasms seeping through the walls were over, and the general awkwardness and heavy atmosphere were a thing of the past.

At last, things were getting back to normal.

FLORENCE HARTGROVE OPENED the door to Emily with a bunch of keys in her hand. In the hallway, a suit jacket hung from the handle of a carry-on suitcase standing next to the coat rack.

'I've only just got home,' the police chief's wife apologised, shaking the profiler's hand. 'The traffic was awful all the way in from Heathrow … I was so worried I would keep you waiting. I was on a business trip to China; it was horrendous. I must look as crumpled as my suit,' she joked, forcing a smile.

She led Emily through to the living room, then invited her to join her on the sofa with all the decorum of a well-bred hostess.

'Leland told me you still haven't had any news…'

Her face began to crack, as if she were about to cry, then lit up again in a polite smile.

'My goodness, I'm so sorry!' she exclaimed, rising to her feet. 'I'm all over the place! Would you like something to drink, BIA Roy?'

'I'm fine, thank you,' Emily replied, with an almost protective softness in her voice.

Florence Hartgrove sat down again on the edge of the sofa, her back straight and her hands flat on her thighs.

'I had Adrian on the phone on my way home,' she continued. 'He's devastated. The girls are waking up at night … having nightmares, the poor little loves. He just doesn't know what to tell them, how…'

She lowered her gaze, shook her head and brought a finger to her right eye to chase away a tear.

'I'm so sorry. I'm such a chatterbox.'

She waved her right hand in front of her face, and another smile appeared, contrasting with the sadness in her eyes.

'Do tell me, how can I be of assistance?' she asked, as she smoothed the edges of her expensive shawl with the tips of her fingers.

'We've established that Julianne wasn't at home on the night prior to her abduction. She was in a hotel, just a stone's throw away. Forty-seven Park Street. We believe she spent the night there. With her lover.'

Florence's lips formed the same *o* shape as the first time they had met. Her eyes locked on Emily's, as they had before, but only for a second before they began to flicker all over the living room.

Emily relished the silence, allowing it to weigh heavily on the other woman for a second or two.

'You're a close friend of hers, Florence. Surely Julianne must have mentioned this relationship to you?'

Again the same *o* appeared, like a sigh struggling to emerge.

Reluctantly, Florence turned her eyes back to meet the profiler's. Eyes that were stricken with pain, and fear.

'The key to her abduction might lie in this secret you're keeping to protect Julianne's reputation; to protect the ones she loves. And the ones you love.'

'You think it's because of that…'

Florence joined her hands together, as if in prayer, and held them to her mouth, pinching her upper lip between her index fingers.

'The most important thing now is to find Julianne. Can you help me, Florence?'

Mrs Hartgrove closed her eyes, then nodded her head a little.

'Don't worry, Florence. You'll see, it's all going to be OK.'

Emily took the commissioner's wife's hands in hers. They were trembling.

'Florence, how long have you been in a relationship with Julianne?'

Florence's eyes widened in surprise.

Those in secret relationships are always arrogant enough to believe they can evade reality. This was the first time anyone had hinted at her affair with Julianne. The first time a light was being shone onto the naked facts; the first time that words had been used to describe what had happened. Now the secret was turning into a lie. Love, sex. Fantasy, adultery.

'Three months last week.'

She lowered her eyes and continued folding and unfolding the hem of her dress.

'It's not … Well, I mean … I had never been with a woman before Julianne…'

She shook her head, then allowed herself a faint, tender smile, tainted with melancholy.

'We'd known each other for a decade. Together with our husbands, we'd spent a lot of time together, all four of us, and even more so once the girls were born. Holidays, birthdays and anniversaries, Christmas … We never, ever thought that we…'

Florence bit her lower lip, staring down at her lap in shame.

'It was unexpected … so completely unexpected, and it happened so suddenly. Well, perhaps not suddenly, but neither she nor I saw it coming.'

She leaned to the side and tucked her legs under her, holding on to the armrest of the sofa as if the ground beneath her had begun to slide away.

'That night, the girls were having a sleepover at a school friend's place. Leland was at a conference in Northampton and Adrian was away on a film shoot. Julianne had come over here for the evening. We'd done that so many times before. Ordered a takeaway, opened a good bottle of wine, laughed our hearts out. But that night, something just…'

She swallowed. Clenched her thighs together. Arched her back.

'I still don't understand how it happened.'

With the back of her hand, she wiped away the tears that were now streaming down her cheeks.

'We were shocked, terrified even. But we just couldn't control ourselves.'

She tried to laugh but it came out the wrong way, more like a groan.

'The desire was so…'

She opened her arms out wide, as if Julianne were now back and running towards her to take refuge in her embrace.

'It was all-consuming. Ever-present. Obsessive.'

She looked at Emily and breathed a heavy sigh.

'I'm sorry. It's indecent … I'm so sorry. This is the first time I've ever spoken about it. The first time I've ever talked openly about Julianne. And myself.'

Another sigh came as deliverance.

'This isn't just sex between two fading forty-something women who are bored, you know. Even though we'd almost rather that were the case.'

'Are you planning to leave your husbands?'

'Do you know the most curious thing of all? I love Leland. I love living with Leland. I love the life I have with my husband. I don't want to leave him. It's the same with Julianne: she would never do that to the girls, or Adrian, not ever. But we hadn't got to a point where we could find the best of both worlds, if ever that were possible.'

Emily gave her a few moments of silence to catch her breath.

'Florence, you're going to have to tell your husband you were with Julianne the night before her abduction.'

Anxiety spread across Florence Hartgrove's face.

'But it's entirely up to you how you explain it.'

Falkenberg
Sunday, 14 September 1980, 1 pm

THE CHILDREN HAD DEVOURED their lunch like little ogres. They inhaled the meatballs greedily as if they were no bigger than raisins, getting tomato sauce all over their faces.

Now they were all huddled together on the velvet sofa in the living room.

Hilda put her coffee down on the side table and sat cross-legged on the carpet. She wedged the book between her thighs and opened it.

On Saturdays and Sundays, straight after lunch, Hilda always read them a story. At first, none of them could sit still long enough; the smaller ones would bound around the room like little goat kids while Hilda continued to read, changing her voice for every character. Gradually, they had grown captivated by her stories and would congregate on the sofa to listen with rapt attention. The youngest ones would gaze at her with eager eyes, as if she were slicing up a cake and giving them each a piece.

'Today, I'm going to tell you the story of Odin.'

She turned the book around towards them and showed them the illustration depicting a one-eyed old man with a long white beard and whiskers, wearing a hat.

'Why is he missing an eye?'

'He gave his eye away in exchange for wisdom.'

'Is he the one with the magic hammer?'

'No, Thor's the one who has *Mjöllnir*, the magic hammer. Odin is Thor's father.'

'What's so magic about Odin?'

'Odin *is* magic. He is the God of all gods.'

'Is he the one who's naked on the cross?'

Hilda couldn't hide her smile. 'No, that's not him. Today, I'll be telling you about our own gods, here, in Sweden. The ones who existed well before the rivers, the seas and the mountains.'

'But I thought there was only one god and that he lived up there in the sky, above the clouds, with a white sheet draped across his shoulders and owned lots of things made of gold?'

Hilda bit her lip so she wouldn't burst out laughing.

'The world is much too big to have only one god. And the gods aren't just up there, in the sky. They're everywhere.'

'Is Odin like the other god, the one on the cross who asks people not to hit back if someone hurts you?'

'No. Odin allows the use of force when necessary and he even gives weapons to the most courageous warriors.'

'Is it him who gave Thor his magic hammer?'

'No, that was a dwarf named Brokk.'

'Oh, just shut up, will you?' Skorpan intervened. 'Let Hilda tell us all about Odin.'

'Don't speak like that to your brother.'

'But they're not letting you tell your story,' Skorpan protested.

'I'm getting there, all right. So, today, I'm going to tell you about Odin, because he's my favourite god. Do you know why?'

The four fair-haired children shook their heads in unison.

'Well, it's because Odin is the god who looks after the world. And there are nine worlds, in fact, in his kingdom. Can you show me how much nine is?'

Screwing up their faces, they all waved a varying number of tiny fingers, with varying degrees of confidence or hesitation.

'Nine is the number of fingers on two hands, less one. Very good. So, Odin is a god who looks after his nine worlds and, in order to do so, he has to travel a lot.'

'He goes on holiday?'

'Odin is a travelling god, but he doesn't take holidays; he is always working. He spends his time flying through the clouds, swimming in the oceans, blowing in the wind, trying to fathom how his nine worlds function. Everywhere he goes, he seeks wisdom and knowledge.'

'Like he's still in school?'

'Except for the fact that he enjoys it,' Hilda grinned.

'So, he enjoys having lessons to learn all the time?'

'Yes, Odin enjoys spending his time learning; he believes that knowledge is nothing if we don't keep on learning.'

'And does he take care of us too?'

'Of course. And he has two friends to help him. Two ravens called Huginn and Muninn. Every day at sunrise, Huginn and Muninn set off to travel around all nine worlds and return the following morning. They land on Odin's shoulders, one on each side, and whisper in his ear what they have seen and heard.'

'It's not good to tell tales, though, is it?'

'Huginn and Muninn help Odin look after the gods and the people he is protecting, the way we look after our family.'

'I'm Muninn!' Skorpan enthusiastically proclaimed, jumping on the sofa.

'And I'm the other raven!'

'Me, I'm Thor!'

'And I'm Odin!'

Skorpan shrugged.

'What are you on about? You don't get it, do you? Can't you see, Hilda is Odin? It's Hilda who looks after us. She's the one who feeds us and looks after the house, the pigs, Sigvard and even the horrible people. That's why I'm Muninn.'

Hilda stood up.

'Come on now, children, let's all go outside and get some fresh air.'

Her suggestion was greeted by general protest.

'No, we want to hear more about Odin and his ravens!'

'Next week. Come on, put your anoraks on, I'll see you outside.'

Three of them obeyed, slipping on their jackets and dashing out of the room. Skorpan followed Hilda, who was heading into the kitchen to put her cup in the sink.

'Is that why you made Sigvard's friend leave? To protect us, like Odin?' Skorpan asked.

Hilda turned around. She gazed for a moment into the blue eyes that were far too serious for such a young child; already damaged before life had even really begun.

'Yes,' she replied eventually, as she poured the dregs of her coffee down the sink.

'I know you didn't really make her leave,' Skorpan added.

Hilda froze.

'You know that?'

'I do. You forgot her shoes. Her socks and her shoes. The clogs she always left under the chest of drawers in the hallway. But don't you worry, I burned them. She really wasn't that nice, was she? And she wasn't a good mum.'

'No, she wasn't a good mum.'

'And no one loved her, apart from Sigvard. But she certainly had good taste.'

THE WATER'S COOL EMBRACE invigorated Emily from her very first stride. She ran in liquid time to the pitter-patter of the rain, sometimes lifting her knees as high as her chest to leap over gnarled roots and uprooted tree trunks.

Julianne Bell and Florence Hartgrove.

This morning, the pain coursing through her legs and buttocks was of no help in clarifying her thoughts. The one thought she was trying to ignore kept rising to the surface in her mind. Emily couldn't help but wonder whether the blossoming relationship between Julianne Bell and Florence Hartgrove could have triggered an intense stress response in the serial killer and led him to commit these crimes. The affair might have been the catalyst for him to start killing again … That would mean the Tower Hamlets killer knew Julianne Bell … Who was he? Her husband? Her brother? A friend? A fan? What if he were an acquaintance of Florence Hartgrove's?

Emily shook her head. That still wouldn't explain why the man had interrupted his killing spree for ten years. No … something was niggling at her. As if she were reading a sentence that needed a comma to make sense; a comma that could change the entire meaning of the sentence, depending on where it was placed.

She blinked away the beads of sweat and raindrops obscuring her vision.

Pearce was in the process of broadening the investigation to canvas Julianne Bell's entire entourage. Not just the make-up artists, hairdressers, friends, colleagues and hangers-on, but also Florence Hartgrove and the commissioner himself. The chances they would dig something up were slim, but this time the DCS couldn't leave any stone unturned.

Emily slowed her pace as she approached a rocky downhill section of the path. When she reached the bottom, she stopped and leaned against a shrivelled tree, and started to do some stretches.

There was one other crucial element she still had no satisfactory explanation for: the feathers inside the victims' ears. In every case, Maria Paulsson included, the killer had used synthetic feathers, dyed black – made in China and sold all over the world. The obstruction of the ear canals could mean one of two things: either the killer was hoping the victim wouldn't hear anything; or he was punishing her for not listening. Either way, it might be a punishment the serial killer had endured himself as a child. But why choose black feathers? The profiler had identified a few theories, but wanted to discuss the matter with her Swedish colleagues before drawing any kind of conclusions.

Her phone vibrated. She pulled it from the plastic pocket of her armband and held it a centimetre away from her wet ear. The conversation lasted barely ten seconds.

Emily unbuttoned her jacket and pulled out her little black box from the inner pocket. She opened it and spirited her nascent theories inside, together with her suppositions and questions, as well as the portraits of all seven victims. She placed her images of Julianne Bell and Florence Hartgrove on top of it all. Then she closed the box, tucked it back into her pocket and started to run back home.

THE CLEAR BLUE SKY ushered in a cold that burned cheeks and hastened people's paces for fear of numbness setting in. It would have been a beautiful day, had the wind not been blowing with such persistent rage. It moaned as it bent and broke the bare branches of the trees, as if ravaging everything in its path was a painful pursuit.

Sigvard's little white van pulled up a few metres away from the barn. As he got out of the driver's seat, he smoothed the wrinkles on his forehead with the tips of his fingers. He stared at the ground in front of him as he tottered his way towards his sister, buffeted by the wind.

He knew Hilda had heard him arrive, but she didn't turn around.

Her thin body seemed rooted to the spot in the middle of the gaggle of pigs happily oinking down their breakfast.

Sigvard glanced at the two mucky buckets on the old plough beside her. Hilda plunged one hand clad in a yellow rubber glove inside, grabbing another handful of chunks of meat and throwing them to the pigs, provoking a crescendo of enthusiastic grunts.

'The police came to see me at the bakery,' Sigvard began, hesitantly. 'They wanted to know if I was with Kerstin ... the night she disappeared.'

Hilda swivelled around. The savage wind blew her hair in all directions, lashing her ponytail against her shoulders and whipping stray curls across her face.

'On the night she disappeared, you were at your golf-club function. I was here with the kids.'

Sigvard's mouth gaped open as he gasped for air.

Hilda gave him a dispassionate look and an incredulous smile.

'Is that what you came home to tell me?'

He implored her with his eyes. His sister's smile widened.

'You should get back to the bakery. Get back to work. I'll see you at dinner time,' she said, as her gloved hands scraped the bottom of the bucket.

Sigvard forced himself to banish from his mind all the terrible images that were running through it, trampling over the life he had built with Hilda and his love for her.

'Sigvard?'

A slap in the face to bring him back in line.

He pulled himself together quickly, kissed his sister on her forehead and drove off again.

'The pig is Scandinavia's sacred animal, the dish with which we honour Odin,' Hilda declared aloud, as she continued to feed the hungry horde. She emptied the remnants in the second bucket on the ground and walked back into the house in silence.

She put the containers away in the utility room, then went into the pantry. Skorpan was sliding the bolt across the trapdoor that led down to the cellar.

'She keeps on screaming. She even spat at me when I gave her the bottle.'

'Open it again, please, *älskling*.'

Skorpan obeyed.

A cacophony of muffled cries surged forth from the opening. Desperate pleas amid a flood of tears.

Hilda sighed heavily.

It was time to silence Kerstin. And to start getting lunch ready.

ALEXIS SAT DOWN with a cup of coffee and a slice of lemon cake at Starbucks, at a round table by the door.

As she nibbled her breakfast, she congratulated herself for passing on the porridge. She had thought about it, but had soon changed her mind. As soon as she laid eyes on the assortment of cakes and pastries, the idea of porridge for breakfast had quickly evaporated, like a bad dream. *None of that horse fodder for me*, she thought, washing her sweet treat down with a mouthful of coffee. Taking better care of her arteries and thighs could wait until another day.

Her meeting the previous day with Oliver Ackermann had been something of a disappointment; she had hoped to find out a lot more from the head of the nursery. But other than the name of Hemfield's acquaintance and a dinner invitation, she'd walked out empty-handed.

'Alexis?'

With her mouth still full of one last bite of cake, she looked up and saw a shaven-headed man in his fifties, wearing a grey hoodie.

He extended a hand covered in paint for her to shake.

'Harvey,' he said. 'Somehow I pictured you as older.'

Unable to summon a reaction to such a candid introduction, Alexis settled for a faint smile.

'It was so much easier for us to meet here,' he said, taking a seat. 'We're running behind schedule on the site, and I'm working all sorts of hours. So, what's this book you're writing? When does it come out?'

Harvey Cowden, a former colleague of Richard Hemfield's, wouldn't have taken the empathy bait; Alexis had had to pretend she was writing a book about Hemfield.

'We haven't set a firm date yet.'

'Ah. So, what was it you wanted to know about Ricky, or Richard, as you call him?'

'Perhaps we could start with how you first met?'

'Hey, we weren't sleeping together! I'm more into girls like you,' he said, with a glint in his eye.

Indeed, thought Alexis. She must be sending out the wrong signals.

'So, who *did* he sleep with?'

'Damn it, you don't waste any time, do you?'

Look who's talking, Harvey, she thought.

'You're the one who brought it up,' Alexis replied, without batting an eye, 'but I was going to ask you anyway. You broke the ice, so why shouldn't I take advantage?'

Harvey Cowden burst out laughing, revealing a set of teeth that would make any dentist proud.

'Ricky was always on the prowl. I never saw him pull that many pieces of skirt, come to think of it, but he was always leering. As soon as a girl came anywhere near him, he was like a dog trying to catch a whiff. I'm sure he'd have gone around sniffing their arses if he could!'

You have no idea how true that is, Alexis thought.

'He often went to those peep shows in Soho, where you look at a girl in a window touching herself, know what I mean?'

No, she didn't – and felt all the better for it.

'Is he the one who told you about the peep shows?'

'No, we bumped into each other in the one on Greek Street. Caught each other red-handed!'

Another peal of laughter bared his ridiculously white teeth again.

'So, that aside, what sort of man was he?'

'That aside, he wasn't one to go out on the town. He was more the quiet type. Probably preferred to chat women up on his own.'

'How did you come to meet him?'

'I'd been putting up shelves at the café where he worked. He was such a great help, I persuaded my dad to take him on whenever we needed an extra pair of hands. Now, I've taken over the business. Well, my wife runs it. Right now, we're busy with a big home renovation we have to finish up by the autumn. I can't tell you how far behind we are. Anyway, getting back to Ricky, my father ended up calling on him so often that he stopped working at the café. He worked for my dad for six years or more before he went off to set up his own business. But he only did painting and some basic decorating, small-scale stuff. So, he wasn't really a competitor.'

'Did you stay in touch?'

'No. We weren't exactly close friends. We just went for the odd beer or two whenever we worked on a job together, that's all. He was a good bloke, Ricky. I'm sure he didn't do all those things he was accused of. It's a pity I wasn't called as a witness at the trial, because I'd have been happy to speak on his behalf. I still don't understand why they never called me in.'

Alexis knew why: a friend who frequented strip clubs as often as others went to the gym would have been no help to 'Ricky'.

'Did he have any other friends, apart from you?'

'His two flatmates. That's it, I think.'

'And you never saw him have any arguments with workmates, clients, male or female? No rows at all?'

'No, he was clean, I'm telling you.'

'Did he ever talk about his family?'

'Once, he mentioned his bitch of an aunt.'

Alexis waited for him to go on. She nodded to prompt him.

Harvey leaned in closer to Alexis. He laid his paint-stained hands flat on the table, and looked straight at her.

'Back then, we did a lot of work for some businesses in Covent Garden. Refitting a load of stores, restaurants, beauty salons, that kind of thing. One day, Ricky told me that working around there brought back bad memories for him, because his aunt used to work in an Italian restaurant in the next street over.'

'Do you remember the name of the street you were on?'

'Floral or Russell Street. Around there, anyway. But do you know what the poor bloke said to me? That the bitch who brought him up only had one thing on her mind. She was a bloody nymphomaniac! He said she used to bring blokes home all the time and frig herself off when she was on her own. Squealed like a pig, he said! And she'd always leave her bedroom door open so Ricky, would see and hear. He was only five; can you imagine? My son was the same age when Ricky told me about all this. I was sick to my stomach. Poor bloke...'

Not just a nymphomaniac, but a paedophile, Alexis reflected.

'And you never met his aunt?'

'Well, that would have been awkward; she'd been pushing up daisies for ten to fifteen years by then.'

A DISHEVELLED KARLA with streaks of white down her cheeks opened the door to Olofsson.

'What the hell, Hansen! What's happened to you? Mixed up your toothpaste and your mascara, did you?'

'Just give me two minutes, Olofsson. My girls are driving me crazy this morning. Come in. My husband's making another pot of coffee.'

'Muuuummm! She won't give me back my top! Tell her to give it baaaaccckkkk! Daddddyyy—'

More screaming and shouting drowned out the last part of the eldest Hansen daughter's complaint.

'Coffee's tempting, but I'd rather wait outside, thanks.'

Olofsson walked back to the refuge of his car, thanking the gods he didn't have children himself. Why the hell did people have them? It was a crazy world: mums swelled to double their size and dads pushed buggies around like lunatics. Actually, there was a correlation between the two, he realised. And judging by the Hansen tribe this morning, things didn't get much better with age.

The creaking of the passenger door interrupted his thoughts. Karla got into the car with a heavy sigh, more a sign of deliverance than an expression of relief.

'Thanks for picking me up, Olofsson. Our car wouldn't start this morning. What a disaster! My husband's going to have to hire one. Why didn't you come in and say hello?'

'I'll wait for the cease-fire.'

Karla rolled her eyes.

'No, but seriously, Hansen, why do people keep on doing it over and over again?' Olofsson asked, starting the engine.

'Doing what?'

'Having kids.'

'It's for the state benefits, actually.'

'I'm not surprised!'

'Just kidding. You and Nyman are like peas in a pod. You're just as allergic to children as he is!'

'Have you heard anything from him? How's he getting on running the station?'

'It's a madhouse. Poor soul must be on the verge of a nervous breakdown.'

Karla pulled her phone out of her jacket pocket. 'How far are we from Torslanda? About two hours' drive, do you think?' she asked, checking the screen.

'An hour and forty minutes, according to my satnav, which means I should manage it in an hour and a quarter, tops.'

'OK. I'm going to call back home and see if everyone is still alive…'

Olofsson shot a look of outrage at his colleague. 'You're kidding! You're not going to make me sit through some parental lecture, are you?'

'When you're a dad one day, you'll understand.'

'Yeah, right, like that's ever going to happen!'

✦✦✦

Olofsson parked on a gravel driveway between two rectangles of lawn dotted with tombstones, behind a church with a red-tiled roof and plaster walls. It looked more like someone's home than a house of God.

Bergström and *Nicholas-Nordin-Medical-Examiner* were deep in conversation in front of a white tent set up against the side wall of the building. They greeted Hansen and Olofsson with a nod.

'At least she won't have to travel far for her final confession,' Olofsson muttered as they pulled on gloves, protective outfits and shoe covers.

Hansen ignored him. Her colleague had his own way of readying himself for the scene they were about to witness.

Karla was the first to duck into the tent, with the rustling of Olofsson's protective outfit hot on her heels.

The young woman had been seated against the white wall of the church. Her arms hung alongside her body, and her hands rested on the ground, palms turned to the sky. There were two deep, bloody halos in her chest where her breasts should have been. Her thighs and hips had been carved right down to the bone.

'Her buttocks too,' Karla confirmed, kneeling over the body.

Focus on her hair, thought Olofsson, averting his eyes from the gruesome wounds. He stared at the blonde hair that cascaded over the dead woman's shoulders like a shawl. As far as the rest of her was concerned, he just wondered what the whole damned point of having children was if they could end up like this? He didn't even want to think about it.

'Freja Lund. Twenty-two years old,' the commissioner announced gravely.

Olofsson turned around. Bergström and Nordin were standing behind him, beside Hansen. He hadn't heard them come in. The medical examiner had tilted his head to one side and was staring at the body.

'The wounds are consistent with Maria Paulsson's,' he stated. 'As is the ligature used to strangle her. There are black feathers in her ear canals. I don't want to put words in your mouth, gentlemen – oh, sorry, Detective Hansen – but this is clearly the work of the same killer.'

Olofsson stepped outside the tent, and Hansen followed, leaving Nordin and Bergström behind.

'Just like Google predicted,' Olofsson said, yanking off his latex gloves.

'Google? What are you on about, Olofsson?' Hansen asked.

'I mean Lindbergh. Aliénor. Maybe I should start calling her Little Miss *Encyclopaedia Britannica,* so you don't get confused.'

'Oh, such a bad boy,' Karla chided, waving a finger in his face. 'So, what did Aliénor say?'

'She said it was all connected to Jack the Ripper. Where have we found this latest body? In Torslanda. And Torslanda just happens to be where Elizabeth Stride was born. She was the Ripper's third victim.'

AS SHE OPENED the front door of her flat, Alexis was starting to draw up a mental list of the next steps in her research:

1. Check the transcript of Hemfield's trial and interrogation to see whether there was any mention of an aunt.

She set her handbag down on the side table by the entrance.

2. Find the Italian restaurant near Floral Street.
3. ...

Alexis shrieked in surprise. Stellan was standing in the kitchen doorway. He sidled over to her and gave her a long kiss.

'I see you'd forgotten I was arriving today,' he whispered, as he released her from his embrace.

'I...'

'Or rather, perhaps you lost track of time entirely.'

'I'm so sorry, darling...'

As she planted kisses all over his face, she realised she hadn't spoken to her mother, or to Stellan, since she had hurriedly left Falkenberg two days earlier. *Oops*, she thought, *it should be the other way around: Stellan or my mother.* They had only exchanged a few texts following her visit to Broadmoor. Alexis had let them know the encounter had gone well, but told them she didn't feel like talking about it. They had respected her silence, but she wondered whether her father must have hidden her mother's phone to stop her inundating her with questions. Mado Castells must be on tenterhooks. To say the least.

'How did it go?' she asked, shifting two stacks of files from the sofa to the coffee table.

'Very well.'

Alexis stared at him in disbelief.

'How did it *really* go?'

'Very well. Honestly, it was fantastic. I had some good, long chats with your dad, and your mum and I did some cooking together. She even taught me how to make crêpes. Not pancakes, proper French crêpes.'

'A likely story … I bet my mum spent her time grilling you about you and me, not cooking with you.'

'Well, that too…'

'So how did you and my father manage to stop her picking up the phone every five minutes to ask me how it went with Hemfield?'

'We locked her in the cellar.'

Alexis rolled her eyes and held back a smile.

'It was almost better that you weren't there, I think.'

'Oh … why's that?'

'Your parents didn't feel like they had to walk on eggshells, and I wasn't as worried about disappointing you.'

'Disappointing me?'

'Well, I am the first man you've introduced to your parents since … Samuel.'

Alexis stiffened. It was still painful to hear Samuel's name coming from Stellan's mouth.

'So, have you started writing yet?'

'I met up with a former colleague of Hemfield's,' Alexis replied, with contrition in her voice.

'A colleague?'

'Harvey Cowden. One of Hemfield's old flatmates, who happened to be one of the witnesses for the defence, put me in touch with him.'

Stellan nodded.

'And what did you find out?'

Alexis felt as if she was walking blindfolded into a minefield.

'According to the information gathered by the police and the prosecution, Hemfield's parents died in a road accident. Following their death, their son was put in the care of an aunt on his father's side, Angela Hemfield.'

'How did you get hold of those documents?'

'Jon Pierland, the profiler who was with Samuel when he died. He passed them on to me at the time.'

Alexis swallowed.

'But, according to Harvey Cowden,' she continued, her voice growing hoarse, 'the aunt in question died about a year after the parents. I have to find out what actually happened and who looked after Hemfield after his aunt's death.'

'Why?'

It's not just a minefield, Alexis reckoned. *I'm in a war zone.*

'So, you're questioning me now as well, are you?' she barked, standing up.

'I just get the impression you're avoiding me, Alexis. Actually, it's more than just a feeling: you left Falkenberg just as our relationship was shifting up a gear. To hurl yourself headfirst into your past, back to the love of your life.'

Alexis felt a cold rage surge deep within, creeping around inside her like a weed. She shook her head and went off towards the kitchen.

'See, you're doing it again, avoiding the issue,' he said in a calm, yet firm voice.

Alexis stopped in her tracks, then slowly turned around to face Stellan.

'I need answers,' she stressed, fighting the temptation to just walk out on him.

'You're acting like an angry teenager. Would you just come and sit down, please?'

Shame rained down on Alexis. Stellan was right. She had to lower her defences. This wasn't war, just a conversation with the man she was in love with. But it was so damned hard to open up to him.

He took her hand and held it in his.

'I need to … draw a line under everything,' she murmured, casting her eyes over the files stacked up on the coffee table.

'You have to draw the line full stop, Alexis. The Tower Hamlets investigation has nothing to do with Samuel's death. Hemfield is guilty of Samuel's death, and nothing else the investigation uncovers is going to change that.'

Stellan kissed the back of her hand and then stood up.

Alexis felt the grief weighing heavy in her heart.

Stellan returned a couple of minutes later with a bottle of wine and two stemmed glasses. He set everything down on the table between the piles of documents.

'I know that, being French and all, you have strong moral objections to wine bottles with screw caps, but the man in the wine shop assured me this Riesling is delicious. So, what are we looking for?' he asked, as he poured the wine.

Stellan's words took Alexis by surprise. She looked at him for a second before she gave him an answer.

'First of all, I want to go through the transcripts of Hemfield's trial and questioning again to see what information there might be about Angela Hemfield. If we can't find anything, then we'll have to track down the Italian restaurant where she was working before she died, back in 1979. It was in Covent Garden, somewhere around Floral Street.'

'In 1979? You do realise it's probably been closed for years?'

'There is one other line of inquiry. But I'm going to look into that myself,' she said, taking a sip of her white wine.

SITTING ON THE HANSENS' TERRACE with a Carlsberg in her hand, Emily was looking out at Halmstad's futuristic library building, an arc of glass and steel that reached out into the Nissan river. It had just stopped raining and the sun's rays were now piercing through the clouds like an archer's arrows. It only took a minute or two for the sky to clear and take on a deep shade of blue again, in deference to summer.

The profiler swallowed a mouthful of her frothy beer.

Her plane had landed in Gothenburg in the middle of the afternoon, two hours late. Bergström had only just had time to walk her around the Freja Lund crime scene before the thunderstorm had rolled in and chased them away from Torslanda. They had then driven to Karla's house in Halmstad, where the rest of the team was waiting. They were going to do some work and have a barbecue together.

Ada, the Hansens' youngest daughter, barrelled out onto the terrace.

'Are you Emily?'

'Yes, that's me.'

Ada sat down next to Emily, grabbed a fleece throw that was draped over the back of the chair and laid it on her lap.

'I heard Detective Olofsson say to the man with the beard that your brain was as big as my mummy's boobs. And Mummy's boobs are very big. Much bigger than the other mummies'. But your head doesn't look that big. It looks even smaller than mine.'

'Your English is very good,' Emily said with a smile.

'I've been having English lessons for ever. Did you know that Greta Gris in English is Peppa Pig?'

Karla arrived, carrying a tray of *knäckebröd*, butter, cheese and beers.

'Hey, what are you doing here out here, missy? You should be in bed by now,' she told her youngest.

'I'm having a chat with Emily, Mum.'

Karla set the tray down, restraining a smile.

'Oh, really? And what are you chatting about?'

Ada glanced at Emily for support before she answered.

'About Peppa Pig. And I was about to tell her how some Swedish words can't be translated into English, like *mångata*, *fika* or *tretår*. So, Emily,' she continued in English, 'did you know there are Swedish words you can't translate into English? That's what our teacher told us.'

Ada dipped her hand into a bowl of crisps on the table in front of Emily.

'Ada, don't stuff yourself with junk food; have some *knäckebröd* instead. Are you hungry?'

'No. So, *mångata*, that means the ray of light the moon casts on the water that looks like a road,' she explained through a mouthful of crisps. '*Fika* is a kind of coffee break you have with friends or family, and often there's cake too. And *tretår* means you're going back for a third cup of coffee. There are other words like that, but I don't remember them. Did you know that, Emily?'

Emily shook her head.

Karla went about lighting the barbecue, beaming with pride.

'But Mummy, are you still having a barbecue, even though the weather isn't very nice?' a wide-eyed Ada suddenly asked, with crisp crumbs all around her mouth. 'It's so cold out here.' Then she added, in English, 'Swedish people are crazy!'

'They don't call us Vikings for nothing. Come on, it's bedtime, little missy. Hurry up.'

'Mummy…'

'Yes?'

'Where's Daddy?'

'In his study, with Kommissionär Bergström.'

'Which one is Kommissionär Bergström?'

'The man with the beard. He's my boss.'

'What are they doing?'

'Daddy is showing him his books.'

'I'd like to see Daddy's books too.'

'Ada…'

Karla's tone meant business.

Sulking, Ada reluctantly climbed down from the chair. She folded the blanket and draped it over the back of the chair, then dragged her feet all the way back inside.

The two women exchanged smiles, but Karla picked up on a hint of sadness in Emily's eyes and refrained from asking her the customary question, 'So, do you have children too?'

'You wanted to ask me something earlier and we were interrupted,' Karla said, to divert attention from any awkwardness.

Emily nodded. 'What fairy tales do you read to children in Sweden?'

'Hmm … For the little ones, the adventures of *Alfons Åberg* are very popular. When they're a bit older, we usually read the Astrid Lindgren stories. *Pippi Långstrump.* "Pippi Longstocking" in English, I think.'

'Don't you teach them about Nordic mythology?'

'They learn about it at school, but no, we don't normally make a habit of reading those at bedtime.'

'So, you don't tell them the stories of Odin or Asgard?'

'Well, no … Although, since Chris Hemsworth has been playing Thor on the big screen, I must say I've noticed my eldest daughter seems to have taken more of an interest in mythology! Why do you ask?'

'Your husband tells me you're defending your thesis in judicial psychology soon?'

It wasn't so much the abrupt change of subject that surprised Karla, but the question itself.

'That's right.'

She hesitated for a second.

'I've always dreamed of working at the Yard.'

'So, now we find out Julianne Bell was batting for the other team!' Olofsson breezed out onto the terrace, beer in hand, flanked by Aliénor. The detective took a seat beside Emily.

'Quite an embarrassment for a chief of police, I must say! I doubt he'll get over it. I bet he'll end up resigning. Anyway, if she had to seek comfort elsewhere, and when I say elsewhere I do mean the *other side*, I suppose he can't have been that good on the job, if you know what I mean…'

Emily's phone buzzed in her jacket pocket.

'Aliénor, you should be careful not to be seen with this man in public,' Karla joked.

The profiler picked up the call.

'I do my best to avoid him. It's a coincidence we happened to walk out onto the terrace at the same time. I'd just been to the toilet.'

'We'll be there in half an hour,' Emily told the voice on the other end of the line, and hung up.

Karla turned away from her colleagues and looked at Emily.

'Oh, thank you very much, Lindbergh. That's charming,' Olofsson teased, taking a swig of his beer.

Emily rose.

'We have to go to the station for a video conference with the Yard,' she told them. 'They've arrested someone.'

I'm going to kiss my girls.

Their cheeks. Their eyes. Their foreheads. Their braids. Their hands.

Hold them tight in my arms.

One on each side.

Here, right by my breast.

Their heads huddled against my neck.

Their hair tickling my nose.

I'm going to smell them. Sniff them. Breathe them in.

Listen to their music; the music of their laughter and their voices.

I'm going to kiss Adrian, tell him I love him, in spite of everything. Tell him I love him.

I love you too, my Raymond.

I'm going to hug all four of you. We'll be a cluster of love.

We'll want to laugh, but we'll cry. We'll cry as we laugh. We won't be crying with happiness. It'll be more than that. We'll be laughing with love. And relief.

And you, my Florence.

I will finally be able to see you every single day, my Florence.

Every day.

In the light of day.

OLOFSSON UNROLLED THE SCREEN and switched on the projector while Bergström, Emily and Karla made themselves comfortable around the conference-room table. Then, sitting himself down at the computer, he noticed Aliénor huddled up in a corner of the room, gazing at the screen. She was sitting cross-legged on the floor, with her notebook on her knees.

A few minutes later, they watched Pearce walk into the interview room. Olofsson moved his fingers across the keyboard and the screen split into two: on the left, a wide-angle view of the room showing the DCS from the front and the witness's back; on the right, a close-up of Julianne Bell's brother, Raymond.

'Mr Bell, why did you conceal the fact that you were adopted by the Bell family?'

Raymond Bell slowly shook his head from side to side, his eyes riveted to the metal table.

'I didn't think to mention it.'

Pearce remained silent for a moment, staring at his suspect.

'I find it strange, Mr Bell, that it wouldn't come to mind. It makes me think that you didn't want us to find out about your adoption.'

'That's nonsense! Why would I hide it?'

'Because the adoption took place in Sweden and you are Swedish by birth.'

'So? What's the connection with my sister's abduction?'

Pearce planted his elbows on the table and interlaced his fingers. He rubbed the palm of his right hand with his left thumb.

'Is there something you're not telling me?' Julianne's brother was looking increasingly agitated. 'Have you found her? Did you find her in Sweden?'

'Can you tell me about your parents, Raymond?'

Raymond Bell retreated, leaning against the back of his chair.

'My parents were generous, loving, fun people. They died twenty-five years ago, shortly after their elder son…'

Pearce frowned.

'They both died of cancer, eight months apart. More like they died of grief, actually. My brother was killed in a ski accident when he was twenty-two. He had everything to live for. He was bright, devilishly handsome, studying at Oxford … Doors opened for him wherever he went. My parents referred to him as their ray of sunshine. And it was true, William was a brilliant soul.'

'I was referring to your biological parents.'

'My biological parents? Don't you know, true parents are the ones who rock you to sleep and take care of you, feed you and educate you, protect and encourage you … They're the ones who console you, show you the way, nurture you…'

'And love you.'

'And love you, of course. The term "biological parent" is nonsense, Detective Chief Superintendent, it should be banned. There are progenitors, and there are parents. Please don't call the people who brought me into this world my parents. They were never parents to me. My progenitors forgot about me, ignored me and abandoned me. First of all, my "biological" father walked out on us when I was two, then my "biological" mother did the same thing a year and a half later, leaving me behind, of course. So, I landed in the nearest orphanage. That's the wonderful family story my "biological parents" bequeathed to me and that's the story the head of the orphanage told me, not missing out a single detail, as she kindly explained to me that if I didn't stop wetting the bed every single night, no one would want me. And that, to cut a long story short, is essentially what happened: no one came forward to adopt me until the Bells came along.'

'You were adopted by the Bells very late in the day. You were eleven.'

'Maybe.'

'Don't you remember?'

'No.'

'Raymond, you seem to have erased seven years of your life from your memory. From the time you were three and a half until you were eleven?'

'Don't twist my words. That's just insulting! I said I didn't remember how old I was when the Bells adopted me. And that's the truth: I have no memory of it. All I recall is spending all my time with William when I was at the Bells'. It might well be that the adoption arrangements were made late in the day, but I was living with them as a fully fledged member of their family long before I was eleven.'

'Raymond, can you tell me about your foster family?'

'My memories are vague ... I'm not even sure I could tell the difference between being in the orphanage or being in the foster families...'

'There were several?'

'Maybe ... I told you I can't remember exactly. I just recall some faces, some names ... Hilda was one of the women who looked after me, and her husband was named Sigfried ... or maybe it was Sigvard, or something. But what's the connection between my adoption and Julianne's abduction?'

'Do you know Richard Hemfield?'

'The killer?'

'Yes, the killer.'

'What does he have to do with ... Julianne?'

The DCS allowed the silence to set in. A heavy, brutal silence permeated with grief and loss. Deafening.

Raymond Bell closed his eyes momentarily, taking a deep breath before he opened them again.

'Raymond, where is your sister?'

'Where is my…'

He snarled his lips and banged his cuffed hands repeatedly on the table. His wavy hair bounced in time with the swaying of the chain connecting the handcuffs.

'You're wasting your time, Pearce!' he yelled. 'And Julianne's. My sister is everything, absolutely everything to me! Can't you see? Do you know how many times my brother-in-law has accused me of being in love with my sister? Of having some form of incestuous relationship with her? When all I was doing was giving her the tools she needed to build her career. And teaching her how to use them. That's all. Helping and supporting her, as a brother should. That's all…'

He used the back of his hand to wipe away the snot that was dripping down towards his mouth.

'You're looking in the wrong direction, Pearce,' he muttered in a weary voice laced with menace.

SKORPAN GAZED UP at the giant pole in the middle of the field. Topped with a triangle flanked by two circles and adorned with greenery and flowers, it stood proudly in celebration of *Midsommar*, the feast of St John. The whole construct curiously resembled a phallus impaling a vagina; it was so obvious, you had to be truly narrow-minded not to see it.

The first day of celebration was drawing to a close: following the traditional feast of herring and creamed potatoes with chives, and strawberries, the children had done their traditional frog dance around the maypole, and the families had finally gone home to bed. The only souls remaining were those sleeping off the huge quantities of beer and schnapps they had ingested, and those who were smooching – or doing other things – in the shadows.

For some, it would soon be time for a second feast. Anyone with the right appetite would be eager to come to the table, given what was on the menu. Breasts surging forth from cleavages, skirts that left nothing to the imagination, flirty looks that said, 'I want you right now', all washed down with lashings of alcohol. *Yum, yum.*

The piece of skirt Hilda had her eye on came from Kiruna, a town in the north built on an ice field, 'between two penguin colonies', as she had joked earlier. She was one of those air-headed sorts who slept with seven different types of flowers under her pillow on *Midsommar* night, so that she would dream of her future husband. The kind of girl who'd take too long to figure out how her pussy worked and end up with three kids from three different men in the process.

It was crazy to see how many degenerate mothers and depraved whores were around these days, polluting the streets. It appeared to be a universal, timeless problem, and it had been around for ages. Assisted by Huginn and Muninn, his faithful ravens, Odin had journeyed through all nine of his worlds purifying the air, eliminating its tainted atoms. Preventing the contaminated air from entering your house and poisoning you while you slept.

Just as your mother is the first country you come to know, your family is the first world you grow up in. You had a duty to take care of your family. To protect it from the degenerate mothers and depraved whores; to prevent them from reproducing and spreading.

They had to be completely eradicated, and they should not be allowed to nourish the earth with their remains. Instead, they should become fodder themselves, reduced to their primal essence – flesh you could chew on, swallow and digest.

Skorpan ran a tongue across hungry lips. Hilda had prepared a magnificent St John's feast. The pâté she had served was one of the best she had ever made.

The girl from Kiruna was smiling at Skorpan.

Stupid old Sigvard had been seeing her in secret. His taste in women was truly dreadful and, more to the point, dangerous. Since he'd been seeing her, the atmosphere in the house had grown toxic.

The girl from Kiruna twisted one of her curls around her index finger as she cocked her head to one side. The long feathers of the dreamcatchers dangling from her ears grazed against her bare shoulders.

'Say, can you give me a ride back to Morup? I don't really feel up to walking…' she asked drunkenly, eyeing up Skorpan's Vespa.

'If you want me to.'

The girl climbed onto the scooter and hung onto Skorpan more tightly than she needed to.

Ten minutes later, Skorpan was parking the Vespa behind the barn.

'Hey, we're not in Morup yet…'

Skorpan punched her on the jaw, and she fell to the ground.

'No, we're not in Morup.'

Skorpan straddled her, pulling off a thick belt and tying it around her throat.

The girl blinked and, feeling the pressure on her neck, opened her eyes wide. Skorpan allowed a couple of seconds to pass before tightening the belt, watching the fear cloud the eyes of the prey. Her eyeballs looked like they were going to pop out of their sockets.

She was wriggling about like a fish out of water, sticking her pink tongue out as far as it would go in search of the oxygen she was being deprived of. Then, all of a sudden, her whole body relaxed.

Skorpan stared at the girl's face, which was frozen in an expression of horror, then quickly untied the belt and threaded it back through the loops of the jeans. One of the dreamcatcher earrings had landed in the girl's mouth.

There was something devilishly ironic about that. The lucky charms had not done what they were supposed to do. Her worst nightmare had penetrated the protection they should have provided her. And the feathers! They were grazing the poor girl's shoulders, as if Odin's ravens, Huginn and Muninn, had landed there to whisper into her ears that something was decidedly wrong in her world.

Skorpan yanked the black feathers out of the earrings and plunged them into the girl's ears.

Silly little whore. She really should have listened to them.

OLOFSSON STRETCHED AND FINISHED his morning exercises with a yawn. His brain felt jumbled. He was in desperate need of another coffee and something to eat, before Emily got on his wick with all her profiling whatnot.

He was unable to process all the snippets of information she came out with at a mile a minute. If he could, he'd scribble it all down while she was talking. Or even better, record it all to listen to at his leisure at a meeting only he would attend. But he still had his pride. It was a good thing the dream team, Hansen and Lindbergh, were catching the gist of it all, as easily as if the profiler were explaining a recipe. He just didn't want anyone to think he was stupid.

Olofsson glanced at his colleagues. Emily was glued to the board, her eyes locked on the gruesome crime-scene photographs. Bergström was scribbling God-knows-what in his notebook. Hansen and Lindbergh were lost in the files about the Tower Hamlets victims.

No, but for real, who would have thought? Hansen had a rack like a porn star's, minus the oyster-grade IQ that usually went with it. And the other one, she was as flat as a pancake, the type of girl who would prefer freaking tofu salad to a great steak, but she was a looker as well.

The detective looked down at the basket of pastries.

What if, instead of munching away, he pulled up his socks and said something useful for once? Just to show he could think for himself.

Olofsson rose abruptly, his chair scraping across the linoleum floor, and strode with determination across the conference room. He stood next to the board and immediately felt like a brainless TV game-show host. He banished the thought and pointed a finger at the final photo. The ninth.

'Freja Lund, twenty-two. Lived and worked in Torslanda. Medical student interning at the Sjöwall medical practice.'

His colleagues looked up at him, wide-eyed. Except for the profiler. Emily was sizing him up, good and proper. Hell, maybe he should do this more often!

'Freja was last seen at *Stardust*, the bowling alley in the industrial area, last Saturday night at eleven,' he continued. 'She was found six days later at the church in Torslanda, naked and strangled to death, with flesh carved out of her breasts, hips, thighs and buttocks, just like the previous victims.'

Karla's eyes scanned the faces of all nine women. Jeanine Sanderson. Diana Lantar. Katie Atkins. Chloe Blomer. Sylvia George. Clara Sandro. Maria Paulsson. Julianne Bell. Freja Lund.

Freja Lund. With all the arrogance of youth sparkling in her eyes. The come-hither curl of her lips. Her mouth half-open as if waiting for a lover's kiss. Barely into her twenties. Still a child.

'How do you think he spirits them away?' Olofsson asked, turning to Emily. 'There are no marks or signs of struggle on the bodies that could help us.'

'That's the point,' Aliénor chimed in.

'*What* is the point, Lindbergh?'

'Those marks must have been on the flesh that were carved out of the body,' Emily explained. 'We have a clue of sorts in the CCTV footage of Julianne Bell's abduction. The speed with which she was immobilised suggests the use of a Taser or some other device to deliver an electric shock, perhaps to the hips or waist. He then likely injects a sedative, which allows him to carry his prey to his lair with no great difficulty.'

'Which means he must have a sufficiently large space at his disposal where he can confine his victims, cut them up, store the meat…'

'Not necessarily. A small apartment with a private entrance would suffice. As far as the victim is concerned, all he needs is a small bedroom to hold her in captivity, a bathroom where he can cut her up, and a refrigerator with a couple of freezer drawers for storage.'

Emily's explanation, as detached as it was gruesome, was greeted by silence. It took some time for her audience to rid themselves of the awful images she had conjured up in their minds.

The grating of a chair on the floor broke the silence as Karla got up and poured them all coffees.

'Were any of the other victims abducted from their cars?' she asked, as she filled their cups.

'Yes, the fourth victim. Chloe Blomer.'

'There's something odd about this change in his modus operandi, don't you think?'

'Chloe Blomer was a minor celebrity. She was the girlfriend of a footballer who plays for Queen's Park Rangers in London. Julianne and Chloe were likely more challenging prey to get close to.'

'Why target them, then?' Olofsson asked, nonchalantly perched on the edge of the conference-room table.

'Precisely because they were women he could not possess, women whose loose morals meant they could not belong to a single partner, women he could make his own, not by raping them – the act of possession would be too fleeting – but by eating them. Ingestion is the ultimate form of possession. In literal terms, the need to become one is sated. The victim is his feast. She becomes a part of him and inhabits him for ever.'

'Do you think that, of all the things he does to his victims, and by that, I mean the abduction, the confinement and the strangling, the act of cannibalism is the pinnacle for him?' the commissioner asked before taking a swig of his coffee.

'That's certainly when his sexual excitement reaches its peak. But the strangling of his victims might also be intensely satisfying for him; he stands face to face with his victims as he strangles them, as evidenced by the ligature marks on their necks. Like an avid spectator, he savours the moment they pass over the threshold into death and are ready to be consumed at last. Or, rather, the moment when life abandons them. On the other hand, the process of hunting them down is not crucial for him. The victimology indicates he selects the women the way we choose beef or lamb in the supermarket. He doesn't have a favourite type, per se, aside from their gender and skin colour.'

Olofsson slid off the table and made a beeline for the pastries. He plucked out a *kanelbulle* and sat down with his bounty.

'What's the deal with the shoes? Is he a fetishist or what?' he asked, taking a hearty bite out of the cinnamon brioche.

'If he were a fetishist, he would keep the shoes or focus more on the feet. But he protects the shoes and leaves them for the family – and the police, in so doing.'

'Freud theorised that the foot could represent a phallus substitute for women, and was accordingly a symbol of her power,' Aliénor explained, her eyes still glued to the pages of her notebook.

'Shoes also carry a strong form of symbolism, linked to the notion of the couple,' Karla took over the thread of the dialogue. 'Think of Cinderella, whose glass slipper was kept by the prince until he could find a foot to fit it perfectly. And don't Sicilian women sleep with their shoes under their pillows to help them find a husband?'

'I don't think the symbolism here has anything to do with women or couples,' Emily explained. 'Nor do I think it's a cultural thing, even though all the victims' shoes were found either in front of or close to their homes, and the Swedes have a habit of taking their shoes off before they walk into their homes. I think this signature left by the killer is a celebration of his very first crime. The first killing is sacred. By going through with it, he has anchored his fantasies in reality. In my opinion, leaving the shoes behind is linked to something that happened during the initial crime. It might have been something he forgot to do, something that went wrong, or something to do with the victim's reaction. And that something affected the killer to the extent that it became part of his signature. The plastic freezer bag not only serves to protect the shoes, but also to preserve the memory of his first kill.'

'Don't you think that bringing the victims' shoes back to where they live could also be an admission of guilt?' Bergström suggested, leaning back in his chair so he could extend his long legs under the table.

'No, our killer has no sense of guilt. He is a sociopath who is unable to feel any compassion, let alone guilt.'

Emily's gaze lingered on the photographs pinned to the board.

'And we mustn't forget the socks that were carefully folded inside each left shoe,' she continued. 'This is a key element for us to consider, because the killer specifically initiates this particular step in his procedure. He's expressing his desire to link all the victims to each other, as if they were part of a collection. But even more importantly, he's linking them all to the DNA found in the shoes of Jeanine Sanderson, Maria Paulsson and Julianne Bell, the unknown victim zero we haven't yet been able to identify. Or *person* zero, perhaps. That person might be at the origin of all the crimes and is not necessarily a victim.'

'What about the feathers in the ears? That's just plain sick!' Olofsson exclaimed.

The profiler took a sip of her coffee.

'The black feathers make me think of Nordic mythology. Huginn and Muninn were two ravens that would act as messengers for the god Odin. Huginn means "thought", and Muninn means "memory". Every day at dawn, they would fly out to spy on people and observe what was happening in the nine worlds over which Odin reigned. They would return the following morning, land on Odin's shoulders and whisper what they had learned into his ears.'

Karla frowned. 'That's why you asked me yesterday if we read about Nordic mythology with the children,' she muttered under her breath.

'For now, I have no way of verifying this theory,' Emily added, 'but I'm almost certain the story served as some form of inspiration for the killer. Either he doesn't want his victims to hear whatever news Huginn and Muninn have brought back, or he wants to punish them for not listening. In other words, he doesn't want them to recall some particular traumatic memory, or he intends to punish them for not learning their lesson from that trauma.'

'The significance of the feathers in the ears brought to mind Edgar Allan Poe's *The Raven*,' Aliénor commented as she scribbled away. 'This raven who keeps on repeating "Nevermore". I realised I was on the wrong track with that, however. But there is something else for us to consider when it comes to the killer's identity.'

'You always wait for the end of the conversation to reveal your theories, don't you, Lindbergh? Stretching out the suspense, I see,' Olofsson said facetiously.

'We're dealing with either a descendant of Elizabeth Stride, or a descendant of John McCarthy.'

'Who was John McCarthy?' Bergström asked.

'John McCarthy was none other than Jack the Ripper.'

'Now you're completely out of your mind, Sherlock!' Olofsson exploded, spitting out brioche crumbs all over the table. 'Jack the Ripper was never identified.'

'John McCarthy was the owner of Miller's Court,' Aliénor calmly continued, 'where Mary Jane – or *Jeanette* – Kelly, the Ripper's last official victim – or rather, the final "canonical" victim, according to Ripperologists – lived and was killed. There are many elements that support this assumption. First, McCarthy's physical appearance tallies with the various witness statements at the time about Jack the Ripper. Then, he said he saw the liver and other internal organs of Mary Jane Kelly on the table by the bed where she had been left for dead. But how could he have specifically identified a liver in such a dark room, amid all the carnage of the crime scene? And how could he even have remembered such details, considering what an abominable shock the discovery of the woman's butchered body would have been? There's also the fact that John McCarthy's workshop was barely a metre away from the victim's room, which could explain how Jack the Ripper disappeared after Mary Jane Kelly's murder without being noticed. He was likely covered in blood, day was breaking and the surrounding streets were filling up. Add to this that the murders of two other women occurred in Miller's Court while McCarthy owned the property: one in 1898 and another in…'

'Can you give us the short version, Lindbergh, please?' Olofsson roared.

Aliénor looked up at her audience.

'The short version, Olofsson? In English, Jack is a diminutive for John.'

ALEXIS CHECKED HER PHONE quickly. Still no message.

On Sunday evening, after spending all weekend combing through the minutes of the trial and the transcripts of Richard Hemfield's interviews, as well as tracking down the plethora of Italian restaurants in Covent Garden around Floral Street, Stellan and Alexis finally found the pizzeria where Angela Hemfield had worked: Antonelli's, on Garrick Street, which had opened in 1971. The owner remembered Angela well, as over the years, she had become a good friend of his wife's, and the couple had followed the Tower Hamlets affair with great interest. He suggested they contact his wife directly, who was staying with their daughter in Cornwall. Alexis had left a message for Mrs Antonelli at seven the previous evening, and was impatiently waiting for her to return her call.

Alexis reached her arms overhead, interlaced her fingers and stretched her back.

When she had arrived at the psychiatric hospital, her stomach had felt so tight she had found it hard to breathe. She'd had no desire to return to Broadmoor and breathe the same foul air as Hemfield. But if she was to make progress with her enquiry, she had no choice in the matter. Pearce had taken care of obtaining the necessary authorisations, although he pointed out this was a one-off and he was only doing it as a personal favour.

'Miss Castells?'

Alexis looked up to see an imposingly heavy-set man standing in the doorway of the small room where Pat, the hospital's clinical director, had asked her to wait an hour and a half earlier. With no windows – just a square table and two chairs – the room was as bleak and spartan as a prison cell.

'Albert Smith. We met last week,' the man said, nodding to her. 'I was here when you visited Richard Hemfield,' he explained, taking a seat across from Alexis.

He was the fourth orderly Alexis had seen since she had arrived. More so than his psychiatrist, these were the men and women who knew all the ins and outs of Hemfield's daily habits, routines and idiosyncrasies. Maybe even his secrets.

'I remember you, Albert; thank you for agreeing to see me.' Alexis smiled at him.

She certainly hadn't forgotten his apparent protectiveness towards Hemfield.

'How are you?' he asked, his voice warm and welcoming.

The question took Alexis by surprise.

'Very well, thank you,' she hastened to reply.

'Pat tells me you're planning a book about Richard?'

Alexis nodded, aggravating her lie. Never would she write a book about that person. Not ever.

'If he agrees to cooperate.'

'Apart from Detective Chief Superintendent Pearce, you're the only visitor he's ever agreed to meet since he's been here. I think he truly hopes you will forgive him for the death of your partner and would do anything to be granted absolution.'

Alexis's eyes flitted around the cramped room. Moving from the yellowing white walls back to Albert Smith. She had to stay relaxed. If she clammed up, the man across from her would inevitably do the same.

'Thank you,' she whispered, looking down at her notebook.

He gave her a smile full of empathy.

'How long have you been looking after Hemfield?'

'Ever since he was admitted. I've been working at Broadmoor for thirteen years, and on the high-security wing for eleven.'

'Has his behaviour changed over the course of that time?'

'The medication has tempered his impulses – he doesn't put his hand inside his trousers as often as he used to – but it hasn't completely eradicated them. The treatment hasn't exacerbated his aggression, either. Richard is making better progress with his psychiatrist in individual sessions than he did in group therapy, and he is now able to verbalise his desires, or name his impulses, if you will. As you saw for yourself when you were last here.'

Alexis gulped; she felt a lump in her throat just thinking about what Hemfield had said.

'It shocked you, I know, and I'm sorry. But from my side of the fence, it's a concrete sign of progress.'

The orderly shifted his gaze from Alexis to the scratches on the table. His mouth was firmly closed, his lips sealed, as if he wanted to avoid saying another word.

'I must say, Miss Castells,' he finally said with an air of caution, 'I don't believe Richard deserves to be kept in the high-security wing.'

Alexis agreed with him on this point. His place was not in a hospital where he was brought breakfast to his room and he could flit from art studies to music lessons. Richard Hemfield deserved to be in prison.

'How does he interact with the other prisoners?'

'Patients.'

'Sorry?'

'We call them patients here, Miss Castells, not prisoners.'

'Oh, sorry. Patients,' Alexis corrected herself, smiling inside at her faux-pas.

The word left a nasty taste in her mouth.

'In the high-security wing, our interactions with the patients and those between patients can sometimes turn incredibly violent. Richard has been hurt twice.'

'What happened?'

'A patient threw a chair right at his face; he was accusing Richard of having a wasps' nest inside his nose, of all things. On the second occasion, he was unfortunate enough to pick up a newspaper left on a table in the common room: another unhappy patient, who reckoned it was his, threw faeces in his face before beating him up.'

Alexis paused for a few seconds, feigning sympathy.

'Mr Smith, can you give me an idea of Mr Hemfield's daily routine?' she calmly asked.

'Well ... Richard wakes in the morning between seven and seven-thirty. His breakfast is brought to his room between seven-thirty and eight, and his medication is administered at that time. He has lunch and dinner in the common room, at noon and at seven in the evening, together with the other patients from the high-security wing. Bedtime is at nine. Richard has a support group on Monday and Wednesday afternoons, from three to three forty-five. He sees his psychiatrist on Tuesdays, from ten to ten forty-five. He has art therapy on Thursdays from two to four, and music therapy on Fridays, again from two to four. The rest of the time he is free to spend as he wishes, either in his room or in the common room.'

'Do the group activities take place here, in this wing?'

Albert Smith nodded.

'The patients in this wing never leave this building. In that respect you are right, Broadmoor is a prison.'

'What does he do in his free time?'

'He reads the newspaper, watches television.'

'He doesn't read any books?'

'No, never. And I wouldn't say he really reads the newspapers, actually. He only reads one, once a week.'

'Only one?'

'Yes, *The Times*, on Thursdays. In the morning, as soon as he leaves his room. We usually leave a few newspapers at the patients' disposal in the common room.'

'And so, does he read the news, or the sports or politics pages?'

Albert Smith sniggered. His massive shoulders shook as he did so, as if he were about to start dancing.

'No. He reads the small ads.'

Alexis's eyes widened with surprise.

'And, as strange as it might sound, he usually finds it very stimulating to read them … sexually, I mean.'

'You mean…'

'I mean, reading *The Times* gives him an erection.'

Falkenberg
Saturday, 25 July 2015, 11 am

EMILY WAS DRIVING with the windows down.

A heady aroma of fresh, salt-laden sea air breezed into the car from a pebble beach, its frizzy beard of seaweed shaped by the ever-shifting surf.

'Bergström's spoken to Scotland Yard,' Karla said as she hung up. 'They've verified the information Raymond Bell provided.'

'Anything about Julianne Bell's circle of friends?'

'Nothing of note for now. Let's wait and see what the old man has to say.'

Raymond Bell, born Widstradt, had been taken in between the ages of four and eleven by a Hilda and Sigvard Stenson in Falkenberg.

According to Raymond, once he started school, when he was six, he was already spending all his time with the Bells. The family had moved to Falkenberg in 1981 and had settled four kilometres away from the Stensons' farm. Julianne and William Bell had attended the same local school as Raymond. The adoption had only become official in 1986, but it was likely the whole procedure had proven lengthy and fastidious, as these things often are, and the Stensons might indeed have delivered Raymond to the Bells long before the paperwork had been officially completed.

Emily followed the satnav's instructions and turned left, onto a narrow track that resembled a long tongue of dirt rolled out on a field of dense grass.

A hundred metres away, three red wooden buildings formed a U shape in the middle of the field.

Emily parked on a patch of grass bathed in sunlight.

An elderly man wearing a cap was dozing in a rocking chair under an apple tree; the only island of shade in the sea of sunshine.

'Good day, Mr Stenson. I'm Detective Hansen and this is Emily Roy,' Karla said, extending a hand for him to shake.

'You're early,' Sigvard said in a hoarse voice.

True, they were three-quarters of an hour early. Emily liked to catch her witnesses off guard before she questioned them.

'Perhaps you'd rather we came back later.'

'No, now that you're here, you might as well stay.'

The profiler observed Sigvard Stenson: the wrinkles that streaked across his angular face and withered lips; his thin, wiry build; his rough hands gripping the arms of the chair like claws. Emily's Swedish was patchy at best, but body language was universal.

'Your boss, Detective Olofsson, told me you were investigating something about the children Hilda used to look after here?' he said, kicking one leg against the ground to keep the chair rocking.

'That's correct, Mr Stenson,' Karla replied, though she didn't correct the old man's misapprehension. In his mind, she reasoned, Olofsson had to be her hierarchical superior. After all, she was only a woman, wasn't she?

'Another of your paedophile cases, this business, is it?'

'I'm afraid we can't discuss the investigation with you, Mr Stenson. You and your sister Hilda looked after orphans, is that right?'

He slipped a hand inside his trouser pocket and pulled out a little round tobacco tin. He unscrewed the metal top and took out a small pouch of *snus,* which he inserted between his upper lip and his gum.

The old man had no intention of inviting them into his house; that was why he was sitting outside. He hadn't even brought out any chairs for his visitors. Clearly, he wanted their visit to be as short as possible.

'Hilda, yes … may her soul rest in peace,' he murmured, his gaze distant. 'It's been a long time since we've had kids running around out here. But it was mostly my sister who looked after them. God knows why, but she loved having them crowding all around her. My job was to take care of the bakery. I spent the best years of my life working there: up at three in the morning, every day God made.'

He tapped his arthritis-ridden fingers against the arms of the chair.

'Do you remember any of the kids you took in towards the end of the 1970s?'

He sneered, the pouch of tobacco distorting his upper lip.

'You must be joking! I only got home at night, just in time for dinner, and the last thing I wanted was to have kids under my feet. It was my sister who looked after them. She couldn't have children of her own, you see...'

'Do you remember a Raymond Widstradt? He was later adopted by the Bell family.'

'How do you expect me to remember the names of kids I never saw?'

Karla handed a sheet of paper to him. It was a photocopy of a Polaroid Raymond Bell had given to them. The photograph showed him, at the age of eleven, flanked by Julianne and William Bell. The three children were all smiling, standing in front of a Christmas tree.

'It won't cost you to look at it, will it?' she insisted.

Sigvard Stenson glanced at the yellowed image.

'Which one is he?'

'The one in the middle.'

He rolled his head sluggishly from left to right.

'Doesn't ring a bell. Listen, it's not that I'm not enjoying your company, but I'm starting to get hungry for my lunch.'

Sigvard Stenson raised his bony frame to stand upright, pursing his lips. He dismissed them with a nod and went inside.

'What a sour old goat!' Karla humphed. 'I hope his sister was nicer with the kids. What do you think?'

Emily scanned their surroundings quickly.

'I was thinking that Hilda Stenson died on the eighth of October 2004. And that the Tower Hamlets murders started three weeks later.'

ALEXIS DUCKED INSIDE the car to escape the rain. Stellan didn't even give her time to wipe the raindrops off her face.

'So?'

'I have to call Pearce.'

'What is it?'

'Wait. Let me call him.'

Alexis grabbed her mobile and tapped in the number with wet fingers. The DCS picked up almost immediately.

'Jack, I'm just leaving Broadmoor. I got something out of Hemfield, but I need—'

'Alexis…'

On the other end of the line, Pearce bit his tongue and sighed deeply. 'You must stop obsessing about Richard Hemfield. We're just finishing combing through his mail and there's nothing there, Alexis. Nothing. I realise it's hard to accept, believe me … But listen … Emily was the one who convinced me to help you get authorisation for this visit, in the hope it would enable you to move on. You have to let go, Alexis. Take care of yourself, OK?'

Pearce hung up. Frozen in shock, Alexis kept the phone glued to her ear. After a split second, it started to ring. It must be Pearce calling her back, she thought.

'Jack, I…'

'Miss Alexis Castells?'

A woman's voice, with a sing-song accent, pronouncing her Catalan surname perfectly.

'I'm Mrs Antonelli, an old friend of Angela Hemfield's. You spoke to my husband, the owner of the restaurant where Angela used to work.'

'Yes, of course, Mrs Antonelli. Thank you ever so much for calling me back.'

Alexis moved the phone closer to Stellan so he could hear and they could follow the conversation together.

'I'm sorry it's taken me so long to get back to you, but my daughter has just given birth to her third child, and it's an absolute madhouse at their place. I haven't had a single second to breathe. Are you Catalan?'

'My father is.'

'So you speak Catalan?'

'No, only Spanish, much to my father's despair.'

'I can imagine. I'm from Andalucía. I came to London for a year to learn English. I wanted to work in tourism, you see? But then I met my husband, and I never left. A girl from Andalucía in London; it goes against nature, no? So, I hear you want to write about Angela?'

This time it was harder for Alexis to lie.

'I'm working on a book about her nephew.'

'Oh, dear God, what a horrible story ... Let's be thankful she wasn't around to see what her own flesh and blood ended up doing. Well, you know what I mean...'

'Had you known Angela for a long time?'

'Well, I met her when I arrived in London in 1972. We were sharing a flat. She was around when I met my husband. In the summer of 1972, we were both hired as waitresses by the man who would later become my father-in-law.'

'What sort of woman was she?'

'She was a bit of a birdbrain and a little bit off her rocker, but she was adorable. Wore her heart on her sleeve. But when her half-brother and sister-in-law died in a car crash, her life changed overnight, poor soul. She was so miserable; we could see her wasting away. Back then, I'd just had my twins, so I wasn't really in a position to help her the way I'd have wanted. She was given custody of her nephew, a kid she didn't know at all, since she hadn't seen her half-brother in ten years. That child destroyed her life. It wasn't the poor kid's fault … he was as much a victim of the circumstances as she was. But … it just didn't work. She kept on living the single life with the kid in the house, if you know what I mean … At that time, Angela was just not mature enough to look after a little one, and the whole thing was a disaster.'

'For him too?'

'Well, he did end up bumping off a bunch of women and showing off what was left of them in public like pieces of meat, didn't he?'

The sound of screaming kids in the background drowned out her words.

'Hold on, give me a minute.'

Speaking in Spanish, Mrs Antonelli consoled little Susana, who had apparently just been denied a treat by her mother.

'So … where was I? Yes … In the summer of 1979, Angela left for a holiday in Switzerland with some girlfriends and the kid and, when she returned, she told us she'd met the man of her dreams and was planning to move out there to be with him. Just like that!'

'With Richard?'

'Richard? Oh yes, that's his name, isn't it? I don't call him that any more; now he's just Hemfield, or the Tower Hamlets killer. Both of them left together and that was the last I heard of them. *Nada*. That is, until I heard he was arrested. It came as a shock to my husband and me, let me tell you. Terrible.'

'You never heard from Angela at all after they left?'

'No, never. Nothing, no contact at all. As if she'd disappeared off the face of the earth. Bam! God only knows if she even went to Switzerland … No, no, wait … I always mix things up … I always confuse the two places…'

'Excuse me?' a puzzled Alexis asked.

'*No era Suiza, era el oltro … Suecia!*'

'Sweden? You mean that Hemfield's aunt left to live in Sweden with Richard?' Alexis exclaimed.

'Oh, I'm so silly! Sweden, not Switzerland … Well, they're pretty much the same, aren't they? Two countries you wouldn't exactly want to go to on holiday,' she said with a laugh.

Stellan rolled his eyes.

'Do you remember the name of the man? The man she was going to move in with?'

'Sorry, I don't. But I do remember something else.'

WITH HER ANDROGYNOUS BODY and her almost non-existent breasts, Jeanine Sanderson looked like a tiny ballerina. Even her shoes made her look like a dancer. Little golden ballet flats.

But Jeanine Sanderson, twenty-five years old, reeked of sex.

The young woman left the branch of Boots, where she worked, a stone's throw from Bond Street Tube station, and walked up Oxford Street until she reached Oxford Circus. She continued along Regent Street and stopped for a quarter of an hour to nibble on a few makis at a sushi bar. A little further up the street, she cut down Foubert's Place to get to Great Marlborough Street, where her friends from work were waiting for her at the Shakespeare's Head pub.

Drawn outside by the mild weather on the eve of the weekend, crowds of Londoners were sipping their pints, elbow to elbow on the pavement. Jeanine shared a couple of bottles of white wine with her girlfriends, followed by two gin and tonics and a mojito.

When he approached her by the door to the unisex toilets, the alcohol was already slurring her words and slowing her reactions. He slipped the sedative into the second shot he bought for her, just before he suggested they go outside for some fresh air.

Five minutes later, at around eleven-thirty, she agreed to leave with him. They got into his car, which was parked just a few metres away, and as soon as she sat her pretty arse down in the passenger seat, she fell asleep with her head on his shoulder.

He had a few hours to spare before she came to. Plenty of time to get to the cottage, tie her up and lock her in. Then he would wait for her to wake up before the fun could begin.

He pulled her skirt up to her waist and slipped off her thong.

'My dear Hilda, this one's for you,' he whispered to the rear-view mirror.

Then he started the engine.

ALEXIS HAD TRIED SEVERAL TIMES to call Pearce again, to no
avail, and he had not replied to her messages. Her calls to Emily's
mobile had also gone straight to voicemail. Alexis couldn't afford to
wait for ever. She had to see them – and quickly.

First, she had knocked at Emily's door on Flask Walk in Hampstead. Seeing there was no answer, Stellan had then dropped her off
at Scotland Yard, where she had been waiting for Pearce for over half
an hour already.

'Alexis?' asked the DCS, striding down the corridor towards her.
Alexis ran up to him.

'What's going on?' he asked rigidly.

'Just give me five minutes.'

Pearce closed his eyes. 'For Heaven's sake, Alexis!'

'Just five minutes.'

With an exasperated sigh and an impatient wave of his hand, he
agreed to listen.

'I managed to track down a friend of Hemfield's aunt who told me
that in 1979, Angela – that's the aunt's name – went to live in Sweden
with Richard, whom she had custody of, to move in with a man she
had met there. She doesn't remember his name, but the man owned
a bakery and lived with his sister.'

Pearce froze.

'What is it?' Alexis asked, her heart pounding in her chest.

'We've found out that Raymond Bell was adopted by the Bell

family. Prior to his adoption, he lived with a foster family in Falkenberg: a brother and a sister who owned the town's largest bakery.'

Alexis's mouth went dry. She swallowed before she spoke again. 'So, are you going to listen to my theory about Hemfield now?'

◆◆◆◆◆

Alexis and Pearce finished their presentation as breathlessly as if they had just run a hundred-metre sprint.

There was only silence from their audience on the big screen in the conference room – Emily, Bergström and his team – as they digested the information they had just heard.

The commissioner was the first to speak. 'So, Richard Hemfield and Raymond Bell were staying with the same foster family at the same time?'

'That's right.'

'But … where does Raymond Bell fit into all this, then?' Karla asked. 'You certainly rattled his cage when you interviewed him.'

'Well, if what Raymond Bell says is true, that he started living with the Bell family long before his adoption was finalised, it might well be that he and Hemfield barely crossed paths and Bell has no memory of him. But the connection between the two of them can't just be a coincidence. There must be something else. Alexis?'

'I was at Broadmoor this morning, meeting with the staff who work with Hemfield. I thought maybe they would … To cut a long story short, I found out that every Thursday morning, Hemfield reads the small ads in *The Times* – something he finds so satisfying, it excites him sexually.'

'You mean it gives him a hard-on?' Olofsson queried.

'Yes, that's exactly what I mean.'

'What kind of sick perv is he?'

Anyway, it turns out that *The Times* barely publishes any personals any more; some weeks there are none at all. Which means Hemfield is reading either the job ads or the property listings, and somehow,

I doubt he's in the market for any of that. What I do believe is that Hemfield is communicating with an accomplice through these ads, or rather, that Hemfield's accomplice is using them to communicate with him, through coded messages of some sort, to keep him in the loop – keep him abreast of what, I don't know. Some kind of escape plan they're hatching, perhaps?'

'*Helvete!*' Olofsson exclaimed.

'My guys are poring over all *The Times* ad pages published on Thursdays,' Pearce said. 'We started with last Thursday and are working our way back through all three months prior to the murder of Maria Paulsson.'

'I can do that,' Aliénor proposed.

'That's kind of you, Aliénor, but I already have a team working on it.'

'I know I'm kind. But send me all the ads anyway. If there is a code involved, I'll decipher it much faster than your "team".'

ALIÉNOR UNSCREWED THE LID of her Thermos flask and filled her cup with coffee. She opened the tin of Annas *Pepparkakor*, took out two biscuits, then closed it again.

Only now did she allow herself to eat and drink, as she had completed her task.

She bit into the first of her crispy cinnamon treats.

It had all begun with the Abbot Trithemius and his treatise on angelology. No, that wasn't true. It had all begun with a presentation about Herodotus she had seen, back when she was in year 10. In one of the Greek historian's tales, she had come across the anecdote about a slave whose head had been shaven by the king, so that a message could be tattooed on his scalp. The king had waited for his servant's hair to grow back, then dispatched him with the secret message to his son-in-law. It was a genius idea: use the messenger to conceal the real message and escape detection. In this instance, steganography, as the experts called it, went one step further than cryptography, which essentially just jumbled a message and made it initially unintelligible.

Aliénor had then done her homework, reading, studying and analysing everything she could find on the subject, while practising her own steganography techniques on unwitting guinea pigs, first at primary school, and then at her high school. She had gone on to develop a habit of concealing insulting words about the teachers who were making life difficult for her within her essays and presentations.

The actual words – the messages she sent – went unnoticed, something she found immensely satisfying, and it gave her a fleeting sense of victory.

Ten hours earlier, she had received copies of *The Times* small ads she wanted to pore over in the hope of finding a code, if indeed there was one hidden in there. She preferred to work on paper rather than on screen, so she'd printed out the lot, more than a hundred ads, and had set to work.

The most laborious task had been to identify the matrix. She had managed to do that after five hours and ten minutes. The key was simple: the message was formed by the first and the last words on the first line, the second and the next-to-last words on the second line, and the third and third-from-last words on the third line, and so on.

Once she had cracked the code, she had contacted Detective Chief Superintendent Pearce and told him what she had discovered. He had thanked her, adding that his 'team' would now analyse the remainder of the ads and she could go home for a rest. But she had no desire to go to bed. And she didn't. Now she knew the code, she wanted to decipher all the messages Hemfield's accomplice had put together. Which was precisely what she had done. She had sent them all to the DCS a moment ago. Now, all his 'team' had to do was to identify the sender.

Nothing could stop her from going home to bed now.

JUST AS HE ALWAYS DID when he set out on an operation, Pearce had sent Emily a message. He wasn't expecting an answer; it was just to ensure they were connected through their thoughts at that point in time. He harboured a visceral fear of leaving without saying goodbye; he wasn't sure why. No, actually he was. He knew all too well.

'We'll be there in ten minutes, sir,' said the WPC who was driving.

Pearce's colleagues at the Yard were still in the process of analysing the messages sent to Hemfield that Aliénor Lindbergh had deciphered. How incredible was Bergström's intern? The most recent messages told Hemfield about the abductions and subsequent killings of Maria Paulsson and Freja Lund, and were communicated through a series of fake email addresses, the dates of the crimes being concealed in appointment times for visiting apartments to let.

The only grey area they had still not managed to shed any light on was Richard Hemfield's past. He and his aunt had suddenly disappeared in 1979, and he had reappeared in London alone, more than a decade later. If Hemfield grew up in Sweden, why was there no trace of him there? Or his aunt? Was she murdered by her nephew?

If it hadn't been for Alexis's stubbornness – her 'obsession' with Hemfield, as the DCS had put it – none of this would have come to light. Pearce owed her a lot. Far more than she could imagine. Without her perseverance, he might have been on the hook for a monumental judicial error and pressured to resign by his peers and superiors.

The IT specialists at Scotland Yard had traced the breadcrumbs of the ads back to their point of origin. The most recent ones originated from an IP address located an hour or so from London, in Hertfordshire. A house that had belonged for twelve years to a certain Daniel Adams; most likely a false identity. Pearce and his team were on his way there now to scope the place out.

The young WPC followed the Specialist Firearms Command truck, the Yard's special armed-response unit, as it turned onto a narrow, paved road. She switched off her sidelights, and they were swallowed up voraciously by the night. They drove like that at a snail's pace for five whole minutes, before parking behind a line of dense oak trees.

Six men armed with Heckler & Koch MP5s, helmeted, protected by bulletproof vests and wearing night-vision goggles, leaped out of the vehicle with cat-like agility.

Amit Bhatia, the leader of the armed-response unit, gave the go-ahead. They were two hundred metres away from the house, which stood dark and peaceful in the middle of a field.

Pearce led the way, followed by a string of armed officers, through a darkness as thick as treacle, barely scratching the surface of the silence as they moved along.

They came to a halt about twenty metres from the front door, behind a wooden fence.

Amit darted across the remaining distance to the house alone. Once he reached the threshold, he squatted and inserted the digital endoscope under the door. It took him about five seconds to find his bearings, checking the small screen strapped to his left wrist. Then he removed and pocketed the endoscope.

With his gloved hand, he gave another silent signal: the coast was clear. It was time to go in.

Pearce unconsciously rubbed his hand against his bulletproof vest and drew his Glock 17.

Julianne is thirsty. Her lungs, throat and ears are on fire. Every time a shooting pain tears across her face, her dry lips crack; she runs her tongue over them and tastes blood.

She is so thirsty that she drank the blue water from the toilet bowl earlier. It made her throw up immediately, but she did it again all the same. Anything to quell the fire burning all the way down to her stomach that keeps bringing up nothing but bile.

She is no longer being given the bottle. No more water. On the other hand, no more flesh has been carved out of her. Nor has she been given any sedatives. The pain is atrocious. She moans constantly, like a wild dog. Sometimes she screams, but now her throat can cry no more. She manages barely a sound. No more than a whimper.

Suddenly, a shockwave surges through her cell. Even the ground shakes. Another tremor, like someone is banging on the walls, on the...

Someone is smashing the door down. Someone is smashing the door down!

Julianne slides off her mattress to the floor. She knows she is incapable of walking, or standing up, or crawling: her legs and backside hurt too much. She slithers along on her side, trying to reach the cat flap.

She hears a flurry of cries and hurried steps.

What are they saying? What are...

'Police! Police!'

A grimace contorting her face, Julianne tries to stand up, and bangs her determined fists against the door. Screams of rage surge from her throat, lacerating her lungs, bringing blood to her mouth.

'Police! Move away from the door, we're going to open it!'

It's a man's voice.

Julianne lies flat on her belly and drags herself towards the toilet bowl by the strength of her arms, as the metal chain around her ankle clinks along the floor.

'Call an ambulance!' the man shouts.

The battering ram slams into the door.

It slams again.

And again.

The door opens. A man rushes into the room. More people are following him. He runs over to her and drops so quickly, his knees crack against the floor.

'Julianne, my name is Jack Pearce. I work with Leland at Scotland Yard. You're safe now, Julianne. Everything's going to be all right.'

She hangs on to him. Wraps her arms around his neck. He smells of lemon. Of the outside world. She inhales this scent of life. She won't let go of him. She doesn't want to be left alone ever again.

'We're going to get you out of here, Julianne. You're safe, now. Everything's going to be all right, Julianne. Your family is waiting for you. Everything's going to be all right...'

He strokes her hair. Keeps on talking to her. He understands. He understands she can't cope with any more silence.

She wants to laugh, but she's crying. She's crying as she laughs. No, she isn't crying, she's laughing with love. With sheer relief.

Falkenberg Police Station
Tuesday, 28 July 2015, 7 am

ALIÉNOR PUT HER CUP of coffee down on the desk before she answered the phone.

'Hello?'

'Yes … ah, 'ello…'

'Who is this?'

'Ah … my name eez Benjamin. I work for ze IT department at ze Metropolitan Police in London. I'm trying to join Kommissionär Bergström or BIA Emily Roy.'

'So why are you calling me?'

'Because I can't join zem and ze turd number DCS Pearce gave me is, ah, Aliénor Lindbergh's. Is she you?'

'Yes, that's me. But I'm finding it hard to understand you.'

'Ah…'

She could hear him clearing his throat and some rustling on the other end of the line.

'So, can you 'ear me better now?'

'No. I didn't say I couldn't hear you. I said I didn't understand you. You have a funny way of saying "ah" and "ze" all the time, and your words seem a bit odd. Are you OK? Are you unwell?'

'Ah … no. It's … maybe because of my accent. I'm French.'

'Do the French have something wrong with their palates, or their tongues?'

'Ah … no, I don't sink so…'

'Have you just moved to London?'

'Ah … no. I've been in England, ah, seventeen years.'

'How odd. Why are you calling?'

'We've completed our analysis of ze *Times*, ah, small ads and managed to isolate four more IP addresses. Zey are all in Sweden. So, ze DCS has asked us to contact you.'

'Where in Sweden?'

'Malmö, Stockholm, Gothenburg and Uppsala.'

'Give me the exact addresses. Kommissionär!'

Bergström who was hurrying out of his office, froze.

'It's Scotland Yard.'

'Pearce?'

'No, a man who calls himself Benjamin.'

'Benjamin who?'

'A Frenchman in the IT department. He doesn't speak English too well. He blames it on his accent and tells me there's nothing wrong with his mouth, but I don't believe him. I think he's too embarrassed to admit it.'

'What does he want, Aliénor?' the commissioner pressed.

'Sorry, I was just curious what his problem was. He was calling to say they've pinpointed four further IP addresses that were used by Hemfield's accomplice.'

Bergström's eyes widened in surprise.

'Four more addresses?'

'That's what I just said. They're all in Sweden. In Malmö, Stockholm, Gothenburg and Uppsala.'

'Aliénor?' Benjamin asked.

'Hold on, Benjamin, I'm talking to my boss,' she said sharply. 'Detective Chief Superintendent Pearce wants us to follow up on it,' she continued, speaking to Bergström.

'OK. Write down the addresses, but also ask him for a copy of the corresponding ads and the dates those emails were sent to *The Times*. After that, come and join us in the conference room; we have some news.'

Aliénor nodded.

She wrote all the information down in her notebook as Benjamin gave it to her.

'Maybe you have a mouth ulcer,' she said as she hung up. 'I hear calendula mouthwash can work wonders.'

JULIANNE WAS SITTING UP slightly in her hospital bed with a blanket pulled up to her waist. Her arms, sickly thin, like dead twigs, rested alongside her body. Her tousled hair, which had been tied into a messy bun on the top of her head, seemed to dwarf her gaunt features as the occasional nervous twitch shivered across her face.

Adrian laid his hands on his wife's hollow cheeks and planted a gentle kiss on her cracked lips. Julianne sighed heavily, as her shoulders melted into the mattress and her sunken eyes misted over with tears.

She burrowed her nose in her husband's neck, breathing him in, then she started to cough. Adrian moved away, took a glass of water from the bedside table and brought it to her lips. She took a couple of sips. Then her face suddenly creased, and she began to sob uncontrollably. It seemed like the tears were strangling her and burning her throat. She gripped her husband's hand tightly.

A nurse rushed into the room. 'Are you in pain, Mrs Bell?' she asked, checking Julianne's pulse and temperature as she continued to sob.

'She was drinking some water and then she … she suddenly burst into tears,' Adrian stammered.

'Mr Bell, stay close to her, please. She needs to feel your touch.'

'I don't want to hurt her…'

'The wounds are all below the waistline, so hold her gently in your arms. She needs to feel you near.'

Adrian embraced his wife's bony torso, nuzzling his nose against her cheek.

'Shhhhh…' he murmured, gently rocking her in his arms. 'I'm here, my darling. I'm here…'

'There, there, it's all going to be all right, love,' the nurse tried to reassure her. 'You're safe now, it's all OK.'

It took a few minutes for the tears to dry up and for Julianne's breathing to return to normal.

'We gave you a sedative ten minutes ago, Mrs Bell, and that will soon kick in. Everything's going to be all right, you'll see. Press the call button if there's anything at all,' she said to Adrian, before leaving the room.

Julianne's right hand was connected to a drip. She raised it slightly, with great difficulty.

'The girls…'

Her voice sounded broken, slurring and hesitant, like a sick, elderly woman's.

'They're fine, my darling. I've been keeping them out of school so they wouldn't … so they wouldn't hear anything. Antonia, Raymond and I have taken them on lots of trips round London, to distract them. They're fine, Julianne.'

'When can I see them?'

'We're waiting for the green light from the doctor, my love. Soon.'

Julianne swallowed. Her face tensed for a second, then she slowly moved her head up and down.

'Florence…'

Adrian averted his eyes from his wife's, staring at their interlaced hands atop the rough blanket instead.

'She's on her way. I called her.'

ALIÉNOR PICKED UP HER NOTEBOOK and her Thermos, and walked through to the other side of the station. As she opened the double doors and stepped into the corridor, she saw Emily Roy walking into the conference room. She quickened her pace, not wanting to miss out on anything the profiler might be about to tell them.

'...confirmed that Julianne Bell has been found alive. She was being held captive in a room and never saw her abductor's face. That's all we know right now. She's been mutilated and is in a state of shock. She's been taken to hospital. Forensics are combing through the premises. We should have some results by the end of the day, or by tomorrow morning at the latest.'

'She was bloody lucky they found her! Any longer, and she'd have been a Sunday roast!' Olofsson scoffed.

Aliénor breathed a sigh of relief as she noticed that her usual corner was unoccupied and that Detective Olofsson hadn't put his feet up there or left a trail of cinnamon brioche crumbs in her way.

'Hemfield's accomplice has changed his modus operandi. He had already started to carve pieces out of her,' Emily said.

Olofsson squirmed with obvious discomfort.

'What? While she was still alive, you mean? That's just bloody disgusting!'

'Good God, how horrible,' Karla murmured.

'Alexis was right to be so insistent,' Bergström added. 'Hemfield was close to getting away with it.'

Emily knew that was meant for her. She ignored him.

'What else have they found in the house?' the commissioner asked.

'No other victims, and no suspect either. And right now, it appears the only fingerprints present are Julianne's.'

Olofsson cleared his throat.

'But … did they find … the pieces of meat he cut out of her?'

'Some.'

'Bloody fucking hell! The bastard had himself a bloody carpaccio, didn't he? Unbelievable. You think you've seen it all, and then – bam! – you see something a hundred times worse. Can you imagine what the poor woman must have had to endure. Just imagine!'

'Aliénor, what's the latest news from the Yard?' Bergström cut to the chase.

'I'll write it all down,' Karla said, moving over to the board.

Aliénor waited for her to be in position, marker in hand, before she began.

'Four new IP addresses have been identified; that's four new locations from which Hemfield's accomplice sent emails with the copy for small ads for publication. On the seventh of May at 10.05 am from the Apple Store in Stockholm; on the thirteenth of June at 7.07 pm from the Wired Internet café in Uppsala; on the third of July at 8.43 am from the Network café in Gothenburg; and on the fourteenth of July at 1.10 am from the Diplomat Hotel in Malmö.'

'Olofsson, I want you to call the Diplomat and ask them for their guest list for the night of the fourteenth of July,' the commissioner ordered. 'And, even better, find out if they keep a record of connection times, assuming that our man used the business centre to get onto the Internet. Perhaps the hotel reception even supplied him with a specific login or password. Check with the prosecutor's office first in case the hotel tries to palm you off with some stupid confidentiality clause. Karla and Aliénor, I want you to check the two Internet cafés. I'll deal with the Apple Store. We're going to bring this sick bastard down.'

Phone in hand, Emily walked out of the station. She crossed the empty street and sat on a low brick wall.

She needed some time to herself, so she could clear her mind. Strip away the theory and focus on the facts.

The killer hadn't waited for Julianne to be dead. He had started to carve her up while she was still alive. That was a significant, radical change in his signature. Usually a signature remained static, though, as it was a reflection of the killer's fantasy.

Shouldn't she be thinking about killers in the plural, though, since Hemfield had an accomplice? Who, then, had killed the six Tower Hamlets victims? Hemfield? Hemfield and his accomplice? It couldn't have been the accomplice on his own. The accomplice was keeping Hemfield in the loop, so Hemfield must be the one pulling the strings. But neither his profile, nor his reactions, were consistent with someone who was pulling the strings.

The theories must fit the facts, and not the other way around, she kept telling herself.

How had Hemfield acted when he told Alexis about his deviant traits? He had taken off his glasses and closed his eyes. Emily had initially thought this was because he didn't want to see Alexis's reaction. What if it was the other way around? Maybe Hemfield didn't want anyone to see how much *he* was enjoying the conversation. It could have been a way for him to make sure no one noticed what an intense feeling of sexual satisfaction he was milking from the situation.

In no way was Richard Hemfield a fit with the typical profile of a cannibal serial killer, but perhaps *he* wasn't the cannibal. Perhaps he was only the sexual predator, the voyeur and the strangler.

According to her calculations, the profile of this cannibal killer should be a Caucasian male between forty and fifty years of age, a meticulous, organised, charming and socially active man intelligent enough to deceive the experts and those closest to him.

Could the cannibal killer be Richard Hemfield's partner? The strangling would represent Hemfield's signature, and the carving of flesh would be his accomplice's. Each of them in charge of specific tasks, which would explain why they had always committed identical crimes. Neither one of them dominant, nor dominated, but acting as a partnership?

Emily shook her head. It was rare, extremely rare, to come across a duo with no dominant element.

Her phone rang; she picked it up.

'Did you get my message?' she quickly asked Pearce before he could get a word in.

'No, I—'

'Check if they've taken a DNA sample from Julianne Bell's forehead and, if not, get someone over to the hospital fast to do so. Call the hospital and warn them not to clean her up. Call me back after that.'

The profiler hung up.

Her phone rang five minutes later.

'No, they didn't take a sample from her forehead and they did clean her up as soon as she was admitted,' Pearce informed her.

Emily was silent for an instant.

'No prints on the body?'

'Nor the dressings.'

'When will the lab results from the other samples be ready?'

'Around noon. They're still searching the house from top to bottom. Forensics are even taking the electrical sockets apart to look for fingerprints.'

'Are you going to interview Julianne Bell?'

'Yes, the doctor and the husband have agreed to it, but I'll only have ten minutes. I'm at the hospital right now.'

'I need you to ask her this. First, how he cut into her flesh: whether she was awake or unconscious. If she was awake and she says she never caught a glimpse of his face, ask her what he was hiding behind. I also need to know what areas he cut into first. Then, check whether she was raped, and ask the lab if she was wearing underwear; if so, tell them to take a photo and forward it to me. And most importantly, get them to check for prints. I'll be waiting for your call.'

JACK PEARCE WAS KNOCKING on the door of Julianne Bell's hospital room when he noticed Adrian in conversation with a doctor at the other end of the corridor.

'Come in!'

The DCS recognised Florence Hartgrove's voice.

The spacious, well-furnished room with separate living-room area would have given any hotel suite a run for its money, had it not been for the hospital bed and the drip stands.

Julianne Bell looked even frailer than when he had carried her out of the house a few hours earlier. She still had the same look of fear in her eyes.

Florence rose, without letting go of Julianne's hand.

'Jack … you have no idea how thankful we are.'

'I'm not the one to thank, Mrs Hartgrove; quite a few others worked harder than I did to help find and release Mrs Bell.'

The commissioner's wife smiled sadly.

'Adrian told us you had a few questions for Julianne.'

'Is that all right with you, Julianne?' the DCS checked.

She nodded painfully.

'I realise your throat must be terribly painful. I've brought an iPad along so you can type in your answers instead of trying to talk. The keyboard is easier to use than a phone. OK with you?'

She nodded again.

'I don't have a lot of questions, but they're not pleasant ones, I'm afraid. Feel free to stop me at any time, and I'll leave you in peace, OK?'

Julianne blinked to indicate that she understood.

Pearce set the iPad down on the blanket. Florence raised the bed so that Julianne was sitting up, and held the tablet in front of her hands.

'Let's get started. Did he feed you at all?'

She shook her head. Then typed with two fingers.

Just water with lemon and honey

'Did he pass the bottles through the cat flap, or did he open the door?'

Cat flap

'You said this morning you never saw his face.'

She shook her head firmly. Her lower lips shivered, then she began to type again.

Never saw him never came in

'So, you were mutilated while you were unconscious?'

She closed her eyes and nodded. For a second, Florence let go of the tablet and stroked her arm. Julianne began typing again.

Water drugged
Wounds were there when I woke up

'Did you always wake up in your cell?'

Yes always
Don't know if he took me out
Don't know where he

She didn't complete her answer, as her eyes filled with tears.

Pearce had spoken with the doctor, so he knew the extent of her horrific injuries.

'Are you OK, Julianne?' Florence was worried.

'Am OK,' Julianne whispered barely audibly.

She swallowed with difficulty as she caught her breath. Florence helped her drink some more water. Pearce waited a few seconds before he carried on.

'Do you recall any particular smells?'

Only mine bad horrible

'Do you know which part of your body he cut into first?'

Julianne's mouth twisted as she tapped out another word.

Bum

She looked up at Pearce, who was mulling over how to formulate his next question, then reached for the screen again.

Not raped

Florence Hartgrove's face was creased with pain and grief.

Am sure

Pearce lowered his eyes. He was already aware of the fact. The lab had confirmed it.

Finish now tired sorry

'Of course,' he said, with compassion. 'Thank you, Julianne, thank you very much.'

He pocketed the iPad and nodded to them both before walking out of the room.

Jack waited until he was outside the hospital before calling Emily.

'He mutilated her while she was unconscious. He sliced her buttocks up first, and she wasn't raped. Oh, and her underwear was bloodstained,' the profiler said before Pearce could even get a word in.

'So, the lab has already sent you a photo of her underwear?'

'Not yet.'

Pearce smiled. She was incredible.

'She never saw her abductor, Emily. He drugged her before he dragged her out of the room and, I reckon, took her to his workshop where he cut her up on an autopsy table, then locked her up in her cell again. She was only given water with lemon and honey to drink, so he must have drugged her with that. He never gave her anything to eat.'

His explanations were greeted with silence.

Emily broke the silence some ten seconds later. She told him what he needed to do to arrest Julianne's abductor. Because she knew who it was.

'*HELVETE!*' OLOFSSON GROANED, slumping into his chair.

Naturally, he was the one who had been assigned the crappiest research to do, and his efforts were yet to bear fruit. The manager of the Diplomat Hotel was away on business in Switzerland and still hadn't called his assistant back.

Karla and Aliénor, on the other hand, had already made contact with the two Internet cafés in Uppsala and Gothenburg, neither of which had any surveillance system in place – seriously? – and as such were unable to provide any information about search histories, let alone the identity of any of the customers connecting to their terminals. As for the Apple Store in Stockholm, surveillance footage was only kept for a week. What was the bloody point of filming people? And so, the boss and his dream team had wrapped up their homework in a heartbeat and were now watching a live stream of Adrian Bell's questioning. Meanwhile, he was here on his own acting like their bloody secretary, not really grasping the why and the how of it all. Which Bell did they want to arrest? Typical Bergström, not wanting to leave any stone unturned. Problem was, there were no bloody stones left to turn!

The telephone on his desk rang.

'Olofsson,' he barked as he picked up.

'Good morning, detective. Krister Widmark, manager of the Diplomat Hotel in Malmö. I'm sorry I couldn't return your call sooner, but I was—'

'Can you send me a list of your guests on the night of the four-teenth of July, or do I have to get the prosecutor on your case with a warrant?'

'I've had that emailed to you already, detective,' Krister Widmark answered, his unctuous tone turning surly. 'If you require my assistance for anything else, call me at the number my assistant sent you in the email,' he added before hanging up without further ado.

Olofsson grimaced at the phone and quickly clicked on his inbox. Just as he was about to open the document, his desk phone rang again.

'Olofsson,' he answered gruffly.

'Kristian, it's Maja.'

'*Hej*, Maja,' the detective softened. 'How come you're on the switchboard?'

'Hans had to go and pick up his wife. Her car broke down.'

'Don't tell me you're having to cancel tonight?'

'Of course not,' she giggled. 'My place at seven.'

An image of the sublime Maja fulfilling his every fantasy flashed straight from the detective's brain to his pants.

'The commissioner has asked me to forward any calls connected to the Paulsson and Lund cases to you, while he's on the conference call with the Brits.'

'Right on, sweet cheeks. Who is it?'

'Lasse Holt. He works at the Wired Internet café in Uppsala. I through he was a crank caller at first, because his voice sounds so childish, so I called the Internet café back to speak to the boss. He confirmed Lasse Holt does work there. He's eighteen. Lindbergh called them earlier about the emails sent to *The Times* from their IP address, and Holt says he has some information which might be relevant.'

'OK, put him through. See you tonight, sweet cheeks.'

A chuckle preceded the click on the line.

'Detective Olofsson.'

'Yeah … Hey … Lasse … Work … Internet café … Upp…'

'Hey, can you spit out whatever you're chewing on? I can't understand a word you're saying.'

Olofsson heard him spit something out and clear his throat.

'Yeah. I'm Lasse Holt. I work at the Wired Internet café in Uppsala. And I was working on the night of the thirteenth of June. My boss said I should call you.'

'And why's that?'

'Because I know who sent the email at 7.07 pm.'

ALEXIS WAS STANDING BEHIND the one-way mirror.

The adrenaline rush of victory had stirred up a curious mixture of feelings for her. She had butterflies in her stomach, but it was as if a weight had been lifted from her shoulders. She felt like she was floating on air, like a wave of serenity had washed over her. Strangely, these sensations were not dissimilar to the rush of new love. She felt exalted, like a warrior after the battle was over. A powerful metaphor took shape in her mind. She could see herself standing tall, puffing out her chest with pride and snuffing out her enemy underfoot like a dropped cigarette butt. God, she was incorrigible.

She released a long sigh of relief.

Pearce had described Julianne Bell's cell to her, the overwhelming stink in the room, the chain that held her down, the lack of water and temporal orientation. The rest of the small house where she had been detained was just as spartan. From the kitchen to the bathroom, bedroom, garage and workshop – or rather, makeshift butcher's shop – everything was clean and tidy. Immaculate. The DCS had also gone into detail about Julianne Bell's wounds, explaining how carefully the flesh had been carved out of her buttocks, as well as her inner and outer thighs. Several chunks had been found in the fridge and the freezer.

Julianne Bell's scars would be a permanent, everlasting reminder of the hell she endured for eleven days, as if her torturer had tattooed his name all over her body. Which was certainly his intention, as

Emily had pointed out. By committing this symbolic form of rape, his possession of her would be twofold. Through the act of cannibalism, Julianne would live inside him for ever, and he would live in her through the indelible marks on her body.

Alexis was suddenly startled. On the other side of the one-way mirror, one of the two chairs had been hurled against the wall. It fell to the ground with a crash. Adrian Bell kicked the chair in rage, then he started yelling to be released.

Pearce stood, picked up the chair, dragged it back to the table and ordered Adrian to sit down. His mouth still frothing with anger, Julianne's husband obeyed.

BERGSTRÖM FOLLOWED OLOFSSON AS he hurried along the corridor.

'Good God, Kristian, I hope for your sake this is important. They're about to start questioning Bell any time now.'

Olofsson's only answer was to hasten his pace.

'So?' Bergström was growing impatient as they neared the detective's office.

Unusually serious, Olofsson sighed deeply, as if he were about to take a deep breath in preparation for a free-dive.

'Just as I got off the phone with the manager of the hotel in Malmö hotel, I got a call from a kid who works at the Uppsala web place. He told me he was working there on the night in question, the thirteenth of June, and he knew who sent the message to *The Times*, because he accessed the screen after the customer left.'

'Who was it?'

Olofsson opened his inbox in Outlook and clicked on the document attached to the email Lasse Holt had forwarded to him. A photo popped up in a full-screen window.

The commissioner was so stunned, he had to sit down. He couldn't believe his eyes.

'That's not all. The manager of the Diplomat Hotel sent me a list of their guests on the night of the fourteenth of July.'

Olofsson swallowed, catching his breath.

'He was staying at the hotel on the night that email was sent to *The Times*.'

Bergström stared at the photo with thunder in his eyes.

'I'm calling Pearce. Go see the others. Get Emily to try calling Jack too. I'm worried they've already started questioning Bell. Then get everyone to come back to my office.'

'CAN YOU TELL ME what the heck is going on?' a frantic Raymond Bell asked as he hurried into Jack Pearce's office.

The DCS, who was on the phone, thanked the person on the other end of the line and hung up. He motioned for Raymond Bell to sit down.

'Have you arrested my brother-in-law?'

'No.'

Raymond Bell frowned in puzzlement.

'But ... two policemen came to fetch him at the hospital. And my solicitor rang to say that Adrian had called him.'

'That's right.'

'I don't understand.'

'Join the club, Mr Bell. We didn't understand either, not at first.'

'Pardon?'

Jack Pearce's lips curled upward into a confident smile.

'We didn't understand why Julianne Bell was mutilated while she was still alive, or why she never caught sight of her abductor.'

He slid the notebook on his desk towards Raymond Bell.

'Don't insult my intelligence, Mr Bell, and I won't insult yours. I won't try and flatter your overinflated ego by telling you how impressed I am by your intellect, your sense of organisation, and your painstaking care and attention to detail. All I'm saying is that if you write down on this page a full list of the names of the women you've abducted, strangled, mutilated and consumed in cahoots with

Richard Hemfield since your tender childhood, we might find a way of making your future life behind bars less unpleasant.'

Raymond Bell stared first at the notebook, then at the DCS, with the same blank look in his eyes.

'Well, that's the way you want to play it, is it, Mr Bell? Do you remember BIA Roy?'

Raymond Bell's mouth arced sharply downwards.

'Yes, I know, she has that effect on a lot of people. There were several things that struck Emily Roy. First, that Julianne Bell was drugged and never saw her abductor. She found this rather odd, because if your sister, or rather your adoptive sister, was doomed to die like all the other victims, there was no reason for the abductor not to reveal his identity. Also, our profiler found it interesting, and quite revealing, that Julianne Bell was mutilated while she was still alive and was abducted at a time when she had barely embarked on an adulterous relationship.'

Bell's lower lip trembled with a nervous tic.

'Oh, I'm sorry. I should have said *homosexual* too. A *homosexual* adulterous relationship. It's not just adultery that bothers you, is it, Mr Bell?'

Creases began to ravage the man's chin and mouth.

'When we found your adoptive sister, BIA Roy had me check the underwear Julianne was wearing for traces of blood and to determine which parts of her body chunks of flesh had been taken from first. A strange request, wouldn't you say?'

Raymond Bell leaned his head to the side slightly.

'When the lab confirmed that her silk knickers were stained with blood, and I'm referring to traces that correspond to blood spatter, spurts and residual bleeding from the wounds inflicted on her buttocks, BIA Roy deduced – and the forensics team are in full agreement with her – that the underwear was not removed before she was mutilated. The fact that it was not removed suggests the aggressor held his victim in some respect. Which also explains why the person in question targeted Julianne's buttock first. The aggressor wanted to begin his work without having to see Julianne's face because, even if she was unconscious, the sight of her face troubled him, made him overly aware of what he was doing and provoked shame and remorse in him. Are you with me?'

Raymond Bell sat up in his chair, straightening the involuntary curve in his back.

'And this is where things get interesting, Mr Bell. Because, when Julianne was found, BIA Roy immediately asked for DNA samples to be taken from her forehead and her silk knickers, which hadn't been changed for eleven days. Of course, the forensics team would automatically check for DNA on the knickers, but what was all this about the DNA on her forehead, which we would almost certainly have glossed over had Emily not mentioned it? So, why the forehead? Well, the bloodstained underwear, and the fact that the buttocks were the first part of her body to be targeted, suggested to our dear profiler that Julianne's abductor had, as I mentioned earlier, treated her with so much modesty and respect that the only real contact he allowed himself to have with her was both protective and chaste. Think about how we kiss a sick child to check their temperature. A kiss on the forehead, to be more precise. Unfortunately for us, the hospital had already cleaned Julianne up on arrival and we were unable to obtain a DNA sample from her forehead.'

Raymond Bell relaxed his shoulders.

'Wait, Raymond, there's more. Do you know why I'm emphasising the fact that the underwear was made of silk? Well, because it's possible to pick up DNA from that particular material; not with powder, of course, but through a technique known as vacuum metal deposition. And did you realise, Mr Bell, that as Ted, our fingerprint expert puts it, "There's always a time when the gloves come off, always", and that's even more true of a person who, for the very first time, was in a position to approach, look at and observe the delta of Venus of the woman he idolised as much as he worshipped her.'

Raymond Bell's hands gripped the arms of the chair.

'What BIA Roy believes, Mr Bell, is that together with Richard

Hemfield, a man whom you consider to be a brother, since you lived under the same roof until you were eleven – in spite of your highly convincing efforts to persuade us otherwise – you have killed, mutilated and consumed a great many women. And so, in Emily Roy's estimation, when you learned that your adoptive sister, this woman you had spoiled like your own child and who owed her fame to you, was playing away from home, and with another woman to boot, you were unable to bear it any longer and you told yourself you would punish her in a very public fashion, by abducting her and chaining her up in your chamber of horrors, the sinister bachelor pad you once shared with Richard Hemfield. But sadly, we humans are creatures of habit, and routine is what makes us vulnerable. So, when you found yourself confronted with tens of kilos of meat right under your nose, you couldn't resist having a little taste, could you? It was never your intention to kill your dear Julianne. At any rate, not until it came to light that you grew up in the same foster family as the Tower Hamlets killer. But then, as you pulled the wool over our eyes with your little performance, you came to realise that the ravishing Julianne Bell would now have to disappear once and for all.'

Anger darkened Raymond Bell's face.

'Why do I say that?' Pearce continued. 'Because you lied when you told us you'd moved in with the Bells long before your official adoption, and the only person who could have contradicted that was Julianne Bell herself. So, you decided you had to get rid of her. And without the perseverance and the intelligence of one of our … consultants, we would never have discovered how you communicated with Richard Hemfield and we would never have located your chamber of horrors – and Julianne – in time.'

Pearce paused for a smile. A deliberately false smile.

'These are your fingerprints, Mr Bell, that we found on your adoptive sister's silk underwear. And that's not all. We're in the process of taking your country house apart. And not just the house, but also the garden, where we've dug up a pretty suitcase containing the clothes of Jeanine Sanderson, Diana Lantar, Katie Atkins, Chloe Blomer,

Sylvia George, Clara Sandro, Maria Paulsson and Freja Lund. All clothing we are now in the process of testing and on which I am sure we will find traces of your DNA and that of your associate Richard Hemfield.'

Raymond Bell's eyes flickered to the ceiling behind Jack Pearce.

'Yes, you can rest assured, Mr Bell, there are two cameras filming your every reaction.'

Bell looked down at the notebook.

'We had to let you believe that you were still one step ahead of the game, that you were walking into Scotland Yard still in control of the situation. We had to take you by surprise. Inviting you to my office instead of leading you to an interview room certainly helped. You might ask why the element of surprise was so important if we already had material evidence of your guilt. Well, because when we set up the two cameras, we didn't have all the evidence in hand. Only our profiler's certainty, and we were hoping to tease a confession out of you. Now that's no longer necessary. The lab confirmed the fingerprints on Julianne Bell's silk underwear were yours just as you were coming into the room.'

Raymond Bell shifted to the edge of his chair and planted his elbows on Pearce's desk. He wiped the corners of his mouth with his index finger.

'Detective Chief Superintendent Pearce. Jack. If you want to know the names of all the women we've abducted, strangled, fried, boiled, cooked, browned, poached and simmered for more than thirty years, you're going to have to give us something in return. To me and to Richard.'

EMILY, BERGSTRÖM, OLOFSSON AND KARLA were standing behind the one-way mirror, staring intently at the interview room on the other side, as if they were trying to see something in there other than a just a metal table and three chairs.

Behind them, Aliénor sat huddled in a corner like a spider in its web. The silence weighing down on the observation suite reminded her of the terrifying calm that always preceded her mother's outbursts. Instinctively, she was readying herself for the screaming, the violence and the sadness that would ensue every time.

The past two hours had etched agonising lines on their faces and still weighed on their shoulders. Neither Bergström nor Emily had managed to reach Pearce and share the news of their discovery prior to Raymond Bell's questioning. This meant Pearce was unaware that the person who had sent the emails to *The Times*, from the Uppsala Internet café on the thirteenth of June and from the Diplomat Hotel in Malmö on the fourteenth of July, was not Raymond Bell. A third person had been helping Richard Hemfield and Raymond Bell here, in Sweden. An individual who was surely the killer of Maria Paulsson and Freja Lund.

A uniformed policeman opened the door and signalled to Bergström that they were ready. The commissioner heaved a deep sigh before raising an inquisitive eyebrow at Karla and Emily. They nodded stiffly and stepped out of the observation suite and into the interview room.

Karla rested her shaking hands on the table. She moistened her dry lips, swallowing back her latent nausea, and took a seat.

Emily sat beside her, scooching their chairs closer together.

At that moment, the accused was led into the room. In handcuffs. The police officer pulled out a chair and pressed a hand on the man's shoulder to get him to sit.

On the thirteenth of June, Lasse Holt, the Uppsala Internet café employee, had attended a book signing and a talk in a bookshop near the university with his girlfriend. The talk ended up going on for ever and Lasse had needed to leave early to get back in time for a lecture, so he had missed the signing. A few hours later, when he was working his shift at the Internet café, the young man immediately recognised the writer he had seen earlier that day: Dan Hansen. He had been too shy to go over and chat, but once the author had left, Lasse had been curious to see what he had been looking at, so he pulled up the history on that PC. Like most people who used Internet cafés, Dan had cleared his recent history, but Lasse had managed to restore it and had been somewhat disappointed to see that the author had merely contacted *The Times*.

As far as Olofsson was concerned, the presence of Dan Hansen's name among the registered guests at Malmö's Diplomat Hotel on the night of the fourteenth of July was just another nail in his coffin, but he didn't dare say so out loud.

They had no way of determining with any accuracy whether he had been the sender of the emails from the Apple Store in Stockholm on the seventh of May at 10.15 am, or those sent from the Network Internet café in Gothenburg on the third of July at 8.43 am, but Bergström and Emily were in no doubt. Those dates were an exact match with the author's business trips.

◆◆◆◆◆

Dan Hansen's eyes glazed over as he looked up at his wife.

The reality of all this hit Karla like a slap in the face. The pain was crushing her. The love of her life, the father of her children. She wanted to hug him and beat him to a pulp, all at once. She couldn't help the love from flowing beneath the dark anger that was taking hold of her. Her breath quickened, and she had to open her mouth wide to force herself to keep breathing deeply.

Karla pointed an angry finger at her husband.

'Are you the one who did this?'

Her tear-stricken voice faltered at the end of her question. She coughed and spluttered, trying to hold back the wave of tears that was taking her breath away.

Emily, meanwhile, was observing Dan. His rigid posture and stubborn silence.

On the other side of the one-way mirror, Bergström was beginning to wonder whether he had done the right thing by giving the green light for this face-to-face.

Karla closed her eyes for a second before getting back in the saddle.

'So you're the one who helped … those two monsters to … kill those women?'

Karla's pain shot right through Emily like an arrow to the heart.

'Don't you realise what you've done to your family? What you've done to us? And our girls? Our girls!'

Dan Hansen exhaled slowly through his nose. It seemed like he was about to say something, but he didn't open his mouth. He didn't even look at his wife. He seemed transfixed by his own reflection in the one-way mirror. His very presence filled the room with the kind of tension you could cut with a knife, yet he remained absent from the conversation.

'Dan! Are you going to just sit there, in front of me, your wife, and not say anything?'

'Richard and Raymond were my brothers,' Dan finally said in a flat voice, his eyes never wandering from the one-way mirror. 'I grew up with them, at Hilda Stenson's farm. They were my family, all three of them. Richard, Raymond and Hilda. All three of them. I had a duty to help them. It was my duty to help my family.'

Karla wiped her face with the back of her hand.

'I can't ... I can't,' she muttered, shaking her head from side to side, her eyes closed tight. 'I just can't...'

She rose abruptly and left the room, keeping her gaze down.

DAN HANSEN UNBUTTONED the jacket of his pale grey suit with careful deliberation, straightened his narrow tie and sat down to face the judge. Sorry. Madam Justice.

His eyes zeroed in on the heavy pearls dangling from her distended ear lobes. As big as his thumb. His lawyer had advised him to wear a sober, dark suit. For the tie, something more classic. With a looser knot. Just a 'suggestion'.

He couldn't give a damn about the suit, per se. It was having a choice in the matter that he found exciting. This was one sliver of power he could exploit to the hilt. Savour it right down to the bone.

The judge started to speak. She shook her head, and her earrings swayed as if they were slow dancing. Earlobes lolling like tongues.

> *Lobes and mash, home-made style...*
> *Beat two egg yolks and dip the lobes in.*
> *Toss them in breadcrumbs.*
> *Fry them up in parsley butter.*
> *Drizzle them in olive oil and serve with mash.*
> *Lobes and mash, home-made style...*

Dan leaned in to bring his mouth closer to the microphone and give Madam Justice an answer. Spelled out his surname. Paused to brush away a speck of dust from his left shoulder with the back of his hand. Carried on with his given name, date of birth and profession, his mind dwelling on the curious habit he had of unbuttoning his suit jacket when he sat down. A fashion adopted by pupils at Eton or, more accurately, those elected to the in-crowd of their exclusive 'Pop' club. Though perhaps this particular idiosyncrasy went all the way back to King Edward VII, whose fullness of figure demanded the extra space when His Majesty sat on His Royal Backside.

The judge had just asked him to speak. She straightened the lace collar of her robe and shifted some files across her desk.

Lobes and mash, home-made style…

He coughed into his hand. Appreciated the absence of handcuffs. Reflected on how a cage would soon replace them. An image flashed across his mind, slotting into the space between himself and Madam Justice with her lolling ear lobes. A vision of himself hanging from the bars of his cell like a monkey. Still wearing his suit.

He laughed. The sound of it echoed harshly back at him.

Though he was laughing, he shivered as a thin film of sweat spread across the nape of his neck.

'It's not my fault,' he mumbled, as if to himself. 'It's not my fault…'

The judge interrupted him. He couldn't make out the words, just the music of her speech. A crescendo building to a climax. A question.

'It's not my fault,' he continued. 'Hilda was the one who started it … It all started with Hilda…'

'What are you talking about, Mr Hansen?' the judge asked.

'It's all Skorpan's fault…'

'Mr Hansen…'

'But you know the most ironic thing? I should have been Skorpan. I was never Jonathan. Never. I should've been Skorpan…'

'Mr Hansen!'

He clapped his hand over his mouth. He really should keep a lid on it from now on.

BERGSTRÖM, EMILY AND ALEXIS left the courtroom and took refuge in the café next door.

'Olofsson and I went over to Karla's last night,' Bergström explained as he carried a mug of tea, an espresso and a latte over to the table. 'She told me she's been in touch with the Yard about going over to work in your neck of the woods.'

Emily nodded, taking her phone out of her pocket.

'How is she handling things?' Alexis asked, blowing on her latte to cool it down.

'She's OK, but the kids are having a hard time. They've been getting a lot of aggro at school, and they're becoming quite withdrawn. Karla is very worried. She feels they should move away sooner rather than later.'

'I can see that,' said Alexis. 'What's left for her here in Sweden after a tragedy like this? Can you imagine what it must be like for her daughters? With Facebook and all the other social-media crap, a drama like this won't just go away. It's going to hang around like a bad smell.'

Emily passed the headset over to the commissioner, bringing an end to the conversation, and played Dan Hansen's testimony for him, which she had recorded a few hours earlier at the trial.

Sipping his espresso, Bergström translated for them.

'Who are Skorpan and Jonathan?' Alexis asked, once he'd finished.

'They're the two main characters in Astrid Lindgren's tale, *The*

Brothers Lionheart. It's the story of two brothers who had a very close relationship. Jonathan, the eldest, a protective and loving soul, died trying to save Skorpan, his little brother who was ill, from a fire that ravaged their home.'

Emily was staring blankly at Bergström.

'What's wrong, Emily?' Alexis asked, pushing her cup away.

'I'm not sure. But perhaps Sigvard Stenson will be able to tell us.'

THE CAR DOORS slammed shut.

Bergström, Emily and Alexis hurried over to the front door of the Stenson farmhouse, their coats and scarves barely protecting them against the wind and rain.

Sigvard Stenson opened the door and looked his three frozen visitors up and down.

'What do you want?'

'Good evening, Mr Stenson. I'm Kommissionär Bergström. We have some questions we'd like to ask you about Dan Hansen. Perhaps we can talk about this inside?'

Reluctantly, the old man stepped aside to let them in.

'Look, I thought this whole thing was dead and buried,' he grumbled sourly, standing in the gloomy hallway. 'You made my summer a living hell summoning me to your station God knows how many times to talk about kids I never even knew. And that girl, your serial killer's aunt, that ... er...'

'Angela Hemfield.'

'That Angela Hemfield. She never came to live here and, no, I don't know her nephew and I have no idea why he's spinning you all these yarns!'

'We're here to talk to you about Dan Hansen, Mr Stenson.'

'So what? What's the difference? This is all starting to get on my wick. Like I told your beefy detective, I don't remember a Dan Hansen, and I don't remember any of the others. How many times can I keep on telling you I spent my whole life at work? I barely even knew the kid's father. He was a neighbour, of course, but their little shack wasn't exactly right next door to my farm. Not to mention the fact he was a raging alcoholic and a lazy bastard, to boot. No way was I going to spend any time with him, even if I'd had any time to spare.'

'Would you happen to know, Mr Stenson, whether Dan Hansen had a brother?'

'Do you think I know where every kid's father dipped his wick and how many times he hit the target?' Stenson cursed, pulling out his little box of *snus* from his trouser pocket.

'Mr Stenson, at his trial today Dan Hansen mentioned the name Skorpan. Does it sound familiar?'

'Skorpan? Are you testing me on Swedish literature now?'

Kommissionär Bergström took a step towards the old man. Sigvard Stenson had to tilt his head back to look the mountain of a man in the eye.

'Mr Stenson, Richard Hemfield's and Raymond Bell's lawyers are no doubt waiting for the end of Dan Hansen's trial before supplying us with a list of their clients' victims. We'd be willing to bet that your sister, Hilda, who is the common denominator between these three men, was the instigator of their initial crimes. In a few weeks' time, your farm, your land and your old bakery will be examined with a fine-toothed comb in order to uncover DNA fragments of all the young women who were killed, chopped up and eaten. In a few weeks' time, your supposed line of defence – along the lines of "I didn't see or hear anything" – won't cut the mustard, Mr Stenson. I would strongly suggest that you start cooperating with us right now.'

The old man lowered his eyes. He opened his tin of *snus* and inserted a little pouch of tobacco beneath his upper lip.

'Was Skorpan a nickname given to Richard Hemfield, Raymond Bell or any of the other children your sister looked after?'

'I don't know what my sister did. I don't know…'

'Who is Skorpan, Mr Stenson?'

Sigvard Stenson turned his head to the side, as if someone had just called his name, then he cast a vacant stare at the grey wall.

'Dan Hansen's father had a girlfriend. A whore, a bloody good-for-nothing alcoholic, just like him. Her kid looked exactly the same as the kid who played Skorpan in the film of *The Brothers Lionheart*, which Hilda loved. They were like two peas in a pod. That's why she nicknamed the kid Skorpan.'

'What was the name of Skorpan's mother, Mr Stenson?'

'I don't know.'

'Sigvard, Hilda is dead,' Emily intervened, in English. 'Look around you, Sigvard. Look. There's nothing left. No one. Nothing but you and the memory of your sister. Nothing and no one left to protect. So protect yourself.'

The old man's eyes were shrouded in tears as he looked up at the profiler.

'You won't last five minutes in prison, Mr Stenson,' Bergström intervened. 'You might be able to avoid it if you cooperate. Do you understand?'

Sigvard Stenson's chin began to quiver.

'Iris … Sundberg. Skorpan's mother's name was Iris Sundberg…'

KARLA HANSEN GLANCED at the time on the microwave while she cleared the breakfast table. Emily would be there soon.

She looked over into the living room. Her two daughters were snuggled up together on the sofa, engrossed in the TV. They had lost their father, their roots and their bearings. Theirs had become a broken family, and Karla was wondering how the three of them would ever rebuild it. She knew that Pia's and Ada's grief and indifference would soon turn to anger, and that they would blame her for their father's crimes and for him abandoning them. But she had been through worse, and she would keep it together.

Karla had been in touch with Jack Pearce at Scotland Yard. Bearing in mind the excellence of her record at the police training school, she was hoping to begin a new life in England. Emily had said she would back her application.

The doorbell rang. Her daughters didn't blink an eye. Karla went to open the door.

The profiler smiled briefly by way of greeting and shouted out a '*Hej!*' to Pia and Ada, who acknowledged her without turning around.

'Leave them be,' Emily said, as she saw Karla about to reprimand them. 'How are they?' she asked, following the detective into the kitchen.

Karla closed the door behind them.

'Not great. Things aren't going well here at home, or at school. We have to get out of here. It's becoming too much of a burden to stay. Everything here reminds us of Dan.'

Karla tried to swallow it all back, realising how alone she was now.

'We went to see Sigvard Stenson…' Emily said.

'Have Hemfield and Bell given you the list of their victims?'

Emily shook her head as she sat down at the table.

'No, their lawyers haven't sent us anything yet.'

Anxiety gripped Karla's throat.

'It was something Dan said at his trial,' Emily carried on.

Karla closed her eyes for a second, leaning against the kitchen counter for support.

'Dan said something about *The Brothers Lionheart*, Jonathan and Skorpan.'

Dan. Dan. Dan.

She poured two cups of coffee and placed one in front of Emily before she sat down.

'That's why we went to see Svenson.'

Karla looked at the profiler with weary eyes.

'Sigvard Stenson hanged himself in his barn, shortly after we left. We found him this morning.'

'Emily, I … I don't want to keep talking about all this.'

'I know. But this won't take long. Before he hanged himself, Stenson told us all about a certain Iris Sundberg. Iris Sundberg is the key to the whole thing, Karla. Iris Sundberg was living with Alf Hansen. They had a little house near Hilda and Sigvard Stenson's farm. When they first met, Iris and Alf each had one child: Alf was Dan's father, and Iris was Skorpan's mother. Sometimes they forgot to feed the kids, they often beat them up and they might even have implicated them in their sex games. So, Dan and Skorpan often took refuge at Hilda Stenson's, where they met other children – other abandoned, mistreated, lost souls like them. Among these children were Raymond Bell and Richard Hemfield. Richard had come from London with his aunt, Angela Hemfield. Angela was Sigvard's lover. But the presence of this pretty English rose in their midst sullied the ideal family portrait Hilda Stenson had painted with the children she believed to be hers and her fantasy of a husband, Sigvard's. She felt that her brother should never need another woman. She was there for him, after all. Hilda dealt with the problem by killing Angela Hemfield, and keeping her nephew. The other children came and went, but according to the records, Skorpan, Raymond, Dan and a certain Josef spent most of their childhood and youth at the Stensons'. I reckon this Josef must have died at an early age somehow and Richard took over his identity. Children change as they grow up, but who kept on looking after them? Hilda, and Hilda only. Which is why we lost track of Hemfield for fifteen years. Because he was living in Sweden, under another child's identity.'

Emily pushed her cup away.

'It wasn't easy to find a record of Iris Sundberg, as she died, as you've probably guessed. But Olofsson did a bloody good job.'

The look of affection Emily gave her took Karla by surprise.

'You're Iris Sundberg's daughter, Karla.'

The detective locked eyes with the profiler.

'Skorpan is you, Karla.'

'Me, Skorpan?' she scoffed. 'Are you out of your mind, Emily?'

'Little Skorpan, that's you. When Hilda died, Richard Hemfield and Raymond started to explore sicker fantasies, following new twisted paths, and that's when everything went off the rails. Hemfield, a sexual sadist, wanted to kill for the sake of killing and to show off his trophies; Raymond, on the other hand, had acquired a taste for human flesh and had no qualms turning into a fully fledged cannibal, so they figured out how they could operate together. I'm fairly certain it's Hemfield's aunt's DNA that was found in the shoes of Jeanine Sanderson, Julianne Bell and Maria Paulsson. She wasn't actually his aunt, by the way. Angela Hemfield and Richard's father had become brother and sister following their parents' marriage. Anyway, I believe that Angela was your initial victim. Your first time. You kept her belongings as trophies – which is a usual thing to do for a first crime – and Richard used her socks when he murdered Jeanine Sanderson. You know how the rest of the story goes.'

Karla folded her arms across her chest.

'But Hemfield managed to get himself caught,' Emily carried on. 'So Raymond turned to you, Karla, and Dan, because he had to get Richard, your brother, out of prison. Coincidentally, at the same time, you and Dan had become parents, and your career in the police was only just beginning, so you wouldn't have been able to get involved in the investigation. So, you were the one who decided to wait until you had all your ducks in a row before you tried to get Richard out of Broadmoor; in any case, he had to serve time for the killing of Samuel Garel and would never have been released straight away. It was a simple plan: to make people believe that the murders were still ongoing, and that the real killer was still on the loose. You dumped the first body on your own patch, Karla, knowing that Johansson, your police chief, was out of commission. You knew you were the one who would be placed in charge of the investigation, which would enable you to misdirect it in any direction you wished. You kept Richard abreast of your progress through *The Times* small ads, while he continued to be a model prisoner, claiming his innocence while awaiting his eventual release, a game which probably amused him a lot. But Raymond slipped up; he attacked his own adoptive sister, and that was when it all began to crumble.'

Karla lowered her eyes.

'When you saw your husband at the police station, you weren't questioning him, you were telling him what to do. You asked him to spare you so that you could keep on bringing up your daughters. I quote "So you're the one who helped … those two monsters to … kill those women." Then you said to him, "Don't you realise what you've done to your family? What you've done to us?" telling him that it was his fault, that he hadn't been careful enough and hadn't taken proper care of his family. *His* family, in other words, his wife, Richard and Raymond. You then added, "And our girls", referring to your children. Then you repeated, "Our girls!", this time meaning your victims, the women you killed together, first with Hilda, then without Hilda. You ended up saying, "Are you going to just sit there, in front of me, your wife, and not say anything?", which was tantamount to ordering him to confess. Which he obediently did. Your husband said so, Friday, at the trial: he was more "Skorpan" than "Jonathan"; you were the protector, the one who took care of him, the one who made the decisions. What I find interesting is that you and Dan have chosen the same kind of childhood for your daughters that you had. You've made the same mistakes as your parents. At the end of the day, you're not giving them any more than your mother gave you.'

Karla waved a menacing finger in Emily's face.

'Don't you compare me to Iris Sundberg,' she spat out, her mouth contorted in anger. 'I am a mother. A wife. A sister. Iris Sundberg … would grab hold of Dan's father's cock and shove it down my throat. She was not my mother. She was a freak of nature who should never have procreated. It should never have happened. She was a whore and a degenerate, just like Hemfield's aunt. And all the others Hilda served us for dinner.'

RICHARD HEMFIELD OPENED the zipped bag. His part of the bargain in return for the list of their victims. His reward.

The tights had been cut up into seven pieces for security reasons: hips and buttocks, thighs, legs and feet.

Carefully he took out the shreds of material, turned them inside out and arranged six of them around his pillow: a thigh, a leg and a foot on each side. Gently, he stretched himself out on his bed and placed the final piece over his face, the crotch covering his mouth and nose.

He closed his eyes and inserted the shred of material into his left nostril. The sweet, spicy aroma soon enveloped his tongue. A scent of rancid butter and honey … a hint of damp leather … such a unique aroma. Like a fine wine, the tasting experience began long before you ever took a sip.

Midsommar night, 1988 … The girl from Kiruna … Hers had smelled of damp leather and rancid butter too…

Hemfield pushed the crotch of the tights into his other nostril.

They had all come out to meet them when they heard the purring of the Vespa. Already straddling their prey, Karla had tightened her belt around the girl's milky throat. She had stared at the five of them in horror before her pink tongue had emerged through her lips, lolloping out like a dog's.

Raymond and Dan had helped carry the girl to the cellar. Karla had undressed and cleaned her, Hilda had carved her up, and then they had gone upstairs to eat. They usually kept the girls for a few days before feasting on them. Once they had calmed down, their meat was more tender and far tastier.

Still, they had tucked in with a healthy appetite. These feasts elicited a form of … oral orgasm, as if the essence of sexual pleasure now resided inside their mouths, their throats and stomachs. Only the discreet sounds of chewing and swallowing interrupted the rattling of the cutlery against the plates, like muted moans of pleasure during the act of love.

Hemfield groped around and picked up another shred of the tights from his right side. A foot. He cleared one of his nostrils and jammed in the new shred of nylon.

'The gods have delivered you to me,' Hilda had often said … They both had English blood running through their veins, after all.

That night, she had caught him masturbating over the girl from Kiruna's clothes. She had merely smiled and closed the cellar door behind her. Hilda realised the meals weren't enough for him. She understood that Richard's needs resided elsewhere, and she did not judge him for it. She even allowed him to experiment…

Hilda…

He grasped two more fragments of material and inserted them into his ears.

Raymond had begged him not to leave the bodies of the girls in Tower Hamlets. But he had refused to listen. He enjoyed the spectacle of the distorted, mutilated whores spread out across the pavement. The pleasure was so heady and intense … So complete.

But Hilda would never forgive him for taking Karla down with him.

Hemfield grabbed hold of the final shreds of the tights.

Hilda would never forgive him for taking her little Skorpan down with him … Her beloved Skorpan…

He stuffed the pieces of material into his mouth and forced them down his throat.

But he understood Hilda … and did not judge her.

ALEXIS STRETCHED OUT and relaxed on the sofa, laying her head on her niece's chubby little legs, as the child combed her dainty fingers through her aunt's hair.

Alexis had delivered the manuscript for her book on the Ebner case four days earlier, and fatigue was catching up with her now. She felt like a mother after giving birth, simply desperate for sleep. Her sister, the mother of two young children, had quickly corrected her, chiding, 'The big difference is that you actually get to sleep.'

'Want to veg out with me, Auntie?'

'That would be lovely, sweetie. What is it you're watching?'

'*Peppa Pig*, nah-nah-nah-nah-nah, na-na-na-na-nah-nah … Auntie!'

'Yes, lovie…'

'Can you sing me that funny song?'

'Which one, darling? *Jingle Bells*?'

'No, the one from Stellan's country that goes lalalalala, that you sing when you're drinking!'

'Oh … that one! You'll have to ask him. I don't know how it goes, sweetie.'

'But Nanny does, she can sing it.'

Alexis gave her mother a curious look.

'Well, of course,' Mado shrugged, reaching over to feed Alexis, and her granddaughter, a chunk of nougat. 'I learned *Hell and Gore* to honour our guest.'

'You know how to sing *Helan Går*, Maman?'

'And very well she does, too,' Stellan chimed in, as he walked across the living room behind Norbert Castells.

'Where are you going?' Alexis asked, her eyes closing of their own accord as she succumbed to the softness of her niece's touch.

'Up to the attic. We're going to try and dig out some old Super 8 films of the *Moros y Cristianos* festivities.'

'OK,' she said, allowing sleep to wash over her.

Completely absorbed by the spectacle of Peppa Pig having a whale of a time jumping in muddy puddles, her niece seemed to have forgotten about *Hell and Gore*.

Stellan and Norbert Castells climbed the stairs up to the mezzanine floor.

'I've been wanting to talk to you since we got here, Norbert,' Stellan explained as he closed the door of the recess that led to the attic, 'but I never seem to be able to find the right time…'

'You want to talk to me? What about? Ooooh!'

Alexis's father sat down on a pile of flattened cardboard boxes. Then quickly stood up again.

'Wait, Stellan, wait! Mado would kill me if she thought we were excluding her from this. Just a second…'

Norbert Castells opened the door again.

'Mado!' he shouted out, using his hands as a megaphone. 'There must be thousands of boxes in this attic. I can't find the films anywhere. Where did you put them? I've already emptied two boxes and haven't seen a thing.'

'Oh, for heaven's sake!' Mado exclaimed, hurriedly climbing the stairs. 'You wouldn't find water in the sea, Castells! Let me have a look.'

Norbert closed the door behind her.

'Our young friend wants to talk to us, but you never step away from Alexis for a second.'

'Can't you see she's exhausted? She's as white as a sheet. She's spent all autumn sitting behind her screen with no fresh air and…'

Mado stopped in her tracks, her eyes clouding over.

'What? What is it? Do you have bad news? Are you ill? Is Alexis ill?'

'Of course not, Mado. But if you let him get a word in edgeways, maybe he'll say.'

'OK. *Stella*, what did you want to say?'

Stellan smiled.

'I wanted to ask for your daughter's hand in marriage, Mado.'

Norbert buried his future son-in-law in a bear hug, before loudly kissing him on both cheeks.

Stellan watched his future mother-in-law – or so he hoped – for a reaction, but for once, she was lost for words and emotions.

'I knew it, Bert, I knew it!' she suddenly burst out. 'I knew my daughter was going to move to the Far North!'

EMILY UNZIPPED HER PARKA and pulled her little black box from her inside pocket.

Some weeks earlier, she had kneeled by the tiny plot of earth nestling at the foot of the brick wall at the end of her garden. The little cemetery where she buried her closed cases, once their victims had finally found peace. Fifty-two little black boxes now awaited the next addition.

Soon.

Emily opened box number fifty-three.

She gazed at Angela Hemfield. Jeanine Sanderson. Diana Lantar. Katie Atkins. Chloe Blomer. Sylvia George. Clara Sandro. Maria Paulsson. Freja Lund. She pictured all the as-yet unidentified ones, spread out like a bouquet of flowers. All those still waiting for the lawyers to finish bargaining before they could rest in peace and their families could grieve.

She wasn't shocked to see all the torturers in there as well. Hilda, Sigvard, Karla, Dan, Richard and Raymond. The fates of six damaged, mistreated children, abused by their parents and then by life itself. The errors of their ways had stacked up like pearls threaded onto a necklace, passed down from generation to generation.

At the end of the day, this whole tragedy – these tragedies – had nothing to do with the abominable Jack the Ripper, as Aliénor had suggested. His crimes were the pock-marked reflection of misery in Victorian England, but the world had since seen far worse atrocities.

A thin layer of stray snowflakes now lay at the bottom of the box. Emily was about to close it when she had a vision of herself in there too: an intruder in the victims' midst. The profiler who had worked, chatted and dined with a she-monster and shared her pain without unmasking her.

Emily closed the lid, put the box back inside her pocket and zipped up her parka, under Pearce's loving gaze.

They walked up the path along the edge of the cemetery, their boots crunching through the snow.

Her son was resting alongside a grandmother named Hortense, in a white coffin the size of a crib that she had had to pick out all by herself. Sebastian was right there, just beneath her feet.

Emily delicately brushed the snow from his grave, until she felt the stones beneath her gloved fingers. She placed a grey oblong pebble with black streaks next to the white pebble she had brought with her last summer.

She kneeled and lowered her palms and forehead to touch the icy grave.

Emily spoke to her son about all the love she would have wanted to give him, all the meals they could have shared, all the laughter, the travels, the arguments, the heartache, the tears, the birthdays, the celebrations…

She confided all her regrets to him.

'What is important is not what happens to us, but how we respond to what happens to us.'

Jean-Paul Sartre

Acknowledgments

Just over two years ago, I released my first-born, *Block 46*, into the world. I had always told myself that after it was published, it wouldn't matter if I died … Yes, I know, so terribly tragic, like a play by Racine, but don't forget I'm from Marseille! Well, I was wrong, as *Block 46* made its way into your arms, to you, the readers, booksellers, journalists, bloggers, other writers, all full of passion for noir. Thank you for your warm welcome, your encouragement and your enthusiasm. I can't tell you how many times I cried with joy reading all your messages. I, who have always thought that life was all about meeting people, couldn't have asked for more.

An immense vote of thanks to my publisher, Karen Sullivan, for her unstoppable energy, her determination and the passion she puts into taking care of Team Orenda. She's the real-life Leah Lager of this story!

All my dearest thanks to Maxim Jakubowski, who has done me an honour once again by translating this second novel of mine, which is now ours.

Thanks equally to David Warriner for polishing this book to a shine.

A colossal thank-you to Michel Dufranne and Nicolas Lefort, who propelled *Block 46* onto the small screen in France. Long live scratch-and-sniff T-shirts and British tea!

Thanks to all of you wonderful noir writers for rolling out the welcome mat to me when I was a complete newbie on the scene.

My warmest thanks to the Bragelonne Dream Team: Fanny

Caignec, Stéphane Marsan, Guillaume Missonier, Sébastien Mori-card, Alain Névant, Leslie Pallant and Yolande Rochat de la Vallée: guys, you ROCK!

Thank you from the bottom of my heart to the president of the Étoile d'Asperger association, Elisabet Guillot, who guided me with patience and extraordinary availability when it came to crafting the character of Aliénor Lindbergh.

Thank you to the three writers with whom I dissected Jack the Ripper: Stéphane Bourgoin, Maxim Jakubowski and Michel Moatti (whose theory about Jack's identity I borrowed).

Thanks to Richard Migneault for helping me with the name of the cemetery where Sebastian is buried.

Thanks to the fantastic team at Blossom & Co for the work they did around this novel and to Marcel Saucet and LCA Consulting for their innovative marketing campaign with *Block 46*.

Gracias-mercis-tackar to my homegrown dream team: my four lovely Vikings, my parents and my sister.

Thanks to you, Mattias, my other half, for embracing this new life with your customary good mood and eternal smiles; and thank you for being such an incredible Daddy: you are our rock.

For Maxou, Will and Alex, my little miracles, thanks for being so adaptable and for your love of life: you are my magic Asterix potion.

Thanks to my mother for her unconditional support, her words, her listening ear and her good humour: Mado Castells was born from our mother-daughter madness.

Thank you to my father for all the patient and passionate reread-ings. Thanks for standing by me; for me, writing is something we do together.

My little sister, who always finds the time to journey with me through my often-horrific world and has a talent for analysing my characters' ups and down with her psychological insights: thanks for always being there in spite of the distance. You're an essential part of all this.

And Lilas Seewald, my writing fairy godmother: without you this novel would not exist as it stands, or perhaps not at all... What would I do without you, my Lilas?

London, 8 December 2017

If you enjoyed *Keeper*, you'll love Book 1 in the Roy & Castells Series

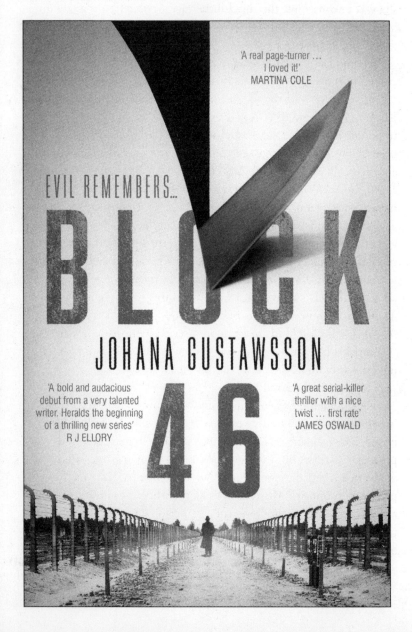

'A real page-turner …
I loved it!'
MARTINA COLE

EVIL REMEMBERS…

BLOCK

JOHANA GUSTAWSSON

'A bold and audacious
debut from a very talented
writer. Heralds the beginning
of a thrilling new series'
R J ELLORY

46

'A great serial-killer
thriller with a nice
twist … first rate'
JAMES OSWALD